A.W.O.L

MERITA KING

Published by Merita King

Eastleigh

Hampshire

United Kingdom

© Merita King 2014 all rights reserved

Cover art by Shardel

A.W.O.L

OTHER WORKS BY MERITA KING

The Lilean Chronicles: Book One ~ Redemption
The Lilean Chronicles: Book Two ~ The Sleeping
The Lilean Chronicles: Book Three ~ Changing Faces
The Lilean Chronicles: Book Four ~ Avalanche Effect

Floxham Island ~ Sinclair V-Log AZ267/M
Bygora Vandos ~ Sinclair V-Log LB734/A

Delectus Morbidium

ABOUT THE AUTHOR

Merita King has loved the science fiction and fantasy genre in both books and movies since she was a young child. She has been greatly inspired by years of watching movies and reading books and has wanted to make a contribution to this genre for many years. Her stories all contain a spiritual thread as she believes that spirituality is universal and crosses all boundaries. She believes that the creative process is largely intuitive and can be very effectively blocked by too much pre-planning. "Plot lines, characters and events all come to me intuitively," she says, "and this makes the act of writing a constant pleasure." She lives alone, with her vivid imagination, in Hampshire, UK.

DEDICATION

This work is dedicated to all who wish for love, all those who believe
themselves unworthy of love, and all with love to give.
When two hearts are destined to become one,
no distance is too great, no time too long, and no price too high.
However infinite the universe should turn out to be, no power within it
has a greater force for change, than love.

A.W.O.L

CHAPTER ONE

"If you don't get them to me within the hour, you'll be in trouble so you better get on with it."

Risa sighed and tried to calm the dark knot of despair she felt flutter into life deep inside. Her heart sank a little more, as it did after every exchange such as this and she wondered how much further it could sink, how much worse she could feel, and how she would cope with feeling so low. She was determined never to let Lorella see her upset, so she forced a smile.

"You'll have them, don't worry."

"Stupid bitch," Lorella muttered as she turned and left, not bothering to shut the door behind her.

"Who rattled her cage today?"

Risa turned and saw Gage, her colleague and fellow stores hand peering round from behind a stack of boxes.

"Me, as usual," she replied with a shrug.

"Sisterly love huh?" Gage grinned. "You sure you both got the same parents Risa?"

"I wish it were not so," she said. "Come on then, let's have those stores manifests or you'll all find yourselves vying for my job when she sacks me."

"Will it mean a raise?" he grinned.

"Yep," she nodded. "And of course you'll report directly to her on a daily basis, instead of me."

"Oh, on second thoughts, you can keep your job," he laughed.

"I thought that might change your mind."

"Seriously though Risa, why do you let her bully you so much? What's her damn problem?"

"She's always been the same, ever since I can remember. I can't really remember anytime she was ever genuinely nice to me without some ulterior motive."

"Maybe she didn't like not being the only child anymore," Gage offered.

"Maybe," Risa shrugged. "I guess that's a question only she can answer."

Twenty minutes later, Risa made her way across to the Administration office to hand her sister the stores manifests. She looked up into the sky as she walked and sighed deeply, aware of the loneliness that had seeped right through to her bones over the last few years since her parents died. Risa was born on the base twenty-two years ago and had never left Luzel 2, despite her parents having a holiday home on the neighbouring planet, Luzel 3 and up until just recently, she had never wanted to leave. This place was the only home she had ever known, and she had been happy when her parents were still around as a buffer of safety and comfort between herself and Lorella. Somehow, their presence made her sister's torments easier to cope with, and with them both dead, that comfort had gone. Within a couple of years, she had gone from a happy young woman who enjoyed her work and was content with her life, to a shell, empty of joy. When she looked into her future, she felt nothing but dread and had almost forgotten what happiness felt like. The thought of spending the rest of her life here with Lorella tormenting her on a daily basis was too much to bear, but at the same time, this was all she had ever known and she mourned for the joy that had died alongside her parents. Not knowing why Lorella treated her so cruelly was worse than the treatment she endured at her sister's hands, and she often wished someone would one day tell her. In all of the years though, Risa had never had the nerve to ask Lorella directly, for she feared the answer at the same time as craving for it. She felt the sting of hot tears prick the back of her eyes and she shook them away as she walked across the base, not wanting to show her sister she was upset.

The base was one of many dotted all over the planet, and just like all the others, it served as a refuelling and restocking station for all manner of spacecraft. From luxury passenger liners to individual personal runabouts and everything in between, they all stopped at Luzel 2. Being in the middle of a major intergalactic shipping lane made it the ideal place to set up a refuelling base and Risa's family had worked for the company for three generations. Risa's grandparents were among the small workforce that set up the very first Luzel 2 base, one that was now being refitted and modernised. When her parents married they moved to base twenty five for a couple of years before both were offered the chance of promotion here at base seven, and both Lorella and Risa had been born here on the base. Although genetically a full-blooded Earth woman, Risa did not feel any connection with the mystical blue planet everyone talked about and always referred to herself as Luzellian, even though there had never been indigenous humanoids on Luzel 2. She felt restless and unsettled as she entered the Administration office and handed her sister the stores manifests.

"Just stick them in the tray," Lorella said without looking up. "I'll get to them tomorrow sometime."

Risa did not rise to her sister's taunt. She had learned self-discipline and never took the bait Lorella waved at her in these moments. Inside herself, Risa wanted to scream but she just put the papers in the tray and left. She and her staff had missed part of their lunch break to get those manifests ready, and now Lorella was not going to bother with them until tomorrow. She was not an aggressive woman at all but sometimes Risa found herself daydreaming about punching her sister for her treatment of her. So many times she wished she could be more aggressive and hit back at Lorella, but she was not made that way. She stepped back into the sunshine and took a moment to close her eyes and sigh, before heading back to the stores to finish unloading the latest delivery.

The sun was setting over Mount Koomo as Risa set out for her daily run around the perimeter wall of the base, the track beaten down by generations of runners before her. Eight point three miles took her a complete circuit of the base and she looked forward to this throughout her daily work at the stores. As she ran, she thought of Lorella and her constant bullying and by the time she passed the refuelling sector, she was in tears of loneliness and anger. Ever since her parents died five years ago, Lorella's treatment of Risa became much worse than had been the norm. What had been simple name calling and teasing was now open hostility and attempts to discredit her. Lorella was outspoken and gregarious, made friends easily, whilst Risa was quiet and a little shy, and consequently did not have a large crowd around her. She spent much of her time alone with her thoughts and her tears, and the smile with which she greeted her co-workers and visitors to the base, was not as genuine as it was when her parents were alive.

The smell of roasting meat came to Risa's nostrils as she ran behind one of the five hotels attached to the base and reminded her of the many laughter filled evening meals she had shared with her parents. Birthdays, anniversaries, and all manner of special occasions were always celebrated with a family meal out, and she had many happy memories of such times. Nowadays, those memories just made her sad, so she tried her best to forget them. She seldom went out in the evenings now, even though the base had a thriving nightlife to entertain the visitors from many worlds who spent a night or two waiting for their ships to be refuelled and restocked, repairs done and travel plans made. She used to go for her evening meal every night, as most base personnel do, but since that awful night six months ago, Risa hadn't dared. She went cold as she remembered.

Gage and a couple of the other stores hands had invited her out for the evening to celebrate a birthday and she accepted happily. They had a delicious meal in the best of the base's restaurants, before heading to the club for drinks. Everything had been going well until Lorella and her friends arrived, already the worse for several drinks. Lorella had been a heavy drinker for as long as Risa could remember and most evenings saw her in the club or one of the hotel bars. Risa knew her sister had something of a reputation as someone who liked a good time and found it very embarrassing. She had bumped into the group in the bathroom and Lorella had started the name calling and insults, urging her friends to join in and before too long, the five of them had Risa cornered and were chanting horrible names and pointing at her.

Within an hour and a half, a group of soldiers from the base's military section came in and Risa's heart leapt as he looked at her and nodded, a faint smile on his lips. She smiled back and watched as he and his friends went to get drinks. Narek Jenn was a Sergeant in the base's military section, responsible for training recruits in survival skills and combat and Risa had fallen in love with him the moment she first saw him, that first day he arrived on the base two years, six months and twenty-nine days ago. From Vendala 4, and six feet three, Narek was well muscled, with light brown skin, black wavy hair and a little curl that always dropped down over his right eye. His large, brown, almond shaped eyes sported long thick lashes that Risa reckoned must make an audible swish to those lucky to get close enough to hear. What always caught her attention though was the flurry of dark brown spots that ran down each side of his neck and caressed the tops of his muscular shoulders before spilling down the centre of his chest and down his spine. She wondered how far down they went.

As Risa sat with her friends and gazed at Narek's back, she saw an arm slip itself through his and she looked up to find Lorella staring at her with a look of triumph on her face, before turning and gazing up at him. She knew her sister had seen her gazing at Narek and was now enjoying teasing her by pretending to be close to him, so she looked away and tried to look as if it didn't bother her. At one point, Gage went up to get more drinks and she clearly heard Lorella speak to him.

"You're not still allowing that ugly little thing to crash your nights out are you Gage?"

Risa could not hear Gage's reply but many people in the bar had heard and were now staring at her. Blood flushed into her cheeks and she wanted to run away but her pride did not allow it, so she sat up, smiled at her companions, and forced herself to join in the boring conversation they were having. By the time Gage and the others decided their celebration was over, Risa allowed herself to follow them outside into the night air. They split up at the corner by the communications centre and Risa began the walk back to her room alone. The air on Luzel 2 was clear and crisp and Risa breathed deeply in an attempt to stem the rising tears she felt within.

Shaking away the thoughts, she headed down the last mile of her run, past the military section. She looked forward to spending the next two hours in the base's staff gym, not only because she enjoyed the discipline of working out, but because it was the only place she knew without a doubt Lorella would never go. Her sister had never been one for keeping fit and healthy and her figure showed her lack of restraint. Drinking too much, eating the wrong things, and precious little exercise had given Lorella a rounded figure that could almost be described as fat. Lorella was everything Risa never wanted to be, so she used her sister's example to help spur her on to ever greater levels of fitness and she now ran the eight mile perimeter wall every day, following it up with two hours pulling weights and working her body's muscle groups. Her body showed her disciplined regime and she had a six pack any man would be proud of, firm thighs, a flat stomach and a taught backside, but still she looked at herself in the mirror each day and grimaced with disgust.

With a grunt of satisfaction, she hefted the weights back onto the rack and sat down to get her breath back. Working out hard each day enabled Risa to channel her emotions into something positive, and made her feel strong and disciplined. She took a long draw of water and wiped the sweat off her brow as the door opened and in walked Narek with two other Vendalan soldiers, deep in conversation in their native tongue, which she did not understand.

"Minach do lampaste ta'kil me na," Narek grinned.

"Pua lang tiliotche," the guy on the left replied and all three laughed.

"Li allimala do Risa," the guy on the right said with a smile and pointed at her.

Risa blushed and smiled as Narek met her gaze and his laugh settled into a smile as his eyelashes fluttered.

"Hello Risa, how are you this evening," he asked, his accent melting her heart.

"Hi Narek, I'm fine thank you. I don't usually see you here at this time of night."

"No, I left my jacket here earlier," he smiled as he reached behind her and retrieved it from a locker. The aroma of his warm body filled her nostrils, like warm baked spice that reminded her of the ginger pies her mother used to make on special occasions, and she ached to reach out and hold him close to drink in that smell.

"We're going to the club for a drink," he said as he donned the jacket. "Would you like to come with us?"

She almost said yes and desperately wanted to, but the thought of Lorella was always foremost in her mind so she smiled and shook her head.

"Uh, no thanks, I have to shower and I have things to do. Thank you for asking me though," she smiled up at him, wishing he would bend down and kiss her.

"Okay, but if you change your mind, I'll buy you a drink huh?"

"Have a good time guys," she called as they left. Alone once more, in the hot and sweaty atmosphere of the staff gym, surrounded by mirrors and chrome, Risa burst into tears and watched a hundred reflections of her own miserable self, wallow in anguish.

Lorella squeezed herself into her red leather skirt and held her breath as she hauled the zipper up. She admired herself in the mirror and smiled at her curves. She always dressed to show her figure and the men at the base appreciated her for it. Tonight she was going to have a good time and she was determined to put her plan of revenge into action. She knew that little bitch sister of hers fancied Narek Jenn and she was not going to allow that little cow to steal the best looking guy on the base. It made Lorella sick to her stomach the way Risa, with her long golden hair and shy smile would catch the men's eyes so easily and without effort. If it were not for the knowledge that Risa would think she was copying her, Lorella would have dyed her hair blonde ages ago but she did not want her thinking she was envious.

She turned this way and that, admiring her reflection, before hitching her breasts a little higher and yanking her top a little lower, then, with a last slick of red lipstick, she sauntered out into the warm Luzel night and headed for the club. On her way, opportunity smiled upon her as she met the little bitch coming out of the gym, all sweaty and smelly. Ugh, she looks more like a man every day, Lorella thought to herself as she looked at her slim figure and cheekbones. She grinned to herself and launched into her carefully practiced act, knowing she had more than enough talent to pull it off.

"Hi Risa," she called and tottered over in her high heels. "It's no good; I have to confide in someone," she puffed. "I know I shouldn't, and you have to promise not to breathe a word to anyone, but I'll burst if I don't' share my news."

"Whatever is the matter Lorella?" Risa replied, wondering why her sister was suddenly being friendly and confiding anything in her at all and immediately suspicious.

"It's happened," Lorella gushed. "Oh it's finally happened."

"What's happened?"

"We're dating. At last, he asked me to be his girlfriend. Oh, I'm so happy I could just die. Oh but you mustn't tell a living soul. It's against his people's rules so no one must know, only you and me. Promise me."

"Dating?" Risa asked, incredulous that Lorella should be dating anyone exclusively. "Dating who?"

"Promise me you won't tell. Promise Risa."

"I promise. My lips are sealed."

"Thank you," Lorella continued gushing. "I just had to tell someone or I'd go mad. Anyway, thanks for letting me confide in you. Now I must dash, I'm late to meet him."

"But who is it?" Risa called as Lorella began tottering away.

"Narek of course, silly. He finally told me how he felt about me this morning and asked if we could start dating, but it must be a secret as his people don't announce a relationship until the two decide to marry, so when other people are around we have to be just work colleagues. You wouldn't believe how wonderful he kisses Risa, oh my god those lips."

Risa watched Lorella turn and go and did not know how to feel. First came disbelief. She knew her sister well enough to know that she would have great difficulty sticking with just one man and with her love of partying and nightlife; she could not see Narek putting up with that for long. Then she remembered that night at the club six months ago, when Lorella had slipped her arm through his and Risa's disbelief began to falter. Lorella and Narek were around the same age and Risa knew her sister's social skills would ensure no man went without her attentions for long. For long moments she could not decide how she should feel about this. On the one hand, it seemed crazy that Narek would go for someone like Lorella. Risa had never seen any Vendalan women though, and had no idea what they were like nor how they lived, and she had to accept the possibility of Narek finding Lorella and her behaviour attractive. One thing she knew to be true. Narek had never been seen with a woman since his arrival on the base, and it was common knowledge that Vendalan custom dictated romance is done privately until the couple know their bond is for life. Lorella had not been lying about that particular thing, so Risa had to admit her sister and Narek could have been dating and no one would have known. As she walked back to her apartment, she felt herself go numb inside at the thought of Lorella and Narek, the man she loved more than anything, dating. She could not cry at her loss, no tears would come to soak her pillow and torment her dreams; she could not wallow in shock nor even scream in anger. All she could do was sit and stare into space as her heart shattered within her breast. The emotional part of Risa seemed to give up and she was almost relieved as she felt the emotions within, wither and die. No more tears, no more self pity, and no more wondering about her future. Something flickered and died within Risa as she sat in her apartment, and coldness took its place.

Narek and his two Vendalan friends entered the club and looked around for the other men in their unit. A wave from the far corner table and Narek smiled and sauntered over.

An hour later the door opened and in walked Lorella Parks and Narek groaned a little louder than he intended to and his friends all heard and grinned.

"Hey Sarge, your girlfriend's arrived. Want us to leave you two in peace?"

"Don't you dare," Narek glared. "If one of you so much as lifts one ass cheek off his chair, you're all on triple cleaning duties for a week."

"But she loves you boss," a red headed man named Doc, with a permanent smile grinned.

"I don't care."

"It's those sexy Vendalan spots that does it," hissed a white haired man with bright blue eyes named Rakshi. "One look at them and every woman is your slave. The rest of us here will have to visit the tattoo parlour out behind the refuelling sector or we've no hope of getting laid with you three here."

"Don't be daft," Narek blushed as he pulled the collar of his jacket a little tighter around his neck, which only made his friends laugh more. He had no desire to tell them that they were right and that the spots that Vendalan men carry always get darker and more prominent when they are in their sexual prime and ready to take a mate.

"Is it perhaps the sight of Lorella Parks that's making those spots stand out like ripe nipples?" a large bald black skinned man asked and everyone, including Narek, burst out laughing.

"No it certainly isn't," he hissed in reply.

"Then who?"

Narek looked down at the table and blushed. He had only ever confided in his Vendalan friends before and he felt embarrassed at the thought of telling his innermost secret to these men, especially as he was their Sergeant and was supposed to be in a position of authority over them. Narek believed in being a friend to those in his charge as well as a leader, as he believed that men would obey someone they liked and respected, quicker and more easily than someone they feared or could not resonate with on a friendly level. He looked up as one of his Vendalan friends named Kaylak, asked him if he wanted him to answer for him.

"Skeshrillie mataksa?" you want me to tell?

"Kiana," Narek nodded.

"Risa," Kaylak whispered.

The whole table gasped. "Lorella's sister?" Rakshi asked.

"That shy little thing with the lovely golden hair?" The black skinned man asked.

"Yes," Narek nodded.

"So have you approached her?"

"No."

"Why the hell not?"

"Because Lorella told me a few weeks ago that Risa has taken a vow of abstinence. It would be against Vendalan moral values to try to make a woman break such a vow. Everyone on Vendala holds those who take such vows in the highest esteem and their moral code is beyond reproach. They dedicate their lives to the service of others or spiritual work and I would be damned to the depths of Kon so Fahl for disrespecting her in such a manner."

"But Risa's not Vendalan Narek," A man with a tanned complexion and black hair named Anjelus replied. "And you've no real proof that what Lorella said is true, have you? Have you asked Risa herself about this vow?"

"No," Narek conceded.

"She may be just saying that to try to stop you and Risa getting together," The black skinned man offered and the others nodded.

"Jack's right," Kaylak said, nodding at the black skinned man. "This may be just an attempt to keep you from Risa, so Lorella can get you for herself."

"Well she's doomed to failure," Narek declared. "That is something I can assure you all with total confidence. That is never going to happen."

"You have to approach Risa, Narek," Kaylak said. "You have to find out. We don't want this to bring you to Kwyam tialash Sakri. We don't want that for you brother."

"What's that?" asked Doc.

"*Kwyam tialash Sakri,*" Kaylak repeated. "It means the eternal bond of souls. On Vendala, when a man has given his whole heart to a woman and knows there can never be anyone else to fill his heart, their souls are said to combine into one for eternity. If one or other should die before they marry, or if one doesn't reciprocate the other's feelings, the person left behind is doomed to live his whole life with only half a soul. In such cases, many of them take the Tal ak Roi to release their half soul from their doomed existence."

"And what is this Tal, whatever?" Jack asked.

"Tal ak Roi," Kaylak said and Jack nodded. "It means willing sacrifice. What you would call suicide."

"What?" Rakshi hissed in shock. "You'd take your own life just because a woman doesn't love you back?"

"It's our way," Narek replied quietly. "A Vendalan man cannot live with half a soul and he would be doomed to Kon so Fahl if he didn't take the Tal ak Roi."

"What's Kon so Fahl?" Jack asked.

"It means the pit of sorrow," Narek replied. "Where those with half souls are doomed to spend eternity if they refuse the Tal ak Roi. Those who refuse to acknowledge the gods' authority go there also, as do those who take the life of another in anger or jealousy."

"Oh," Jack nodded. "Kinda like hell I guess."

"Hell?" Kaylak asked.

"Yeah, it's our version of Kon so Fahl, only ours is a flaming pit full of fire and brimstone where the devil rules supreme and you suffer endless physical torture for your sins."

"Who is the devil? Rakshi asked.

"He's a demon. A nasty, evil looking thing with horns who loves nothing better than maiming, killing and torturing folks. He's the opposite of god in our religion."

"Oh," Rakshi replied. "Back home on Epplon 7 we don't have invisible gods. We believe the concept of God is within all of us, that we are both creator and creation and we worship that part of ourselves that knows all there is to know, even though our conscious side may not know."

"Mind if I join you boys?" the voice cut into the conversation and Narek groaned inwardly. This was the last thing he wanted.

"Actually we're on a um, kind of a boys night out thing," Doc smiled at Lorella and winked. "Another time honey."

"Oh that sounds like fun," Lorella giggled and pulled up a chair. "I can be one of the boys."

"Not tonight Lorella," Kaylak replied in a tone Narek did not often hear. "It's Vendalan custom. Tonight is estrillie doriel and no women allowed. I'm sorry but it's our custom."

"Aww okay boys," Lorella crooned as she got up from her chair, holding onto Narek's shoulder to stop herself from falling over. "But you won't get away so easily next time."

As Lorella tottered and swayed towards the bar and joined in with a group of drunks who were singing a rather bawdy song, Narek tried hard not to laugh aloud. Kaylak and Vronil, the other Vendalan soldiers were red faced by the time they stopped laughing.

"What the hell was that all about?" Rakshi asked.

"*Estrillie doriel?*" Vronil asked and the others nodded. This sent the Vendalans into a fresh fit of almost silent giggles and it was almost a minute before any of them could speak.

"It means you are a doriel," Narek replied as all three started laughing again.

"And what's a doriel?" Doc asked.

"A woman of low moral standards," Vronil replied between giggles. "A woman who will have sex with any man at any time."

"OH, you mean a whore," Doc replied and everyone roared with laughter.

By the time the barman reminded Narek and his friends that it was closing time, they were the last ones in the club. Narek felt better having confided in his friends about his feelings for Risa and with their emotional support, he decided that as soon as they returned from their training exercise, he would find a way to talk to Risa and find out if Lorella's story of her vow of abstinence was true. He knew himself well enough to know that if it turned out to be true, he would take the Tal ak Roi to release his half soul from the Kon so Fahl. He could not face life with half a soul and the thought of even that half soul being damned to eternity in the pit of sorrow was more than he could bear. He decided not to confide this truth to Kaylak and Vronil though, as he did not want them to feel obligated to help him, to the detriment of their own whole souls. He guessed they both probably knew he would do it but so long as he never voiced the intention openly, there would be no obligation on them.

They made their way back to their military accommodations and the three Vendalans said goodnight to their friends, before making their way outside onto a patch of open ground to pray to their gods for guidance and support. For almost an hour they sat there in silent prayer, tears running down Narek's cheeks as they beseeched Alima, the god of love and bonding, for help in this troubling matter. Luzel 2's moon was full and bright as the three friends mouthed the silent words; their belief in their Gods unflinching and despite his anguish, Narek knew Alima was receiving his prayers. As he lay down in bed and tried to sleep, he felt a dark weight upon his heart and he knew trouble lay not far ahead. At the same time, he knew there was nothing he could do to avoid it, that he would be expected to experience something deeply traumatic in return for the God's favour. This was often the price of Alima's intervention. When calling upon the God of love and bonding, one must expect the cost to be high. Narek felt no fear at having called upon Alima, for he knew himself well enough to be sure that he would meet this powerful god's price, whatever it turned out to be. He also felt strength pouring into his soul from somewhere outside of himself, somewhere of infinite wisdom and he knew that whatever fight lay in front of him, he would not perish.

A.W.O.L

CHAPTER TWO

Risa dressed, the early morning shower having revived her a little after a sleepless night during which she reluctantly came to a decision. As she tied her long golden hair up, she knew she had to leave Luzel 2, or at least leave Base 7. The thought of remaining here and having to watch Lorella and Narek together, possibly starting a family, was too much to bear and she knew there was no other man on the base to whom she could give her heart, not with Narek around as a constant reminder of what she had lost. In a way she felt guilty for being upset; she loved Narek and wanted him to be happy, but the knowledge that his happiness did not lie with her, made it difficult for her to be as altruistic as she liked to think herself to be. She decided she would push all thoughts of him from her mind as much as she could and concentrate solely on finding a way out of the base as quickly as she could.

Her footsteps echoed as she descended the stairs from her apartment to the stores building below and went through the empty building to open up. After unlocking and rolling up the shutters, she switched off the alarm and went to make herself a hot drink while she waited for Gage and the other stores staff to arrive. She was early, having not slept at all well during the night, so she thought she would take the time to check the coming day's schedule. Three deliveries were due and one major shipment was to go out. One of the military units was leaving on a survival training exercise and needed two week's rations and medical kits, and the military section kitchens needed their weekly stock up.

The sound of the door opening and closing echoed through the empty stores and Risa went through from her tiny staff kitchen to see who it was. Narek's big brown eyes met her gaze, his lips automatically finding a smile.

"Hello Risa, you're open early today."

"Hi Narek, how can I help you?" she replied, her heart falling. Having only just decided to try to push him from her mind, seeing him so soon almost made her burst into tears. She did not want to see him; she could not help but think of Lorella whenever she thought of him, and as she gazed into his big brown eyes, thoughts of them together filled her mind.

"I've brought the lists from the military section. One for the normal weekly stock up and one for the unit I'm taking out on exercise. I saw you were open early, I hope you don't mind me dropping by."

"Not at all, that's fine," she took the lists from him and checked them. "What time do you need the stock for your unit?"

"We're leaving right after lunch, so if we can be all stocked by mid-day that would be great."

"No problem, I'll make sure the guys do your job first so you should have it by the middle of the morning."

"That's wonderful, thank you." Narek looked into her eyes and Risa saw a slight frown crease his brow. "Is everything okay? You look worried about something."

For a moment, she almost blurted it all out. Those big brown eyes almost broke her resolve but she checked herself just in time by looking down at the list in her hands. "Oh uh, yeah I'm fine. I didn't sleep very well that's all."

"Is there a problem? Can I help with anything?"

Again, Risa found herself tempted to tell him the news Lorella had given her the night before but held her tongue just in time and forced a smile.

"No, I'll be fine once I've had a drink and some breakfast. Thanks for asking though."

"Okay but you can come to me if you have a problem. Remember that huh?"

"I will, thanks Narek."

Before he could press the point, Gage came in, the spell was broken, and Risa sighed inwardly with relief. If Narek pushed much further she would have a problem holding on to her secret. She mentally cursed his ability to notice the subtle changes that gave away people's moods. Gage handed her a paper bag containing the usual morning breakfast rolls and said hello to Narek. Then he looked at Risa.

"You okay girl? You look like you've pulled an all-nighter."

"I didn't sleep too well," she replied. "Must've been something I ate." She tried to smile but Narek knew she was faking it and he was worried.

"Hey Gage, I'm off on an exercise with a unit today, so you take care of this girl okay?"

"I will Sarge," Gage replied and gave a very bad salute. "Sir yes Sir," he shouted and Narek could not help but laugh. He turned and left, knowing that

Risa had lied about being all right. He wished Gage had not come in; if they had been alone a moment longer, he might have been able to encourage her to open up to him. His brow creased with worry as he walked back to the military sector to rouse his recruits for their training exercise and knew that this coming two weeks would be agony for him.

Lorella smiled as she made her way to the stores. If all went as it should, today would see Risa's plan to snatch Narek from her, finally fail. The building seemed quiet as she entered and she wondered where everyone was. Footsteps behind her made her spin around.

"Hello Lorella," Risa said. "How can we help you?"

"Here's the manifest for the delivery today," Lorella replied, handing Risa a three-page document. "It'll be a couple of hours late. Apparently the ship had a problem with its main drive and they had to make a hasty repair."

"Okay, no problem, thanks," Risa replied and turned away, heading for her office.

"Can I share something with you?" Lorella asked.

Risa was surprised and annoyed that her sister had followed her into her office rather than take the hint and leave, but she feigned another smile.

"Sure, what's up?"

"Last night, he gave me this," Lorella grinned and handed Risa a small photograph. "It was taken out the back of the club where no one could see us so it's a bit dark, but he wanted to capture the moment." Risa looked into Narek's handsome face as he snuggled up to a grinning Lorella, the floodlights giving them both a strange cast to their skins. Her heart breaking, Risa smiled as she handed it back.

"That's lovely Lorella, congratulations."

"He told me he loved me. I thought I was going to faint."

"I'm not surprised," Risa replied, unable to restrain herself from wondering how she would react in such a situation.

"He's so handsome and so loving. He just loves snuggling and kissing. We're going to be so happy together."

"Spare me the icky stuff please," Risa said in an attempt at light heartedness that she did not feel.

Once Gage returned from overseeing the military section's delivery, Risa went out to buy something for her lunch. She saw a small crowd gathered at the fence that separated the military section from the rest of the base and went to see what was going on. Narek and his unit were stocking their ship for their training exercise while wives and girlfriends stood at the fence, waving goodbye. As she turned to leave, she noticed Lorella amongst the crowd, waving frantically. Risa hurried away, she could not face another conversation with her sister about how wonderful Narek's kissing was.

With her sandwich in hand, Risa exited the shop and headed back to the stores to await the main delivery. The sound of an engine overhead made her look up and see a military ship heading away from the base.

"Goodbye Narek," she whispered silently. "I love you."

The afternoon dragged on and Risa tried to occupy herself so that thoughts of Narek would not intrude upon her mind. Once the main delivery turned up she found herself sufficiently busy for several hours and it was closing time before she remembered his smile again. She said goodnight to Gage and went upstairs to her apartment to get changed for her run and workout. Four hours later, tired and sweaty, she showered and got herself a high protein dinner from her nutri-vend machine and logged into the galactic web to research possible opportunities to leave Luzel 2.

The days wore on, one very much like another and by the end of the week, several people had noticed her change of mood and asked her if she was okay. She was able to brush off their concerns with anything from a sleepless night to a stomach bug and so far, no one had pushed the point. Each night she searched the galactic web for any ideas as to how she could get away from Luzel 2 but so far, she'd come up with nothing. It was not until the seventh day after Narek's departure on his training exercise that her solution presented itself and at first, she turned away from it in fear. As she was returning from delivering the week's manifests to her sister in the administration office, she saw a large area of the military section being cleared and fenced off. People were standing around watching and she asked someone what was going on.

"It's that time of year again Risa," the woman said. "They've come back again. Doesn't time fly huh?"

"Who?" Risa asked.

"The Fa'ahlima," the woman replied. "They're here on their yearly recruiting drive."

Risa stood, everyone around her disappearing as an icy shiver ran down her spine. The base went silent and it was as though she were the only person on Luzel 2 as thoughts raced around her head, melded into an idea that she instinctively drew back from in fear. The Fa'ahlima visited many planets on a roughly yearly cycle to recruit volunteers to go with them to their planet Fa'ahla to work. No one knew what work they did and no one knew anyone who had ever returned. There were countless rumours, many of them involving tales of slavery, torture and all sorts of miseries but no one knew the truth. No one knew much at all about the Fa'ahlima as they tended to keep themselves to themselves. Risa had become used to this yearly event but still the sight of them instilled fear into her, even though they had never given her reason to fear them.

Although obviously humanoid, the Fa'ahlima were very different from the humanoid races Risa had met and it was this that caused most people's initial fear. They were tall, nearly seven feet and their heads and faces were strange. The Fa'ahlima have pale grey skin with a waxy appearance and very large, totally black, oval eyes. Their faces have a distinct ridge down the front, making the nose and chin seem very protuberant, their cheeks and eyes therefore being ever so slightly side facing rather than front facing. This very alien appearance made it hard for other races to feel comfortable with them and so most people just avoided them when they could, the rumours of their treatment of volunteers giving weight to the people's fears. Every time the Fa'ahlima had visited, the routine was the same. Arriving on a roughly yearly cycle, they stayed for two days, the rear hatch of their ship guarded by two guards. They used the base's facilities freely and were always polite to everyone. Whilst on the base, their ship was refuelled and restocked with supplies and they spent their evenings sat around campfires talking with the cargo of volunteers they had gleaned from the other planets they had visited. On the morning of their departure, the rear hatch opened and the guard doubled to four. One hour before departure a horn would sound, the low sonorous note continuing for the whole hour and signalling that they were ready to receive volunteers. Anyone wishing to go with the Fa'ahlima would simply walk through the gap in the fence and state their intention to volunteer to the guards, who would indicate for them to enter the hatch. Once volunteered, there was no going back and as far as anyone knew, no one ever returned.

At first Risa was horrified that the thought had even occurred to her but as the next day and night passed, she began to wonder about these strange people. They were always polite, she had never heard anyone talk of them fighting or being rude or aggressive, and she began to wonder if all the rumours she had heard about them were true or not. The following morning she decided to try to get to talk with one of them and see how she felt then. Her chance came when she went on her daily lunch trip, where she found herself almost bumping headlong into one of them as she exited the shop with her sandwich.

"Oh I'm so sorry," she said in a rush. "I wasn't looking where I was going. Forgive me."

"There is nothing to forgive," a distinctly male voice replied. "You were deep in thought, not reckless."

"Yes," she nodded. "Very deep just lately." Despite her best efforts, her eyes misted over and she felt a lump rise in her throat as she gazed into the huge black eyes of the Fa'ahlima man.

"You find yourself at a crossroads in your life," he continued. Risa nodded sadly. "There is much pain in your heart." She nodded again. "Whichever way you choose, you know some pain will have to be endured." Another nod. "The answer lies in knowing which pain is the lesser, not looking for a way without pain. Once you decide that, you will know which road to take." Risa's eyes widened and her mouth opened as the wisdom of his words sank in and he smiled.

"Thank you," she replied quietly. "You have helped me to know what to do."

The strange man with the huge black eyes put a hand over his heart and bowed his head forward to her. As she walked back to the stores to continue her afternoon, she felt a small weight lifted from her shoulders and a new purpose take shape within her mind. When Gage looked up from the boxes he was entering into the manifest, he saw a smile on her face he had not seen in days. Risa tried hard to concentrate on work during the afternoon but her mind was far away and many times she found herself staring into space when she should have been working.

She ran the perimeter fence in her best time ever, her mind full of questions, and her heart heavy but resolved. She was fearful, terrified even, but glad to have found a new direction, one that would take her far away from the pain she knew she would be unable to endure for much longer. Nothing could be worse than staying on Luzel and watching Narek and Lorella getting cosy, and so she controlled her fearful imaginings. She spent extra time on her workout, unsure if she would ever get the chance to enjoy another, and by the time she was back in her apartment, showered and had eaten her dinner, she knew what she was doing was the only solution open to her. The decision having been made, she resolved to look upon it as the right thing to do.

She slept surprisingly well that night and awoke more refreshed than she could remember in weeks. After packing a couple of changes of clothes into a backpack, together with a few precious possessions, she took a last look around her apartment and headed downstairs to open up the stores. Once Gage arrived with the usual breakfast rolls, she slipped out to the communication office and posted the letter, before heading to the administration office to collect the delivery schedule from her sister.

"I was just about to come over with them," Lorella said, surprised to see her sister smiling and looking happy.

"Oh not to worry, I thought I'd save you the bother."

"Here they are, just one shipment today. It should be here by mid-day."

"Okay, thanks."

"By the way," Lorella whispered. "The night before Narek left with his unit we umm, you know," she raised her eyebrows in emphasis. "Our first time and wow, Narek is wonderful."

"Good," Risa replied. "I'm glad for you Lorella. Enjoy him and be good to him, please. He's a very sensitive and caring man with a huge heart and he doesn't deserve to be hurt. I wish you both every happiness."

"Thanks," Lorella replied, taken aback by Risa's comments.

Risa was finishing a hot drink when the horn sounded, making her jump so hard she nearly spilt the hot liquid down her front. Her heart leapt in her breast, pounding with apprehension. The moment had arrived, this was it. Should she do it or should she allow her fears to control her? Could she remain here with Narek and Lorella so close? She remembered what the Fa'ahlima man had told her; decide which way is the lesser pain and that is the way to go. She sat there and finished her drink, listening to the low sonorous note of the Fa'ahlima horn and watched out the window as the crowd gathered, as it always did each time this strange race visited their world. Everyone wanted to see if this year, someone would volunteer and leave with the Fa'ahlima into a secret world of rumour and speculation, never to return. No one from Luzel 2 had ever volunteered, not in Risa's memory anyway and she suddenly felt embarrassed at the knowledge that the whole base would be watching her in a few minutes. With a sigh, she got up from her seat and reached for her backpack, swinging it onto her shoulder as she took a last look around the stores and headed for the open main door.

"Goodbye Narek," she said quietly to the silent room. "I hope she doesn't break your heart. I will always love you."

The crowd gasped in shock as they saw Risa, head high and shoulders back, striding purposefully towards the Fa'ahlima guards. Silence fell upon the base until nothing but Risa's soft boot steps could be heard. She approached the guards and looked first at one, and then the other, square in those huge black eyes.

"I want to leave with you."

The moment Narek and his team landed on their return from their training exercise, he knew something was wrong. There was a feeling of heaviness in the atmosphere that touched his mind the moment he stepped down from the ship to help his men unload. He reported to his commanding officer and sent the men off to unpack in their quarters, before heading to his own room to unpack and shower. Everyone he spoke to seemed subdued, as if they had something on their minds that prevented them from giving him their full attention. He answered a knock on his door to find Kaylak and Vronil standing there, their eyes brimming with tears.

"Come on in guys," he said. "What's up? You both look awful, what's happened?"

"Estriwa eialla manuk," Kaylak whispered. "I'm so sorry brother."

"Mwara manuk, mwara?" Narek demanded. "What brother, what?"

"Reliopale, reliopale," Vronil replied. "She's gone, she's gone."

"Reliopak? Kwana?" Narek demanded. "Gone? Who?"

"Risa. Reliopale." Risa. She's gone."

Narek felt the breath leave his lungs and a chill curl its fingers around his heart at Vronil's words. Where had she gone and why?

"Reliopale? luaiya, li situ?" he asked when he could speak. "She's gone? Where, with who?"

"Reliopale maiy ko Fa'ahlima," Kaylak said. "She's gone with the Fa'ahlima."

This was the last thing Narek expected to hear and the shock hit him like a bullet in the gut. He stumbled and sat down on his bed, his eyes still wide as he tried and failed to comprehend why she would do such a thing.

A.W.O.L

Kaylak and Vronil sat with him and told him all they knew, which was precious little; just that Risa had left with the Fa'ahlima five days ago and had told no one of her plan. They told him how they saw her approach the guards and exchange brief words with them, before they stepped aside to let her pass. They told him how they tried to run from where they had been watching to catch her and stop her, but the window of the mess room was on the other side of the military compound. By the time they got there, the guards blocked their way and no amount of pleading would persuade them to let them through to talk to her.

"Estriwa eialla manuk, estriwa eialla," Kaylak said as he cried. "I'm so sorry brother, I'm so sorry."

The three sat for over an hour discussing every reason they could think of as to why Risa would do such a thing, but the only explanation Narek could come up with, was that it had something to do with the vow of abstinence Lorella had told him about. Kaylak was about to suggest they spend an hour praying to Laminawa, the Vendalan God of knowledge and understanding, when there was a knock at the door. Vronil went to answer it and found one of the civilian mailroom employees standing there.

"Yes?"

"Letter for Sergeant Jenn," he said, offering Vronil the small envelope and a data input pad. "Sign for acceptance please Sir."

"Thank you," Vronil replied as he signed and handed back the data pad. He closed the door and handed the letter to Narek. Narek did not recognise the handwriting; he seldom got letters from anyone. His family back on Vendala always used the military vidicom channel to send video messages. Apart from a couple of anonymous love letters a couple of months ago, which he had ignored, this was his first letter in nearly a year. He tore it open and read it silently. By the time he dropped his head into his hands and cried, the letter was stained with his tears.

"Manuk?" Kaylak enquired. "Brother?"

Narek handed him the letter and Kaylak read it aloud.

'My darling Narek.

This is my fourth attempt at writing this letter and somehow, the words always come out wrong. It's no easier telling you in a letter than I imagine it would be face to face. I have three things to tell you. First, I want to thank you for being so beautiful that you light up my whole day whenever I see your face and the way you smile. You have always been nice to me and I want you to know I will remember and treasure every word you've ever given me. Second, I have to tell you that someone has betrayed you and your culture and as you are someone I care about, I can't let you go into something so important without being fully informed. I have researched Vendalan customs and I know how important honesty is between a man and the woman he chooses for his own. I also know it is your custom to keep a romantic relationship secret for the first little while, until you decide it is the right time to make a public announcement about it.

I'm sorry Narek, but Lorella betrayed you and told me about your relationship with her. I'm telling you this because I know her very well and I don't want you to be hurt before you can't back out of the situation. She showed me a photograph of the two of you together and she told me when you first made love. She swore me to secrecy but I have betrayed her confidence, as she betrayed yours. Be happy Narek, be happy with the one you have chosen, but be careful. Please be careful. I will be gone from Luzel 2 by the time you get back and I will not be returning. I cannot remain here seeing you every day, knowing you and Lorella are together.

Yes Narek, that's the third thing I have to tell you. I have loved you since the first day you arrived at the base and got lost when you were looking for the communication centre, remember that? You asked me for directions and as I looked into your beautiful face, I knew I would never be able to love any other man. So often I've wished that you would ask me out or show some interest in me, but you never did and I was too shy to make the first move, and always assumed that you weren't interested. That's okay, I understand completely. I'm nothing to look at and have no social skills whatsoever, so why would someone like you choose me? I'm strong enough to wish you and Lorella every happiness, and mean it from the bottom of my heart. When you genuinely love someone, you want them to be happy and if that happiness can only be found with someone else, then I wish you love and happiness. I'm not strong enough to remain here and see you doing it though. That would be beyond my strength, so I have decided to volunteer to leave with the Fa'ahlima, who arrived seven days after you left with your unit for the training exercise. Please remember me with affection Narek, that's all I ask.

Be happy in all that you do. I will always love you.
Risa Parks.'

A.W.O.L

Narek felt the anger rise in his gut, twisting his insides into a painful knot. He clutched his hand to his belly and groaned aloud, his eyes squeezing shut as the fire swept up through his heart and roared out of his mouth in a scream of anguish. Kaylak and Vronil sat with him and shared his anguish, promised to be at his side as brothers and pledged their souls to help him heal as his own soul broke into two pieces. Narek wanted to take the Tal ak Roi right there and then, to end his life so his own half soul would not be doomed to the Kon so Fahl for eternity, but Kaylak and Vronil beseeched him to hold on and share their own souls until they could find out if there was anything they could do. Narek knew he could not refuse their gift, for to do so would be to damn their souls alongside his own, so he accepted and allowed them both to bond their own souls together with his own half soul. An hour later, Kaylak and Vronil placed a clipping of their hair and a drop of their blood onto a circle of fabric, gathered it together and bound it tightly with cord. After sharing prayers, Narek allowed them to tie it around his neck. In this simple but ultimately binding ceremony, Kaylak and Vronil shared their souls with him and kept him from the Tal ak Roi. Narek felt their strength filtering into him as he gave himself up to the bond he knew he could never break without damning his friends to the pit of sorrow, and felt his anguish move a little further back.

"Swan kiahi manukichi. En niahai sakrichi." he whispered. "Thank you brothers. I feel your souls."

The club was crowded when Narek walked in with Kaylak and Vronil. Lorella looked up and grinned, her crudely red lips splitting her face in half as she slid off her stool and staggered towards them, arms open wide. Before she was halfway across the room, Narek exploded and the bar fell silent.

"Don't you come near me. Don't ever come near me."

Lorella stopped mid stride, her arms dropping to her sides as her smile faltered. She looked around the room and realised everyone was watching her. Despite herself, she felt her cheeks flush with embarrassment.

"What's up guys? I just wanted to welcome you home."

"How could you do such a thing?" Narek demanded, taking a step nearer. "Why? Tell me why?"

"What?" Lorella asked, despite having a sneaking suspicion that she knew what was coming.

"Is there a problem here guys?" the barman asked.

"This woman," Narek said, pointing at Lorella. "This, Doriel, this whore, told Risa that she and I were dating and now Risa has gone with the Fa'ahlima and will never return."

Audible gasps went around the room and despite Lorella's protestations, her blushing told them the truth. Narek took another step towards her and this time, Lorella took one back.

"There is only one woman I could ever give my heart to, and now she's gone and I am doomed to the Kon so Fahl for eternity. Now I have only half a soul and it is all your fault. You disgust me. Estrillie doriel. You are a whore." Narek turned and left, Kaylak and Vronil by his side and behind them, the bar remained in awkward silence for several minutes. Lorella returned to her stool by the bar but found the soldiers she had been drinking with, mysteriously disappeared.

Narek and his friends walked back towards the military compound in silence until a voice calling his name stopped them in their tracks. They turned to see a young man running towards them.

"Narek, stop a minute please."

"What?" Narek replied.

"I uh, I was blackmailed by Lorella into helping her with her plan to dupe Risa into believing you and she were dating. I uh, I made a mistake and some funds went missing a while back. I paid it back eventually but Lorella found out and said if I didn't help her out, she would report me and I'd lose my job. I didn't want to but I need this job, my wife is sick and needs expensive medication and without this job she'll die."

"What did you do?" Kaylak asked.

"She made me fake a photograph of you and her together. I took one of the shots from your military file and pasted a shot of her into it so it looked like you and she were embracing. I'm really sorry. I hated doing it but she had me by the balls. Please understand."

"Thank you for your truth," Narek said. "You paid for your mistake twice over. Now you won't make the same mistake again."

"Never."

"Can your wife not be treated by the base hospital?" Vronil asked.

"I can't yet afford to bring them here from my home world," the man replied. "I send most of my pay back so my son can buy her medication but that doesn't leave me much to save for a transport here."

"Where is your home world?" Kaylak asked.

"Coroptima 8."

"Give me your name and home address," Narek asked. "I'll have a word around and see if I can help."

"You'd do that for me? After what I did to you?" the man asked, his eyes welling up. "I don't deserve that."

"You're wife deserves it, and your truth has earned it," Narek replied.

"I don't know what to say," the man said as he handed Narek his name and home address. "But I can tell you that the Fa'ahlima always call into Coroptima 8 around now. I remember my son telling me that several people from my town have volunteered over the past few years. Maybe they've gone there straight from here. Is that information of any use to you? Maybe you could chase after them or something."

Narek's eyes opened wide as the man's words filtered through to his consciousness, allowing a spark of hope to come into being. He took the man's hand and gripped it tightly.

"Thank you my friend. Thank you."

Merita King

CHAPTER THREE

"No Sergeant, absolutely out of the question." The Base Military Commander glowered at Narek.

Sergeant Major Cable had been appointed Base Commander just six months ago, his untarnished record within the Inter-Galactic Military Force assuring him the position for the last five years of his career. Originally from Earth, Cable, as Base Commander, had the right to address his men by the military designations he recognised if he so wished, and always addressed Narek as Sergeant, despite him being a Lashen in the Vendalan Army.

"You're off with a unit tomorrow for survival training. There's no way to find another Sergeant at such short notice without calling someone off leave, and the only two other Sergeants we have are both off world right now."

"But Sir," Narek began but Cable cut him off by raising a hand.

"Narek. Sit down. Let's drop the formalities for a minute huh? You're my best Sergeant and I give you far more leeway than anyone else on this base. I know I can trust you and your decisions and if it was possible to find someone else, I wouldn't hesitate to allow it."

"Thank you Beganzi," Narek nodded, using the Vendalan term for his boss's military designation. "It's just that Risa has gone and I didn't know she felt the same way as I do, and if I can't find her, I'll be damned with half a soul for eternity. Kaylak and Vronil did a soul binding with me last night to keep me from the Tal ak Roi, which means I am doomed to the Kon so Fahl when I die. They are good men, honourable brothers and first class soldiers and I want to release them from their binding."

"I won't disrespect you by pretending to know much about Vendalan customs Narek, but I will look you in the eyes and tell you I respect any man with a strong faith in God, no matter what name he gives to his deity. Despite this grizzled face you see before you, I also have some experience in matters of the heart, so I can honestly say I empathise with your predicament."

"So how am I to proceed?" Narek pleaded.

"Like I said, I cannot approve your request for time off, I'm sorry. You are to take your unit for the scheduled three week survival training exercise as planned."

"But Sir."

"But," Cable commanded. "Hear me out Sergeant. As is your right, as commander of your unit, where you take your men for this exercise is your choice. Historically, we've always used the more remote areas here on Luzel 2, but there is no ruling that says you must follow suit. Do you understand me?"

"Oh yes," Narek whispered, his eyes welling up. "I understand completely. I will do as you command Sir."

"Good," Cable nodded and extended a hand, which Narek shook. "I knew I could rely on my best soldier."

"Thank you Beganzi, you honour me with your trust."

The eight soldiers stood to attention and waited for Narek to address them. Kaylak and Vronil, as Narek's Tinash and Prelam, the Vendalan equivalent of Corporal and Lance Corporal, stood slightly to one side, one at the end of each row of four men. Narek walked up and down the two rows, checking their dress and weapons, correcting a collar here, a cap there, before returning to the front to address them.

"For the next three weeks you will all be required to pull together as a team. Your survival depends upon it. One day you will be active soldiers and may be required to enter war zones on worlds very different to those you may have experienced before. Surviving not only means finding food, water and shelter, it can often mean interacting with the indigenous population in such a way as to get you to your goal. That goal may be simply to return to your unit, it may be to get off the planet safely, it may be to observe an enemy's movements or gain information. There will be times when you will need to think quickly and act without hesitation when you don't have the luxury of time enough to ask your superior officers for advice or orders. You may be the only survivors of a military ship that has crashed on a planet where the indigenous population are extremely hostile, or there may not be an indigenous humanoid population at all. You could be faced with all manner of dangerous creatures bent on having you for breakfast. This is your first basic survival exercise, so we will assume that you eight men are the only survivors of a large company. You will not be doing solo survival on this trip so don't worry, but you will need to pull together, elect a leader in the absence of a superior officer and then follow his orders without question. As that elected leader, you will need to be able to make fast decisions for the defence of your men; you will need to inspire them to trust your judgement and follow your orders, knowing that those orders are the correct ones for that situation. Any arguments and internal jockeying for position could cost men's lives. Any questions?"

"Where are we going Sergeant?" a young lad named Dodge asked.

"We will be going first to Coroptima 8. Your mission there is information gathering. We won't know our next destination until your mission on Coroptima is completed."

"What information are we seeking Sarge?" a big lad named Esclan asked.

"We need to know two things," Narek replied. "First, we want to know if the Fa'ahlima have been there. Second, if they have been and they've since gone, we need to know where they went."

"The Fa'ahlima Sarge?" Dodge called. "Why are we chasing them?"

Narek faltered at this question. Although this unit of men had become like friends to him, he was not sure about letting them know about Risa and his feelings for her just yet. Kaylak noticed his hesitation.

"We are going to try to retrieve, or at least speak with Risa Parks. There was a situation between her and her sister Lorella a few days ago that resulted in Risa leaving with the Fa'ahlima. To cut a long story short, Risa was lied to, and because of those lies, she left Luzel 2. We feel it is right to inform her of the truth so that she can rethink her decision. Then at least if she continues on with the Fa'ahlima, it will be on a basis of truth rather than lies."

"I saw her leave Sarge," a tall thin man named Ciorrin said. "She looked real sad when she spoke with the guards and I thought at the time that it seemed as if she wanted to escape something. It was weird; it wasn't that she looked like she was going on an exciting adventure, like you'd expect, but as if she was running from something."

"You are very observant," Narek nodded. "She was running and that is why we want to find her. Okay then let's be off, who's first at the stick?"

"I am Sarge," a big man named Noro replied. "We've agreed four hours in the pilot's seat each. Is that okay?"

"That's fine," Narek nodded.

The ship headed up into the light cloud of the Luzel 2 sky and headed for the upper atmosphere. Narek flipped the comms switch when he heard the crackle from the intercom.

"LMB72 this is Luzel 2 Base 7 Air Traffic Control. We have you on our scanner as leaving the atmosphere. Our data has you on a scheduled training exercise. Please state your destination."

"Luzel 2 Air Traffic Control, this is LMB72, Sergeant Narek Jenn confirming. We are headed for Coroptima 8 to begin our training exercise."

"Safe journey Sergeant. See you in three weeks. Luzel 2 Air Traffic Control out."

The void of space opened up around them and as always, the men looked out of the ship's windows and all fell silent for a moment. Narek looked and smiled. No matter how often a man travels the cosmos, it is always a humbling experience, he thought to himself as he remembered the first time he went into space as a raw recruit in the Vendalan military. His friends in his unit had teased him for months about how he cried when he first saw Vendala 4 shining below him from his vantage point at the tiny window of a military shuttlecraft. He was a sensitive man and felt it right that everyone be made aware of their insignificance from time to time.

"Never let that sight become anything less than a wonder to behold," he said aloud. "It is in a man's nature to regard himself as the highest of beings in creation, but never let yourselves forget that we are but a speck in an infinite universe. It will help to keep your ego in check when it tries to get out of hand, as it tends to do sometimes. Perspective my friends."

"It's amazing Sarge," Esclan said quietly. "When I first left Amintep 6 when I joined the military, I never imagined my world was so beautiful. Everyone knows space is big but its, well Sarge, it's just too big to put into words."

Narek nodded. "I had the same experience myself."

"We're clear of Luzel 2 airspace Sarge," Noro called from the cockpit. "Ready to engage the TFC."

"Go," Narek replied. "Time is of the essence so let's not waste any." Noro pressed a switch and the Trans Wave Flow Core began to spin. Within seconds a quiet hum echoed softly through the ship and rose in pitch until, with a ping, the ship leapt through space at top speed.

"How long till we reach Coroptima?" Narek called.

"Thirty one hours at top speed Sarge," Noro replied.

"Okay. First we work out a pilot rota, then a cooking rota," Narek said. "Then I vote we have a meal and discuss what we know about the situation and how to proceed. Noro, yell if you need anything."

"Yes Sir. Course is laid in and autopilot is on. She's flying herself really."

"You'll be relieved in four hours. To the mess room guys," Narek smiled.

Over a basic but filling meal, they discussed what they knew of the Fa'ahlima, which was precious little. The conversation yielded only what everyone knew about this secretive race; that they visited worlds on their chosen route roughly once a year and took volunteers away with them. The rumours surrounding what these volunteers did were many and varied, and all made Narek scared for Risa and desperate to find her.

"We obviously need to find out more about the Fa'ahlima if we can," Narek said and everyone nodded. "So I want two volunteers to spend our time on Coroptima doing some discreet but thorough research."

"I'll do it," Ciorrin said. "I was going to be a research scientist before I saw a movie about a guy who went into the military to escape his boring life, and had the most fantastic adventures, all involving beautiful women. That kinda turned my head I guess."

"I'll go with him," a serious looking man named Ribas said. "I know a bit about computers so if there are any records, I might be able to bypass any security."

"Great, thanks guys," Narek nodded. "Now our cover story is that we're on a survival exercise but we stopped on the way to sort out some emergency military transport for the wife of a base employee on Luzel 2. He helped me out the other night with information that the Fa'ahlima usually call in around this time of year, and he told me his wife is sick. Her medication has to be bought off world as it's not manufactured on Coroptima and is hugely expensive. If she could go to the base with him, his costs would be reduced enormously and the base hospital may even be able to help her."

"I'd be good for that Sarge," Dodge offered. "As head medic of this unit, my word might carry a little weight."

"Good thinking," Kaylak smiled.

"Okay," Narek said. "Dodge, Kaylak, Vronil and I will liaise with the military and try to persuade them to arrange an emergency transport for her. The rest of you guys get the ship's cells refuelled and get us stocked with fresh water. We're fine for food and ammunition but always keep the ship charged and the water tanks full. I know it's basic stuff, but remember that in future, fuel and water are your first supply priorities. You can survive without food for a good long time but you must have water and fuel will help you escape."

"Yes Sir," they replied in unison.

"Once we've secured the transport, we'll go visit the family and let them know so they can prepare. Hopefully we'll be in and out in no more than a day."

During the afternoon, Narek, Kaylak and Vronil tested the men on military regulations, gave them various scenarios and had them discuss how they might proceed as a tight unit working together. When Narek told them that all of them but Dodge, as head medic, had fallen victim to some strange affliction on an uninhabited world, Dodge's reply had them laughing aloud.

"I guess I'd put them all out of their misery, steal the ship and become a Merc," he replied with a shrug. "After giving them a decent burial of course."

"You're all heart buddy," Ciorrin laughed.

"Well done guys," Narek said. "Now let's relax for a while before we eat."

"Anyone fancy a few games of Tapshots?" Esclan said, taking a pair of dice from a pocket.

"Not me," Narek said. "I lost too much the last time I played with you. I'm going to write up the day's report. Call me if you need me."

Narek got up and walked the corridor to his bunk, sitting down with a sigh. Closing his eyes, he thought back to his last exchange of words with Risa and cursed himself for not pushing her to tell him what was on her mind. He knew she was worried about something; he had always been able to read people's emotions from their facial expressions and no one could lie to him convincingly. If only he had asked her what was wrong, asked her for a coffee so they could talk longer, maybe she would have told him the truth then and all this could have been avoided. The day he returned from that training exercise, he had known something was wrong the minute he stepped from the ship. His hand found Risa's letter in his pocket and he read it again, his tears splashing onto the floor of the ship.

"*Estriwa eialla re chalosa. Reil filamak, reil laiwai re shinal. Reil tilariwa.*" he whispered. "I'm so sorry my darling. I will find you, I give you my word. I love you."

Wiping his eyes, Narek carefully folded the letter and put it back into his pocket. An hour later, he switched off his digital console and stretched his back before getting up and going to find the men. Kaylak grinned with triumph when he reported how he had won a substantial sum of money from three games of Tapshots and Narek clapped him on the back.

"Well done Manuk. You fared better than I. Now I must remember never to play you at that game either. My social opportunities are getting smaller by the day."

"It was just luck Sarge," Dodge declared. "I'll get it all back and more besides, you wait and see."

"It was not luck," Kaylak replied. "Well not totally. Maybe a little."

"It was sheer luck Manuk," Vronil grinned and everyone laughed.

After their evening meal, Ribas started to sing, his deep velvet voice ringing throughout the ship and everyone listened in silence. Although the words were foreign to them all, the heartfelt emotions came through to each one and Narek knew it was a song of heartfelt love between the singer and his chosen one.

"That was beautiful," he said when Ribas finished. "Tell us what the words mean."

"Thanks Sarge," Ribas replied. "It is a traditional wedding song from Nepsilus 2, where my wife is from. During the wedding ceremony, the man sings the woman a song, telling her how much he loves her and what he promises her for their life together. In this song, the one I sang to my wife when we got married, the man tells her she is the breath in his lungs and without her, he would not be able to breathe and would die. He tells her she is the wind that carries the clouds across the sky, that she is the sun giving warmth to life upon the world, and that she is the rain falling from the sky that gives life to everything. He tells her that just as the world cannot survive without the warmth from the sun, the water from the rain and the blue sky visible only when the wind takes away the clouds, he cannot survive without her. He promises always to protect her from harm, to be the stable foundation beneath from which she can grow and flourish, and to worship her body that gives him joy and blesses them with children. He pledges his life for her love and promises himself to the fulfilment of her joy."

"That's lovely," Narek said. "If I should ever be able to marry the woman I love, will you sing that for us at our ceremony?"

"I'd be honoured Sir," Ribas nodded.

"With a voice like that, you could be an inter-galactic singing star instead of in the military," Damir said and several heads nodded in agreement.

"You'd certainly earn more," Vronil said.

"Oh the celebrity life is not one I hanker for," Ribas smiled. "I've always wanted to be a soldier. My father served, my grandfather served, as did the previous eleven generations of my family. It's all I've ever wanted to do. Singing is something that gives me pleasure and brings joy to people. It should never be thought of as a job. That would somehow kill its magic, don't you think?"

"I never thought of it like that before," Kaylak said, "but you have a point."

"Well how about a movie before we hit the sack?" Noro suggested and everyone nodded.

"What do we have on board?" Marikos asked as he got up and went over to the portable vidicom player.

"Anything that's not going to keep me awake all night," Vronil said.

"Okay, so no monsters," Marikos replied and everyone laughed.

"And no screaming women either," Dodge called. "I can't bear women that spend the entire movie screaming."

"How about this," Marikos said. "This is from way back. It's a historical thing from back before vidicoms or holographic streamers. Some superhero tale about a guy from another planet who can fly through the air and who goes around capturing bad guys and saving his home world from destruction. Oh but on second thoughts, it'll probably have screaming women in it. How about this one then. Population Zero. Some guy has to find this other guy who has stolen some dangerous pathogen from a lab and is threatening to let it loose."

"Isn't that one of that Elloway guy's movies?" Damir asked and Ciorrin nodded.

"Yeah," Ciorrin said. "And it's one of his best too. No monsters and not too many screaming women either. Just those famous blue eyes and six pack that always saves the day."

"Okay, let's have that one then," Narek said. "Anyone object?"

Narek climbed into his bunk at three in the morning, after doing his four hour turn in the cockpit and tried to settle his mind enough to sleep. His thoughts, as always, were of Risa. Whatever may have befallen her at the hands of the Fa'ahlima, he could not imagine, and he worried for her so much that it hurt. All the stories of the Fa'ahlima's treatment of their volunteers raced through his mind and he prayed that she was not being harmed. If she died while in their employ, he would take the Tal ak Roi and no torment his half soul could endure would be sufficient to take away his guilt at having caused such a tragedy. His last thought before a troubled and fitful sleep overcame him, was to beseech the god Alima to reunite him with Risa.

Narek awoke to someone gently shaking his shoulder.

"Manuk, wake up," Kaylak said as Narek opened his eyes and yawned. "I've saved you some breakfast. I got the men onto some unarmed combat practice to keep them occupied."

"Huh? Okay, thanks Manuk," Narek groaned as he dragged himself up. "What time is it?"

"Just after nine."

"It feels like I only just went to sleep."

"I know," Kaylak said. "Try not to worry too much. We will find her. One way or another, you will have your moment with her. Leave the worrying until there is no other choice okay?"

"How can I not worry? I caused all this. If I had spoken to her earlier, none of this would have happened. What is she going through with the Fa'ahlima? She may be in some terrible circumstance with them; she could even be dead by now."

"We cannot know. No one knows anything about them or how they treat the volunteers. Don't let all the rumours and fireside stories trouble your mind. Every time they've come to Luzel 2 they have been friendly and non-violent haven't they?"

"Yes, they've never caused any trouble with anyone that I know of," Narek agreed.

"Then keep that knowledge at the front of your mind and forget those silly rumours. You know people; when you've looked into the faces of the Fa'ahlima, have you ever seen violence or cruelty?"

"None," Narek replied. "They always seem wise and friendly to me. Despite their secrecy, I would trust them if I had to."

"Then trust them now, and remember Vronil and I have bonded our souls with yours. You do not suffer alone with this."

"*Swan kiahi Manuk. Amliokril ashmiraksi.*" Narek nodded. "Thank you so much Brother. I will try to remember."

After eating his late breakfast, Narek joined his men in unarmed combat practice and sparred with them. It helped him forget his woes for a while and the physical exertion helped expunge some of the anger he still felt within. The dark knot in his gut was becoming physically painful and made him feel ill. The exercise made him feel a lot better and when they finished, he was sweating heavily and breathing hard. Several of the men would carry bruises for a few days from the experience, but all would benefit from the challenge. Once everyone was showered and dressed, Narek told them to relax until they reached Coroptima.

"Relax now guys. I hope I didn't hurt anyone too much."

"Not at all Sarge," Damir said. "I welcome the challenge of sparring with you."

"Same here," Ciorrin called and several heads nodded in agreement.

"Good work guys," Narek smiled. "I'm going to take an hour to pray. Call me if you need me."

"Sarge," Domlin called over the intercom. Narek opened his eyes and rose from the ground where he was sitting with Kaylak and Vronil, deep in prayers to Salifkan, the Vendalan god of triumph through adversity.

"Yes?"

"I'm sorry to interrupt your prayer time Sir but we're approaching the Coroptima system. I'm disengaging the TFC now."

"Thank you, we're on our way." He clicked off the intercom and rushed to the cockpit, Kaylak and Vronil hot on his heels.

There are fourteen planets in the Coroptima system, but only the seventh and eighth planets are in the habitable zone around their huge star, and Narek was relieved to finally be here.

An hour later, the intercom crackled and Narek flipped the comms switch.

"Unidentified military vessel, this is Coroptima Air Security, you have entered Coroptima airspace. Identify yourself immediately and state your intentions."

"Coroptima Air Security, this is LMB72, Sergeant Narek Jenn of the Inter-Galactic Military Force, Luzel 2 refuelling station, base 7 responding. My unit and I are on a scheduled military survival training exercise and have stopped here to arrange an emergency military hospital transport for two of your people. Sending you our military and DNA data now."

A.W.O.L

"We have your signal LMB72 and confirm you have permission to land. Sending you landing coordinates now."

"We have them, thank you." Narek flipped off the comms switch and sighed. "Okay guys, ready to party? Remember the Base Commander here uses Vendalan military designations, so refresh yourselves with the correct terms. You refer to him as Beganzi, I am your Lashen, Kaylak is your Tinash, and Vronil is your Prelam. A regular soldier is called Dahlit. You have five minutes to practice before we land. Don't offend anyone by getting it wrong."

It was cool on Coroptima and Narek felt chilled as he stepped down from the ship and pulled the collar of his uniform jacket tighter around his neck. Although not a shy man, he was aware that being Vendalan and carrying a flurry of spots down his neck and across his shoulders would make him stand out in any crowd. The spots of Vendalan men react to their emotional state and sexual arousal. Becoming darker and more prominent during times of emotional stress and when they reach their sexual prime and choose a mate. The chemicals released by their brains during times of high emotion, such as anger, fear or falling in love, make it obvious how they are feeling and Narek was uncomfortable about being on this world where no one knew him, with his spots reacting like that. Vronil noticed and nudged Kaylak, who smiled.

"Anwaha Manuk," Vronil said quietly. "Be proud of them brother."

"En anwaha," Narek replied, blushing. "I am proud."

"Me dinshae," Kaylak said. "But you hide."

"En flakja," Narek grinned. "I'm cold."

"Kiana, Manuk," Kaylak laughed as he and Vronil laughed loudly. "Yes brother."

Narek looked up and saw a large bearded man approaching them, his uniform and insignia telling him that this was the Base Commander. He called his unit to attention and saluted.

"Welcome to Coroptima 8 Lashen. I'm Beganzi Meelia."

"Lashen Narek Jenn Sir. Thank you for allowing us to land. This is my Tinash, Kaylak Prian and my Prelam, Vronil Seng. This is Dodge, our head medic."

"Gentlemen," Meelia nodded at Kaylak, Vronil and Dodge, who all saluted. "Come with me and let's talk about why you're here."

"Thank you Sir," Narek replied. He turned to his unit. "Oversee the refuelling and restocking guys and wait for us inside the ship."

"Yes Sir."

The base was huge, much bigger than the base at Luzel 2 that Narek had come to know as home during the past two and a half years. He estimated there must be several hundred soldiers based here at any one time and he realised he had become used to the easy life back on Luzel. He had seen plenty of action in his military career in the Vendalan Army and had fought for his life on more than one occasion, but found the opportunity of being permanently involved in the training of new recruits to be very appealing. After several years on active duty in the Vendalan Army, he gave up his active role to sign up for the Inter-Galactic Military Force, the galaxy wide military force peopled and run by all the worlds who were part of the Inter-Galactic Treaty, for a single, united goal, the preservation of peace. He cared very much that there are soldiers out in the field, trained by himself and knew that he had instilled each one with a measure of humility and compassion. He did not care whether others viewed his role as glamorous or not, he just wanted to make a difference and the best way to do that, he thought, would be to encourage within the future generation of soldiers, the right qualities to make them good peacekeepers.

Narek saw a group of soldiers as they walked across the base. Some were obviously brand new recruits being taught how to march, salute, and stand to attention. A smile crept across his lips as he remembered his first days in the Vendalan Army, and how confusing it all seemed at first. There had been a time when he feared he would never get the salute right, and twice had been disciplined for his sloppiness. A friend took him under his wing and had spent hours practicing with him and that kindness had started a strong bond of friendship between them. He turned and looked at Kaylak and smiled as he remembered how patient he had been back then, teaching him how to fold his fingers back at the correct angle to make the salute. Kaylak looked round and saw Narek looking at him.

"What?" he whispered.

"Look, over there," Narek pointed. "They're learning how to salute. Remember that night?"

"I remember," Kaylak grinned. "You really didn't have a clue, no wonder you ended up cleaning the cookhouse so many times."

Narek laughed. "Only twice."

Another group of soldiers ran passed them, each weighed down with full kit and Narek remembered doing many such training runs himself. Some of them did a double take when they noticed three Vendalans walking across the base with their Commander, all three carrying the famous spots that always seemed to beguile their women so. Narek resisted the urge to pull his collar tighter around his neck and kept his head up, proud of the markings that singled out his race and always made them a talking point wherever they went. The image of his friend Rakshi from back on Luzel 2 came to him, and the way he always joked that the other men would have to visit the tattoo parlour in order to catch the eyes of a woman when the Vendalans were around. Narek had actually known a man who had a tattoo of Vendalan spots done on himself and grinned as he remembered seeing him for the first time. The man had been given the name Crishnira after that and all the Vendalans laughed and called out this name whenever he was around. It took him months to persuade them to tell him that it meant imposter and he was quite upset about it. The spots did not suit him at all, and had not improved his social life either.

Merita King

CHAPTER FOUR

"You're Vendalan I see," Meelia smiled and Narek nodded. "I'm married to a Vendalan woman and live there with her. I like to use Vendalan military designations here on this base, is that okay with you Lashen?"

"Oh yes Beganzi," Narek replied. "Swan kiahi." "Thank you very much."

"Good. Now sit down and tell me what you want me to do for you."

Narek and his friends sat down and relayed the story to Base Commander Meelia.

"We come from Base 7, Luzel 2 refuelling planet, and one of our civilian personnel is from here. His wife and son are still here, but his wife is very sick and her medication is very expensive as it has to be brought in from off world. He sends all the money he can to pay for it, but it doesn't leave him enough to save for a hospital transport to bring them to join him. Back at the base there is a state of the art hospital, with experts from many worlds who may be able to treat her, or even cure her, and her medication is much cheaper there. We are here to ask if you can provide this transport for her."

"He's a civilian you say?" Meelia asked and Narek nodded.

"Yes Sir. He's not military but he," Narek faltered.

"He what?"

"He did me a great service and as my unit and I were passing by his home world, I thought it was worth at least trying to repay his kindness. I'm sorry Beganzi; this isn't an official military request. I just want to thank someone who helped me when I needed it, and his family deserves it more than most."

Meelia looked down at his desk and let his mind ponder the situation. This request was out of order and he should report Narek to his superiors for trying such a trick, but something about the Vendalan man before him got through to his heart. He thought of his wife and wondered how she would react. She would not hesitate to beg him to agree and would be upset if she found out he had denied such a request. He looked up and smiled.

"I tell you what Lashen," he said. "I'm sending a unit of recruits over to you on Luzel 2 for some basic survival training in a month's time, so I'll arrange for a couple of extra seats."

"Swan kiahi Beganzi," Narek smiled. "Thank you Base Commander."

"You know this is strictly off the record, don't you Lashen?"

"Yes Sir, we are very grateful for your kindness. May we be allowed to inform the lady and her son?"

"Yes of course," Meelia nodded. "Try to encourage her to keep it a little quiet though, as it's unofficial. If you'll give me their names and the address, I'll arrange for one of our base medics to pay her a visit to assess her needs for the trip and give her all the details she'll need to be ready."

"Oh sure, here," Narek said, handing over the piece of paper.

"Ahh, yes. This is not far away. Come, I'll show you how to get there on the map of the city."

The house was small and the garden in front, overgrown and wild. Narek knocked on the door and the four waited. Eventually the door opened to reveal a pale drawn face with wispy yellow hair and black ringed eyes.

"Yes?"

"Are you Jalien Talko?" Narek smiled.

"Yes. What's the problem?"

"Oh don't worry, there is not a problem at all. I am Narek Jenn from Base 7 on Luzel 2, where your husband works."

"Oh no," she cried, her eyes widening in horror and her hand going to her mouth."

"He is okay," Narek assured her. "He is well and happy. Please don't worry. I am here with good news for you."

"He's okay? Are you sure?" she asked, wiping her eyes.

"I'm sure," he nodded. "I promise you he's all right."

"Come in please," she said as she shuffled aside. "Forgive me my manners."

"Thank you very much."

"When you said you are from Luzel 2, I automatically thought something awful had happened to him. I cannot lose my husband, not with things being the way they are at the moment," she said as she showed them into her kitchen. "Sit, please. Would you all like some Bonja juice?"

"That would be welcome, thank you," Narek nodded. "Can I get it for you? I know you are not well, let me help you."

She went to protest but then sighed and sat down heavily. "It's just over there in the cooling unit. Help yourselves."

A.W.O.L

Narek poured five glasses of the dark red liquid and handed them round. It was delicious, at first dry and sharp but then sweet and smooth. He looked at Jalien, felt great sadness for her, and was very happy to be bringing her good news.

"I am very happy to be able to tell you that you and your son will be going to join your husband on Luzel 2."

"We are?" she replied in shock. "But how? We don't have the money. The medication takes all of our money."

"Your husband was very helpful to me when I needed it. He told me something that just might help me to find someone very special to me and bring her home. I have been able to secure military transportation for you and your son in a month," he smiled and watched the tears fall down her sunken cheeks.

"I don't know what to say," she said as she wiped her eyes and blew her nose. "Thank you so much."

"You are very welcome," Narek replied. "A military medic will be calling on you to assess your needs for the journey and to give you all the information you need to prepare. I umm, have to ask you to keep this to yourselves if you can. The Base Commander is doing us a favour here; it's not strictly official, if you understand."

"I understand completely," she nodded. "I won't tell a living soul."

"Will your son be able to keep this to himself do you think?"

"That might be a problem," she admitted. "He is not doing well at the moment."

"What is the problem?" Kaylak asked.

"He finished his education a few months ago and has fallen in with a bad crowd. He spends most of his days out somewhere with them and doesn't come in until all hours of the night."

"I went through a year like that myself when I was fourteen," Vronil said.

"I try to discipline him but he doesn't listen to me anymore," Jalien said. "I fear he will end up in prison, or dead in some alley out beyond the canal."

"What time does he usually get home?" Kaylak asked.

"Not before midnight."

"Okay, so here's what we will do," Narek replied. "I'll call my unit to come here in a hover cab and we'll spend the rest of the afternoon doing this place up for you. You go and have a shower and lie down. Dodge here is our

43

medic, and he will give you a quick check over and look after you. Vronil is an excellent cook so he'll do dinner and by the time your son comes home, the whole place will be fresh and you can stop worrying at least about that. How does that sound?"

"Oh you can't do all that, you're busy."

"We have to stay here at least for today anyway while two of my men try to find some information I'm looking for, so we might as well use the time constructively. Now, where is your power meter and how is the credit on it?"

"It's under the stairs and it's almost empty I'm afraid. We have to watch what we spend on power these days."

"Well not today," Vronil said as he got up and fished his inter-galactic currency card out of his jacket pocket.

As the sun set over Coroptima, Narek made drinks for all his men. Everyone was tired and dirty but the house and garden was clean from top to bottom. Faulty lights now worked, temperamental heating outlets now hummed into life, the broken food stasis unit worked for the first time in months, windows gleamed and even the garden looked under control. Noro folded freshly washed and dried laundry while Vronil prepared to serve dinner. Two of the men went out for food supplies and returned laden with bags and boxes, enough to last the whole month. Narek learned that Jalien's medication had long ago soared in price, beyond the reach of her husband's money, and that she had been taking short measures for several months. He was horrified and immediately went to the dispensary and bought all of the back stock that had built up because of her reduced circumstances. As she joined them for dinner, fresh from a shower and the proper amount of medication administered by Dodge already improving her colour, she burst into tears and Narek hugged her.

"I don't know how to thank you," she sniffed. "You are wonderful men and I am very grateful to you."

"You're more than welcome," Narek replied and all heads nodded in agreement and many were accompanied by grunts of approval.

The meal was wonderful and to Narek's surprise, Jalien ate heartily and seemed to grow stronger with each mouthful. He could not help but wonder how little she had been eating lately and was very glad to have been able to help her. He thought of his own mother and could not imagine allowing her to suffer this way. As Kaylak stacked the dishes in the cleaning unit a knock at the door made them all jump. Narek got up and opened the door to find a neighbourhood security officer on the doorstep, his hand firmly upon the shoulder of a scowling boy of roughly fifteen years or so. Narek stepped aside and bade them enter. Jalien got up, her face once again creased with worry as she looked at the boy.

"Calin, what have you done?"

"Nothing," the boy hissed as his face darkened. "What are all these aliens doing in my house anyway?"

"Calin," Jalien exclaimed in shock. "Don't speak like that. These men are our friends."

"Filthy alien screets," he hissed at Narek, before the security officer squeezed his fingers just a little tighter into the boy's shoulder, quietening him immediately.

"I'm so sorry for his language Narek," Jalien sobbed.

"Do not worry yourself Jalien," he replied and put a hand on her shoulder. "I will take care of this, with your permission?" She nodded and Narek approached the security officer. "Lashen Narek Jenn of the Inter-Galactic Military Force," he smiled and extended his hand, which the officer shook and nodded.

"Endar Prolse, neighbourhood security force. Happy to meet you Sir."

"What has happened with the boy?" Narek asked.

"He was observed exiting a house a few streets away in the company of several other well known gang members. My men and I have been keeping watch on this particular gang for several weeks now, due to the high number of burglaries being reported recently. When my colleagues and I apprehended them, we found jewellery, currency cards and other valuables in their possession. After initial questioning, they could not give adequate reasons as to why they should be in possession of such items, all of which were identified as belonging to the dwelling's owners."

"Calin, you were stealing?" Narek asked.

"Don't question me, filthy alien screet," the boy spat as he tried, and failed to extricate himself from the grip of the big security officer.

"Now then Calin," Prolse said. "Such disgusting words are not welcome in my hearing, or your mother's I would guess. I'm afraid Lashen that as the boy has been caught stealing on two previous occasions, I have no choice but to detain him and he will undoubtedly be formally charged this time."

"What would his punishment be for such a crime?" Narek asked, thinking quickly.

"Most likely hard labour in the Rodmium mines for a couple of weeks," Prolse replied. "As this is his first official detainment."

"And will he have a permanent stain on his record?" Narek asked and Prolse nodded.

"Oh yes. His first entry into the public record of offenders, and the first of many I don't doubt."

"Calin, how could you do this?" Jalien sobbed. "We are a good family. Your father will be heartbroken."

"Well he'll be heartbroken on some swanky rock somewhere then won't he?" Calin yelled back. "Instead of being here, he's having a party with his new friends and doesn't give us a thought. Why should I care what that idiot thinks?"

"Because he works very hard and sends nearly all of his pay home to you and leaves himself with almost nothing to live on," Narek yelled back and took a step towards Calin. "He trusted you to take care of your mother while he works to pay for her medication and how do you repay his trust? You run around with criminals and let your mother suffer alone and her home fall into disrepair. She gave you your life, cared for you all the time when you were totally dependent upon her and asked nothing from you in return except your love, and you can't even give her that. I would be ashamed if you were my son."

"And don't think you'll have it easy in the mine Calin," Prolse added. "The men that work there are rough and won't enjoy the company of a boy who thinks he's tough because he can steal jewellery from a woman and let his mother suffer alone when she's sick. You are not going to enjoy the next two weeks, believe me."

"Sir," Narek said. "Would an entire month basic training in the military base be an acceptable substitute for two weeks in the mine? I can guarantee that he will be made to work and learn to take orders and respect his elders. Anytime he steps out of line, the punishment will be swift and appropriate. Would it be possible for us to arrange something here? Jalien and Calin will be leaving Coroptima in one month to join their father on Luzel 2, so he won't be a problem for you anymore."

"What?" Calin exclaimed in shock. "Leaving? Since when?"

"Since I arranged it for you," Narek replied. "So your mother can be looked after in a state of the art hospital facility where doctors from many worlds will help her to get well and her medication is a fraction of the cost. Your father will be able to spend time with his son, and you will have many opportunities to learn skills that you can use throughout your life. There are many other children of all ages there, from many worlds and you will be as alien to them as they are to you but they will accept you as a brother because that is how we are. There are no screets on Luzel 2."

Calin did not know how to respond so he looked down at the floor, embarrassed. Prolse smiled.

"I'm sure I can persuade my boss to accept your proposal Lashen, after Calin here has spent a night in a cell to see how he feels about it."

"Thank you," Narek smiled. "I'll speak with Base Commander Meelia and let him know he has a new recruit on the way."

Narek was impatient to find out what Ribas and Ciorrin had found out on their information gathering mission. They were waiting with hot drinks when they returned to the ship.

"What did you find out?" he asked.

"Well Sarge," Ribas began as he handed Narek a drink. "Not much is known about the Fa'ahlima but we went to the local archive and discovered the same sort of rumours that we're all used to hearing ourselves. What we did find out was that the Fa'ahlima do indeed visit Coroptima every year around now, and that they left here just four days ago."

"Poshash," Narek cursed and thumped the bulkhead.

"But," Ciorrin continued, "we also found out through the military records which Ribas here was able to access, that they also visit Stalinoka 7 around now. The timings of their visits seems to indicate that the Fa'ahlima year is three hundred and eighty six days long. That's why they're always a little later each year for those planets with shorter years and a little early for those with even longer ones."

"So we need to go there next," Narek said. "How far is it?"

"For us? Seventy eight hours at top speed but for them in a bigger ship, much less probably, which means they will have probably been and gone from there by the time we arrive."

"Poshash," Narek yelled. *"Poshash."*

"One more thing Sarge," Ribas said. "We also found out the last eight planets they've been to before coming here to Coroptima, and knowing they're most likely headed for Stalinoka 7 next means we've been able to plot a possible direction."

"How does that help us if we're always several days behind them?" Kaylak asked.

"It means we can stop chasing them and go wait at their next probable stop, which is Abdelia 3," Ciorrin replied.

Narek's jaw dropped open as he took in Ciorrin's words. He went over and put a hand on each of their shoulders.

"Now that is excellent work guys. That is strategy, tactics. That's the kind of thing that can give you a great advantage in a situation. Well done. You've both earned an extra point for that."

Ribas and Ciorrin smiled, proud that their idea had earned them an extra point that could help their placings at the end of their training period and help ensure they got the postings they wanted.

"Thanks Sarge," they replied in unison.

"Now we all need sleep," Narek said. "Base Commander Meelia has arranged bunks for us so let's go. Thanks for all your work today, all of you. It might not seem like the work of a soldier but you've all learned what real soldiering is about today. You have to be able to interact with indigenous populations and get them to trust and accept you, before they accept and trust your enemy. You guys did fantastic work at the house today and that woman now trusts all of you as her friends. She will tell her friends about it and they will think well of you. That's how you get indigenous people on your side in a hostile situation, by befriending them. In addition, you two came up with a plan that might save us several days and could mean we succeed in finding the Fa'ahlima and rescuing Risa. Good job guys."

Narek woke his men at dawn and after a shower, they all headed down to the mess for breakfast. He had slept well, despite dreaming of Risa calling to him all night long. He found himself running through a dark forest towards her anguished cries, desperate to reach her; branches and roots tripping him repeatedly and awoke with tears on his cheeks. Although he worried for her, he was rested and ready for the journey to Abdelia 3.

"What do we know about Abdelia?" he asked over breakfast. Everyone looked blank and he sighed. "Okay, well let's ask Meelia before we leave."

A.W.O.L

"Abdelia?" Meelia asked and Narek nodded. "Well it's not part of the Inter-Galactic Military Force, so you'll be on your own. We won't be able to help you or give you any back up. Why go there for survival training? Wouldn't it be easier to go somewhere within the IGMF?"

"Things aren't always easy in hostile situations Beganzi," Narek replied, "and I want to give these guys as realistic an environment as possible."

"Well, I can understand that," Meelia nodded. "Okay, let's see what I can tell you," he said as he reached for his data console and tapped the screen. "Ahh, here we are. It's a nice looking place. Idyllic really, look." He handed over his console and Narek saw lush greenery, waterfalls, rocky outcrops and open valleys carpeted with flowers of every colour imaginable.

"Looks beautiful," he nodded, handing back the console. Meelia continued tapping the screen.

"The indigenous population are fairly primitive and haven't quite made it into space yet. They're not known to be hostile to visitors, so you shouldn't have too many problems. The only thing is though, as I said just now, if you do get into difficulty, you can't expect any back up without causing an inter galactic incident. Be careful."

"We will. Thank you very much for your help and hospitality Beganzi," Narek said. "We are very grateful." He stood and saluted, followed promptly by Kaylak and Vronil. Meelia gave the customary acknowledgement and smiled.

"Tell me Lashen," he said. "Off the record, so if you want to tell me to mind my own business, go right ahead. This isn't strictly a training exercise is it? This is something more." Narek hesitated and Meelia nodded. "I thought so. I can see you have umm, something on your mind other than work," he nodded towards Narek's neck and his very prominent spots. Narek blushed and put a hand to his throat. "Don't be embarrassed Narek," Meelia continued. "Just be careful."

"I will Sir, and thank you."

They made their way through the complex of buildings, passing groups of soldiers who all nodded to him. He nodded back, saluted those of higher rank and smiled at the woman cleaning the floor. Rounding a corner, he found himself looking at a batch of fresh recruits being given their first talk by the Officer responsible for their intake group. Narek smiled as he remembered his own experience and how frightened he was as the Sergeant yelled and told them all the rules and regulations they were to follow, and the punishments for breaking them. He was about to turn away when Vronil nudged him and nodded towards the group.

"Manuk, ruliksa?" he whispered. "Brother, you see?"

Narek looked and saw Calin Talko amongst the group, standing with his shoulders back. He seemed to be paying attention and Narek smiled.

"Binna. Swan binna," he replied. "Good. Very good."

"LMB72 this is Coroptima Air Security. You are clear to leave the atmosphere. Safe journey Lashen."

"Coroptima Air Security, this is LMB72 confirming we are leaving the atmosphere. Thank you for your hospitality."

The journey to Abdelia 3 took eighty-three hours and passed without incident, apart from Narek's pacing, his constant worry over Risa and his dreams, which became more disturbed as each night passed. Always he would find himself running towards her desperate cries for help and always, he awoke before he reached her. One morning, he woke to find Kaylak shaking him awake, a worried frown creasing his brow.

"Manuk, lasmeriel. Lasmeriel." Kaylak said. "Brother, wake up. Wake up."

"Uh? Mwara. Mwara do ko ishtiol?" Narek groaned. "What? What is the problem?"

"Teliasharal." Kaylak sat down on the side of the bed. "You cried out."

"Poshash. Eialla." Narek swore as he sat up and yawned. "Shit. I'm very sorry."

"Illiomaral?" Kaylak asked. "You were dreaming?"

"Escrolichi. So Risa." Narek nodded. "Nightmares. Of Risa."

"Shle filamadri. Shle filamadri." Kaylak assured him. "We will find her. We will find her."

"Dosriloi do tioho kirilestwa. Li mwara chaliya?" There is no guarantee. And what then?

"Chaliya todirashrula kiyo palim." Then we will honour your choice.

"Palimarik ko tal ak roi manuk." I will choose sacrifice brother.

"Chaliya todirashrula kiyo palim." Then we will honour your choice.

As the ship approached the Abdelia system, Narek ordered the covert modulation unit be switched on so they might avoid being seen on any scanners the population of the planet, or any visitors that might be down there at the time, might have. He felt it unlikely, as Meelia had said the indigenous population were not that advanced, but he wanted to be extra careful. He did not want to risk anything scuppering his plan to reach the Fa'ahlima and tell Risa he loved her. Even if she should choose not to return with him, he knew he must at least tell her what lies within his heart. He wondered how she was being treated and prayed every night that she was well and unharmed.

"Okay guys," Narek said as they reached orbit around Abdelia 3. "We know that the Fa'ahlima have a huge mothership that waits in orbit around the planets they visit, and that they send shuttles down to the five major centres of population. So, we need to land near to one of the five largest populated areas. What do the scanners show?"

"I'd say these five here Sir," Esclan replied from the pilot's seat. Narek went to look.

"Okay, let's go to this one. It's not the biggest but it's not the smallest either and there is a large area of forest and hills to the south, which will give us a quiet place to land and make a base. Can anyone see what is also good about this choice? Come on guys, come on over here and take a look." The soldiers all crowded around and perused the scanner. Some faces had frowns and a few heads were scratched before Domlin looked up with a smile.

"It's on the night side of the planet Sarge," he said and Narek nodded.

"Right. It's night time in that place, and that will give us more cover to help ensure our arrival goes unnoticed."

"Damn," Ciorrin cursed. "That's so obvious. Why didn't I see that?"

"You will from now on my friend," Narek smiled. "Now, Esclan. Find us an area a few miles from the populated area that offers us cover for the ship, but not too far away so we waste time hiking into town okay?"

"No problem Sir. There are some rocky outcrops in that area where the forest starts. We'll be invisible amongst the rocks and trees."

"Good," Narek nodded. "Now everyone, check your weapons but take only small arms. We don't want to frighten anyone but we need to be able to defend ourselves if necessary. Remember, this planet does not recognise the authority of the Inter-Galactic Military Force so we can't go in looking like we're taking over."

The ship descended invisibly into the Abdelian night and headed for the forested area to the south of their target area. The many rocky outcrops and buttresses, surrounded by trees and brush, afforded them good cover and after an hour of carefully arranging brush and broken branches, the ship was almost invisible to anyone who might happen to fly over or pass through. It was cold and Narek suggested everyone dress warmly, before putting on an extra jacket himself and leading them out towards the city, the location device on Damir's wrist beeping quietly and leading them north towards the centre of the populated area. Three hundred yards into their four mile walk, they rounded a huge boulder and found themselves staring into twenty-five laser rifle barrels.

Narek raised his hands and indicated for his men to do the same.

"We are here as tourists," he said but got no reply. One man stepped forward and used his gun to indicate for them to kneel. Narek and his unit obeyed. The man stepped forward and pointed at Narek's military badge that showed him to be a member of the IGMF, before glaring at him accusingly.

"We are here as tourists," he repeated. "We are on leave and came here to relax and see the country as none of us have been here before." He looked the man right in the eyes in the hope that the eye contact would give his words weight. The man was not impressed and yelled at Narek in a language he had never heard before.

"I'm sorry, I don't speak your language," he said, first in Vendalan and then in the common language adopted by those worlds that had become a part of the Inter-Galactic Union of Worlds. Neither got him any response and the man spoke with his colleagues. Narek observed them as closely as he could in the dark but brightly moonlit night, and was convinced they were arguing between themselves. This pleased him as it told him they were undisciplined and might not have a plan for such an occasion as this. He decided this was useful information and as the men relieved them of their weapons, ordered them to stand and marched them into the Abdelian night, Narek hoped that this lack of planning would make their escape easier.

"How the hell did they find us?" Ciorrin hissed and Narek shrugged.

"I've no idea," he admitted.

"That's how," Damir said and nodded to their left. The faint glow of a campfire a few hundred yards through the trees greeted their squinting eyes and everyone swore under their breath.

"Trust us to land right by their camp," Noro said quietly and Narek grinned, despite the seriousness of the situation.

"It was rather bad luck," he agreed. "Let's just try and turn it into something positive. They might become very helpful once they've assured themselves we're no threat. What does your training tell you to do in this situation?"

"If we're out gunned and have no choice but to surrender," Ribas said, "then we obey them but give them only our name, rank and number."

"Correct," Narek replied, "but?"

"But what?" Ribas asked with a frown.

"But we've told them we're not here as soldiers," Dodge said and Narek nodded.

"Well done. So what should we do?"

"We obey, try to convince them we're not a threat and hope they let us go," Esclan said.

"And what if we fail?" Kaylak asked.

"We take the first opportunity to break out and get away before they recapture us," Noro suggested.

"Making sure we harm no one in the process," Dodge cut in, "seeing as how this world isn't part of the Inter-Galactic Union of Worlds and doesn't recognise the authority of the IGMF."

"Good, well done guys," Narek said as one of the men yelled something he couldn't understand but which they all took to mean, "Shut up or else," and jabbed him in the back. They spent the rest of the journey in obedient silence.

Merita King

A.W.O.L

CHAPTER FIVE

Dawn broke and Narek awoke, his back stiff from lying on the floor of the cell within which his captors had installed him and his unit the night before. The hum of the laser cell bars was ever present and annoying and everyone had complained of a headache within an hour of their incarceration. There was a toilet in one corner but no basin in which to wash themselves and Narek already felt sticky and uncomfortable. As he forced himself into a sitting position, he groaned a prayer to Salifkan, the Vendalan god of triumph over adversity to bring him an opportunity to escape. Trying not to awaken his men, he crept over to the toilet for a pee and then decided to do some exercises to untie the painful knots in his muscles. It had been a while since he had to rough it on active duty and he realised how much he missed his comfortable bunk back on Base 7. An hour later the entire unit was awake and doing martial arts training to get their muscles working and use some pent up energy. It was difficult in the confined space of the cell, so they took it in turns and Narek was impressed with their performance.

The sun was shining through the small window of the cell when the door opened and four men walked in, two of whom Narek recognised from the night before. A big man with a black beard and a huge stomach was obviously in charge and Narek guessed an interrogation was about to begin. The big man said something to what Narek guessed was his second in command, who got up and pressed a switch on a panel by the door. A column rose from the cell floor, eighteen inches square and made of some shiny metal. Two feet of it rose into the air, forming a barrier between the first three laser cell bars, eighteen inches wide. A third man placed a bucket into the rear of the column and indicated to Narek. A small button on the front of the metal structure revealed an inner compartment, containing the bucket. Narek pulled it out and was delighted to see it contained water and a cup. The column sunk back into the floor and the lower three laser cell bars continued their journey uninterrupted.

"Thank you very much," he nodded and looked towards his men. "It's water."

"Is it safe to drink do you reckon?" Ciorrin asked.

"Without our testing equipment we can't know for sure," Ribas replied.

"It won't hurt us if we have a wash with it though, will it?" Noro asked.

"We can't go for long without water," Narek said, "but it could be poisoned. Do we risk it or not?"

"I vote that one of us try some and the others wait to see what happens. If everything seems okay in, say, an hour, then we assume it's safe."

"That's a good idea," Marikos nodded. "But who wants to volunteer to be the one to try it?"

"I will," Narek said immediately. "As your Sergeant, I can't delegate that task when there's danger to your lives."

"No Sarge," Domlin said. "I'll do it. I'm the least useful here so it makes sense that I do it. The guys need you and you have to find Risa anyway, you can't come all this way only to choke on poisoned water on some rotten hell hole out in the middle of nowhere. Dodge here is the best medic we have, Noro is the best pilot apart from yourself and Ribas is a computer whizz who can get access to stuff that would be hidden to the rest of us. The other guys here have girlfriends and wives back on Luzel. I've no family and I'm just a regular foot soldier without any special skills, so I'm the obvious choice. I've had a good life overall and don't regret anything. All I ask is that if the worst does happen, then you arrange for me to be repatriated back to Earth so I can be buried alongside my parents."

"You're wrong soldier," Narek said. "You do have a very special skill."

"I do?" Domlin asked, a frown creasing his brow.

"Courage," Narek said.

Domlin smiled and nodded, then reached into the bucket and took up the cup. It shook a little as he raised it to his lips and after no more than a moment of hesitation, he drank it down in one go.

"Well it taste's just fine," he said. "If it is poisoned, it's undetectable. You should maybe find out what it is, it may be useful for our armoury back at the base."

A loud laugh made Narek and his men turn to see the bearded man holding his belly and laughing, his head thrown back as his whole body shook with the effort.

"Vendala," the man said and Narek's eyes widened.

"Yes," he nodded and pointed to himself, Kaylak and Vronil. "Yes, we are from Vendala."

"Why you come here?" he said in the common language adopted by all worlds within the Inter-Galactic Union of Worlds, of which Abdelia was not a part. Narek was surprised to hear it spoken here, and his surprise showed. "I think you spy for Rachioma, yes?"

"No," Narek said. "I am not a spy. I am a soldier," he pointed to his insignia to emphasise his point. "We come to find the Fa'ahlima."

"Manuk?" Kaylak hissed. "Who or what is Rachioma?"

"I haven't a clue," Narek shrugged. "But since he thinks we're spying, my guess is that it's a who. Probably the leader of a rival faction."

"So we've landed in the middle of a civil war," Ribas exclaimed. "Great."

"Why you want the Fa'ahlima?" the man asked, leaning forward with interest. This was obviously not the answer he was expecting.

"A woman," Narek began. "She go with the Fa'ahlima," he continued, using gestures to illustrate so the man would understand. "I love her and want her to come home."

"Ahh, woman run away from Vendala man huh?"

"No," Narek replied. "Woman run away from other, bad woman."

"We not have soldiers like you here," the man glared, his smile instantly gone. He pointed towards Narek's IGMF badge. "You not welcome here."

"We are not here to be soldiers," Narek spat, trying to remain calm despite the rising anger he felt within. He knew his anger was affecting his spots, which would by now, be almost black but he did not care.

"Vendala man angry," the man laughed and then said something to his own men in a language Narek could not understand. They looked at him and laughed, before touching their own necks and Narek flushed with embarrassment.

"*Wiatan Manuk, wiatan,*" Vronil whispered. "Relax brother, relax."

Narek closed his eyes and sighed deeply, trying to force his emotions under control.

"So why you spy for Rachioma, Vendala man?" the man continued.

"We are not spies," Narek replied as calmly as he could. "I do not know Rachioma. I want to find the Fa'ahlima, get my woman, and leave."

"You will bring us much money when we tell Rachioma that Vendala man is very bad spy."

"Are the Fa'ahlima here yet?" Kaylak asked.

"They come two days ago," the man replied. "Before the next dawn, they leave."

"Let me go to them, please," Narek asked. "Let me speak with Fa'ahlima, and then we go home."

"I speak with Rachioma first. If he admit you are his spies, then maybe I give you to Fa'ahlima myself." He got up and left the room, followed closely by his three colleagues.

Narek dropped his head into his hands and sighed. Knowing the Fa'ahlima were here but not being able to get to them was agony for him and he did not know how to handle the feelings. He wanted to cry out but he knew he could not be seen to lose his self control with his men watching.

"Did you mean what you said Sarge?" Esclan asked. Narek looked up and frowned.

"What did I say?"

"That you love Risa?"

Narek blushed. "Yes," he nodded.

"So that stuff about Lorella," Ciorrin asked. "Was that true?"

"Yes, that's true," Narek replied. "Lorella told her that she and I are dating. She got Jalien Talko's husband to fake a photograph of the two of us together and showed it to Risa to make her believe it. Risa wrote me a letter before she left, telling me she loved me and couldn't remain and watch Lorella and me together. I have to find her to let her know the truth, I have to."

"Okay," Marikos said suddenly. "So here's what we'll do. We have no longer than another day before the Fa'ahlima leave and we'll hear their horn anyway so we'll know when we're down to one hour. As soon as it's dark outside, we break out of this shit hole, down those assholes and get out of here."

"We can't harm them," Kaylak replied. "Abdelia is not part of the IGMF, so if we harm anyone it could start a whole shit load of trouble. We have to do whatever we do without harming them."

"That's fine," Dodge said. "I know the right pressure points on the body to cause unconsciousness. Come here, I'll teach you all so we have some defence until we can get our stun guns back." For the next three hours, Dodge taught Narek and the men where the pressure points that cause unconsciousness are and how to utilise them to their own advantage. They practiced on each other, pressing just hard enough to cause pain but not to render themselves unconscious, and by the time the door opened again with a delivery of food for them, they all felt sure they would be able to use the new skill in combat.

"Dodge?" Narek said as he drank some water, having assumed that if it had been poisoned, Domlin would be showing signs way before now. . "You're amazing. That's earned you a couple of extra points. Well done."

"Awesome, thanks Dodge," Ribas said and the other men nodded. They all decided not to eat the pale cream coloured slop they had been given. A day without food would cause them no harm.

The afternoon wore on and Narek got increasingly anxious as the hours dragged by. Kaylak and Vronil tried to calm him and the men tried to keep him occupied with martial art and unarmed combat practice, but by late afternoon, he was pacing.

"Narek," Kaylak said. "Come and pray with me, please brother."

"I cannot," Narek replied. "I cannot calm myself enough to pray tonight. I have to get out and get to the Fa'ahlima."

"Sarge?" Esclan said. "Please take the time to pray Sir. It will help calm you down. We will all need you to be totally focussed tonight when we make our move. We depend on you."

Narek sighed and sat down with Kaylak and Vronil, closed his eyes and tried to find that quiet place within. Suddenly Damir started to sing. He raised his velvet voice in a song of upliftment from his own faith. He sang of a belief so strong that struggle and pain could always be met with an open heart and compassion. He sang of a mighty and powerful deity and a people's unfaltering belief. He sang of love. Love for his deity, love for his people and love for all creation. When he was finished, several of the men sniffed to hide their emotions.

Narek's prayer time was interrupted by the big bearded man entering the room with the same three colleagues that had accompanied him that morning. Again, he sat in front of the cell and questioned Narek, accused them of spying for someone called Rachioma and again, Narek denied it and told him of Risa and the Fa'ahlima.

"We are not spies," Ciorrin said suddenly. "We see nothing. You capture us as soon as we land and bring us here. We are not spies. If we were spies, you would not see us. We would see everything and go tell Rachioma what we see. If we were spies, we would be the best spies on all Abdelia. If you think we are spies, then you are a stupid man."

The big man's beard twitched at Ciorrin's angry words. Narek was sure they were in trouble and would get a beating, or worse, but to his complete surprise, the big man with the beard nodded.

"Grilch not stupid," he yelled at Ciorrin. "I lead many men, I read and write. I clever man."

"Then work it out for yourself," Ciorrin yelled back. "Think man."

Grilch indicated to one of his men to pass the water bucket through. Again the metallic column rose from the floor and Damir leapt forward to retrieve it. He fumbled with the heavy bucket, and then pushed the food bucket from earlier back in, its contents now cold and stiff, a nasty yellow crust covering the top. The column slid back into the floor and Grilch left the room, followed by his three cohorts.

Once they were alone, Damir moved the water bucket aside and crouched down by the laser cell bars, at the place where the column rose from the floor. With agile fingers he began to feel along the thin line in the floor that indicated the top of the column, as if looking for something. His frown turned to a smile as his fingers grasped something and he looked at Narek and grinned.

"What's up?" Narek asked, moving forwards.

"I thought we were getting out of this joint Sarge?" Damir replied.

"Well we are going to try," Narek nodded.

"Then let's get to it." He continued fumbling with his fingers, working his way along the crack in the floor and everyone sat in silence until, over a minute later, a click was heard and the column rose from the floor, creating an eighteen inch long break in the lower three laser cell bars. Narek gaped.

"What in the name of Ashlion did you do?"

Damir grinned and lifted his fingers from the floor and everyone saw the thin Palentadium wire that once belonged in his IGMF badge. The properties of the wire had interfered with the circuitry controlling the column, making it rise from the floor.

"You clever asshole," Ribas grinned.

"Awesome," Marikos said.

"Damir, you are a genius my friend," Narek grinned.

"Can everyone remember the way out?" Kaylak asked.

"Out that door, turn right and follow the corridor until it ends. Through the door at the end, turn left and another short corridor to the door that leads outside," Dodge replied. Everyone looked at him in amazement. "Well I have a good memory for that kind of stuff," he blushed.

"Is everyone okay with this?" Narek asked. "If one person doesn't want to go, we will all stay together. All of us or none of us, no splitting up." No one replied and Narek nodded. "Right, let's go."

It was a bit of a squeeze for Narek but he finally managed to haul himself through the narrow column. Being a big man, he was afraid he might get stuck when he found his shoulders wedged, but with a wriggle and a push from his friends, he made it through. Kaylak and Vronil followed, being the next biggest and once they were safely through, the others followed easily. Narek approached the door and listened. When he heard boot steps approaching, he indicated for his men to hide behind the door. Two minutes later the unconscious body of a guard was left to sleep it off in the cell, having been roughly shoved through the column.

Narek led them along the corridor, aware of the fact that if someone approached, they had nowhere to hide. He reminded them to be ready to defend themselves. As they passed a door on their left, he pressed his ear to the wood and listened. No sounds came so he opened it and peered into the small room filled with supplies and arms.

"Jackpot guys," he hissed as he entered. "Come in and shut the door." Inside what was clearly the group's storage room, were food and cleaning supplies, medicines, arms, ammunition, and the arms their captors had taken off them the night before. They re-armed themselves and were about to leave when Esclan noticed something among the armoury supplies.

"Look Sarge," he whispered. "Smoke flares. These won't kill anyone but might be useful to help us get away if we need some cover."

"Great," Narek nodded. "Everyone take as many as you can carry comfortably. Okay, let's go."

They entered the corridor and continued their journey as it bent around to the left and ended in a door fifty yards ahead. They ran silently to the door and listened. Narek's heart fell as he heard many voices within, raucous laughter and arguing.

"There must be at least twenty of them in there," he said. "Poshash," he cursed.

"How the hell do we get out?" Ciorrin exclaimed. "We can't take that many on, even with our stun guns. We're outnumbered."

"Not with these," Narek said, holding up a smoke flare.

The men inside the mess room cum meeting room just had time to register the door had opened when the room suddenly burst into a cloud of smoke that burned their eyes and tore at their throats. In too much pain to act, they ran around like mad things, eyes streaming and clutching their throats. Tables scraped across the floor as blind men bumped into them, chairs fell and grunts and oaths filled the air as the men bumped into one another in their panic. Narek and his men ran into the room under cover of the smoke, held their breath and dashed for the door that led out into the fresh air. Once out in the relative safety of the dark, they bolted as fast as their legs would carry them towards the brush and scrub they remembered lay ahead. Shots rang out and Damir yelled in pain and fell. Ciorrin and Kaylak yanked him to his feet and hauled him along with them, diving for the cover of a painfully prickly bush.

"Who fell?" Narek demanded.

"Damir," Kaylak replied, puffing with the effort of running and hauling his wounded colleague.

"Let me through," Dodge ordered and everyone moved aside as best they could without being seen. "It's not too bad, just a flesh wound to your side. It'll hurt like hell but you'll live." He ripped off his shirt and tore it into pieces, binding Damir's abdomen tightly. "There ya go, that'll do you till we get back to the ship."

"Thanks," Damir said, wincing in pain.

More shots hit the soft earth around them and Narek readied his stun gun.

"Okay guys, just stun remember. Put them to sleep but don't kill them."

The firefight lasted no more than five minutes but seemed much longer to Narek and his men. By the time they decided it was safe for them to make another dash away from the compound, several of Grilch's men were unconscious on the ground. Narek guessed that some of the rest were probably making their way around to surprise them from the sides and behind, so he decided it best they make a run for it.

"Let's get going before we're trapped. You okay Damir?"

"Yes Sir, I'll be fine. It's my side that hurts, my legs are as good as ever."

"Great, let's go and be quiet. We may have company from either side so keep a sharp eye out."

"Which way are we going?" Kaylak asked. "Where are the Fa'ahlima?"

A.W.O.L

"We'll head for the town or city or whatever it is they have here and no doubt we'll find out when we get there," Narek said.

"I hope the sight of our uniforms don't upset anyone else," Dodge said.

Narek was about to reply when a noise cut through the darkness, sending them all into silence. The low sonorous sound was instantly recognisable to Narek and his heart fell.

"The Fa'ahlima," he exclaimed. "We have just one hour. We must run. Listen, why don't you guys head for the ship and I'll run towards the sound."

"Now Sarge, you said all of us or none of us remember? No splitting up you said," Marikos reminded him. "You're not going to disobey your own command I hope."

"Okay, come on then," Narek said and headed towards the sound. Through dense brush they ran, leaping boulders that tried to snag their ankles, and as they were approaching the first few houses that signalled a populated area, the low sonorous note of the Fa'ahlima horn stopped dead, sending everyone skidding to a halt. Narek sprinted for all he was worth but before he got a hundred yards further on, a ship rose from the ground several miles ahead and flew towards them, soaring over their heads and away into the dark Abdelian sky.

Narek fell to his knees and screamed in anguish. Kaylak and Vronil ran to him and held him, spoke to him of their binding ceremony and reminded him repeatedly that he shared their souls. They begged him not to give up hope and urged him to hurry back to the ship so they could give chase. When finally, Narek was calmed, they set off back in the direction of their ship and it was as dawn was breaking that they saw the three men standing guard. Kaylak, Vronil and Esclan shot them with their stun guns and within ten minutes, Narek and his men were lifting off the ground and heading up into the night after the Fa'ahlima. Several shots hit the ship and Narek guessed Grilch and his men had caught them up and were trying to shoot them down.

"Put your foot down Ciorrin, as far as you can. Get us out of here."

The void of space opened up around them and everyone breathed a sigh of relief.

"Can you follow the Fa'ahlima's trail?" Narek asked.

"No problem at all," Marikos said as he configured the scanner in front of him. "They're leaving a very clear trail of Exotran particles. I'm configuring the scanner to follow them."

"Fantastic. I'm going to take a shower," Narek said. "Yell if anyone wants me."

"Same here," Kaylak nodded, followed immediately by Vronil and soon, Ciorrin was alone in the pilot's seat as all the others rushed off to shower and change their uniforms. Once everyone was comfortable, Domlin took over at the cockpit, allowing Ciorrin to go and freshen up. Seated around the table over the first proper meal in over a day, Narek thought back to their last minutes on Abdelia and came to a decision.

"I need to apologise to you guys," he began. "As your Sergeant, I shouldn't have lost my focus like that back there. I'm supposed to inspire you to trust my judgement and I let you down."

"Hey Sarge," Damir said. "May I speak freely sir?" Narek nodded. "That's bullshit. You're a person not a robot and I for one feel more at ease with a leader who I can see has real feelings like the rest of us, than someone who doesn't show emotions at all. Any man who loves, fears, laughs, angers and despairs is someone who is more likely to be compassionate and understanding with my feelings. I feel safer under your leadership because of that, not despite it."

"Thank you buddy," Narek smiled.

"It certainly makes me feel easier about how you're likely to react if I hesitate because I'm scared or unsure," Ribas nodded. "Sure you'll let me know how I did wrong and the possible consequences of my hesitation, but knowing you'll understand it makes me feel easier. I know I'm likely to get a fair report at the end of this exercise, even if I do fuck up."

"We all learn best by fucking up from time to time," Vronil said and everyone nodded.

"Now I vote we all catch up on some sleep," Narek said. "Do we have the pilot rota worked out?"

"Yeah, I'm up next," Kaylak replied. "Then Damir after me and Esclan after that."

"Okay, then let's hit the sack guys," Narek said. "See you all in a few hours."

After checking in with Domlin to assure him that Kaylak would be taking over the stick in four hours, and to remind him to call if there was a problem, Narek headed to his bunk and lay down. Sleep evaded him and he found his thoughts drifting back over his life. He remembered his childhood back on Vendala, and how his parents had always made every day a joy for him. Vendalan parents worship their children, seeing them as the most important symbols of their continuance as a race and they make sure that they instil those qualities into them that they regard as most important. He remembered how his mother wept on the day he left Vendala to join the Inter-Galactic Military Force. He smiled as he remembered how his father explained later that Narek need not feel guilty, as his mother's tears were tears of joy at how fine a man her son had become, and how proud she was that he was representing their home world in such an important role. His parents sent him vidicom messages every couple of weeks and he always replied, letting them know how he was getting on, that he loved them and that he was still holding to his Vendalan faith. He had not yet told them of his feelings for Risa; the Vendalan custom forbids any announcement of a romantic union until both feel that their union is for life. He knew he would have to tell them if he could not find Risa, or if she should choose not to return his love. Having already chosen to take the Tal ak Roi and end the suffering of his half soul, his parents had the right to know and be there with him during his last moment. To deny them this right, even to keep them from the pain of losing him would be a deep betrayal.

The day Narek landed on Base 7 on Luzel 2 had been just like any other, until the moment he lost his way when trying to find the communications centre and asked Risa for directions. He felt as if she had melded right into his soul as she gazed up at him with her big green eyes and her long hair the colour of polished Rodmadium glinting in the afternoon sun. He had been unable to prevent himself from smiling at her and knew right away that he wanted to get to know her on a closer emotional level. The problem was that he had been too shy to declare his feelings to her, and she never showed any particular interest in him, other than the normal friendliness she showed to everyone. As he lay there on his bunk, flying through the cold void of space, Narek wished, just as he wished so often, that he had told her how he felt. There had been so many chances and his shyness prevented him from taking any of them. He cursed his shyness and vowed never to waste a moment again, should they be reunited. Then he sent a prayer to Alima, the god of love and bonding and begged for help in finding Risa, before finally falling asleep.

It seemed like just minutes later when the ship lurched violently and Narek awoke after bumping his head painfully against the bulkhead. He rubbed his eyes as he came to his senses, leapt from the bunk and raced to the cockpit. On the way, he met Kaylak and by the time they entered the cockpit, the whole unit was behind him.

"What's going on?" he demanded.

"I don't know Sir," Esclan replied as he struggled with the controls. "It seems we've lost most of our manoeuvring capability."

"How are the fuel cells," Narek asked as he leapt into the co-pilot's seat and studied the digital readout on the console before him.

"They're fine," Ribas reported from the back, his eyes fixed firmly on the fuel supply gauge.

"Then what the fuck is wrong?" Narek hissed.

"I don't know Sir," Esclan said, "but I'm losing the ability to manoeuvre her. We need to land so I can do a proper diagnostic. If we carry on as we are, the problem could get worse and then we may not be able to fix her up at all. There's a planet below us. I strongly suggest we put her down."

"Okay, do it," Narek said, trusting Esclan's judgement implicitly.

"Right Sarge," Esclan nodded. "Give us a hand would you? The stick feels like it's been embedded in pure Altogantium."

"No problem," Narek replied. "The rest of you guys, strap yourselves in huh?"

"Okay boys, on your asses and buckle up. Go go go," Kaylak yelled.

The next two hours were amongst the most frightening of Narek's life and as they emerged from the ship after a not too elegant landing, he sat down on the rough grass and sighed.

"Poshash," he cursed aloud. "It's been a long time since I've done that. I've gone soft."

After checking everyone had survived intact, and congratulating Esclan on handling an emergency landing so well, he went back into the cockpit to scan their immediate surroundings. The star maps showed him that this planet was the fifth planet in the Kelmat System. There was precious little information about this world, except that the indigenous humanoids were very primitive, the atmosphere was safe to breathe, and that the single, huge landmass was violently volcanic. It was quickly dismissed by the Inter-Galactic Union of Worlds and the IGMF as non-viable for settlement, as deep scans showed its core to be extremely unstable, and the top scientists agreed that it would probably blow itself up within a couple of hundred years. Narek wondered if plans had been made to relocate the indigenous humanoids and decided to try to find out, when the opportunity arose.

A.W.O.L

CHAPTER SIX

Kaylak ran his fingers over the ground and examined the fine grey powdery residue left on his fingers. The stuff was everywhere and the air smelled funny, although everyone was able to breathe normally and their testing scanner showed the air to be adequate for their needs.

"What's all this grey powder?" he asked, guessing that none of his colleagues would know the answer.

"I was wondering that too," Damir said.

"I bet I know what it is," Marikos said as he too, rubbed some of the powder between his fingers and sniffed. Everyone looked up at him. "I reckon it's volcanic ash," he said. "There must've been an eruption in the not too distant past."

"Oh yeah, of course," Narek nodded. "It must be."

"I hope that doesn't mean we're gonna be fighting back rivers of lava," Domlin grinned.

"That's not funny," Narek glared.

"Sorry Sarge."

"Don't worry, I'm only kidding," Narek grinned. "Okay now, can you assess the damage Esclan?"

"Not until the fuel cells cool down Sarge, and that will take several hours. I'd say it looks like late afternoon here so my best guess would be to run a full diagnostic in the morning."

"Right," Narek nodded. "Is anyone hurt from our landing?" He looked at his men but all shook their heads and he inwardly sighed with relief. "Great, that's one piece of good news anyway. Well since this is supposed to be a survival training exercise, who can tell me what our first job should be?"

"Set up a perimeter Sarge," Domlin said.

"Good job. How do we achieve that?"

"Secure the immediate area with a defensive fence or other structure, according to available materials," Esclan said.

"Well done. So what do we have available?"

"I'd say our best bet is the trees," Ribas said. "Cut em down and use the trunks to build a fence, even if it's just a pile of logs we can hide behind. It don't have to be pretty, just functional."

"Good. What dangers must we be aware of?"

"We don't know what the animal or humanoid life is like here," Dodge said. "It would be advisable to avoid contact with all animal life and if we encounter the humanoids, use body language to show we mean no harm."

"Good," Narek said. "The information I read said the local indigenous humanoids are very primitive, so what body language do you think we should adopt?"

"Open hands and no pointing weapons at them," Ribas said.

"Eye contact and smiles," Esclan offered.

"Gentle tone of voice," Domlin added.

"Never accept a gift of a flower," Marikos said."

"What?" Narek said, a frown creasing his brow.

"What are you on about?" Domlin said.

"It's not a joke," Marikos grinned. "I saw it in a movie once. This guy goes to some island somewhere where the local people have never met another race of people before. This one beautiful chick offers this guy a flower and he takes it but finds out later it means she's offering him marriage. When he finds out, which is long after he took her to bed, and decides he's not ready to settle down just yet, he has to make a hasty getaway, which the local tribe feels is insulting to them. The locals chase the guy and try to kill him and he only just gets away in time."

"He has a valid point actually," Vronil said when everyone had stopped laughing. "We've no idea what customs any people here might have and although a beautiful woman can be a temptation, we don't want to upset anyone and I for one am certainly not yet ready to settle down."

"Okay so be careful when accepting any gifts," Narek grinned. "Unless the gift is offered to us all at the same time, then I'd advise accepting. If any one of you is offered something that none of the others are offered, even if it seems silly, remember what you could be getting into. And don't come crying to me when she nags the pants off you and you want a divorce."

Before he could give the order to begin setting up a perimeter, a yell from the tree line made them all turn, their weapons at the ready. Another yell and they all heard the sound of someone trying to run through heavy brush and undergrowth, followed by a sound that reminded the three Vendalans of the Brolks back on their home world. These huge fearsome beasts are Vendala's most dangerous predator, easily taking down a grown man and all Vendalan children are taught to avoid areas where they are likely to be found.

A.W.O.L

A man suddenly appeared from the undergrowth, running in obvious fear from something, frequently looking behind him. He sprinted across the open ground for twenty yards before the creature leapt from the brush and galloped towards him, both as yet oblivious to the soldiers. The creature was half the size of the man, its rear half covered in thick grey brown fur that Narek guessed must give it excellent camouflage in the dappled light of the forest. Long narrow jaws sprouted from the front of a huge blocky head and he saw the huge curved fangs that told him this was a carnivorous predator.

"Okay guys, take it down," he ordered and all took aim. The creature dropped and the man fell to the ground, startled by the loud cracks of the laser rifles. Narek ran towards the man, his men behind him and stopped ten yards from where he still lay, terrified on the ground. Narek put his rifle away and opened his hands to the man.

"It's okay, we won't hurt you," he said, knowing the man would not understand him but hoping his friendly tone would convey his non-aggressive stance. He reached a hand towards the man and after several long seconds of eye contact, the man took Narek's hand and allowed him to help him up. Narek pointed towards his own chest.

"Narek," he said as he pointed. "Narek." He nodded to Kaylak and the others, who each introduced themselves in a similar manner.

The man nodded and pointed to himself. "Ablan," he said pointing. "Ablan." He looked over to where the creature lay dead and wondered over, wary in case it leapt up and attacked him.

"It's okay," Narek said. "It's dead." He walked over and lifted the creature's enormous head up, examined it closely and then dropped it. Ablan came over and crouched down by the creature, examining the dark spots of damage done by the laser rifles. He touched the dark spot and sniffed his fingers, before looking up at Narek. Narek showed him his rifle and pointed to the dark spots and Ablan nodded and smiled. He stood, cupped a hand around his mouth and made a high pitched whooping sound towards the trees. Within two minutes, faces appeared from the tree line, nervous at the sight of these strangers. Ablan shouted to them and they stepped forward tentatively. He pointed to the creature and then to Narek and his men and the ten or so men muttered to each other.

One young looking man pointed towards the space ship and said something, looking at Narek with his eyebrows raised.

"It's our ship," Narek said, knowing he would have difficulty explaining this to people who may not have encountered visitors from space before. He started towards the ship, turned and beckoned them to follow. He led them in through the hatch and showed them around, sat on chairs, and lay down on bunks in an effort to illustrate the basic facilities to show that this was their home. Ablan and his men looked on in awe and tentatively tried sitting on the chairs and lying down on the bunks, grimacing at the level of discomfort.

"I wouldn't advise allowing them to sample the nutri vend Sarge," Damir said and everyone grinned. "They might kill us in revenge."

The tour continued and Narek hoped this was helping to show Ablan and his men that they meant no harm so they could rely on their friendship whilst stranded on this planet. As they went back out into the afternoon sun, a low rumble shook the earth beneath their feet.

"Cabisha," Ablan yelled and he and his men fell to the ground and wailed, raising their hands to the sky in a beseeching gesture every few seconds.

"Earthquake," Ribas said.

"Just as we thought," Narek replied.

"What are they doing Sarge," Domlin asked.

"I think they're praying to their gods to stop the earthquake. They probably believe a spirit of some kind is causing it."

"I hope they don't think the spirit is angry because we've arrived," Kaylak remarked.

"Oh please Manuk," Narek begged, "make that not be so."

The rumbling stopped and Ablan stood, his men wide eyed and frightened. He turned to Narek and said something in his own language. Narek did not understand but Ablan's smile told him it was friendly. He watched them jog across the open ground and haul the carcass of the dead creature away with them. As they disappeared into the trees, he hoped that they would have a rewarding and positive experience with these people.

"Okay guys," he sighed. "Let's get that perimeter going."

It was dark by the time Narek and his men had finished and all were dirty and sweaty after hauling armfuls of brush and fallen branches into a five-foot high hedge around their ship. Six regularly spaced openings in the hedge allowed them to pass through if necessary and ensured that there were enough men to police the area. Long burning flares lit the area in an eerie yellow glow that kept the cloying black of the night away enough to stop them being creeped out too much.

"We must be aware of the danger of night creatures," Narek reminded them. "So guys, knowing the dangers and the area we have to protect, how would you arrange the watch rota for the night?"

"Watch in pairs," Marikos said.

"How many pairs?" Kaylak asked.

"Four pairs of men, north, south, east and west of the ship," he replied.

"And how long for each watch?" Vronil asked.

"Four hours."

"So," Narek said. "Four pairs. That's eight men for four hours. Four hours will take us into the middle of the night. There are eleven of us and with eight on watch, that leaves three sleeping and ready to take over the watch in the middle of the night."

"Shit," Marikos said. "Sorry."

"Don't feel bad," Narek replied. "You are learning to do your job. That is something to be celebrated not apologised for."

"Yes Sir."

"So," Narek continued. "How do we approach this problem? Anyone?"

"I reckon we should have two teams of five," Dodge said. "Space em out around the ship so they're not too far apart to feel all alone and vulnerable, and so they can yell to each other if there's a problem. Watch for six hours, then another five take over. That leaves one with nothing to do."

"Not a bad suggestion at all," Narek nodded. "Anyone else have another idea?"

"We could have three pairs," Ciorrin said. "That makes six men. I reckon the first half of the night is the most dangerous and if the men watch for six hours, it'll be not long before dawn by the time the other five take over."

"Another great suggestion," Narek said. "So what are the pros and cons of each?"

"Well Sarge," Domlin said. "If we do Ciorrin's idea, the six first and five later, that means all of us will be engaged in doing something and no one will be spare. I reckon it would be better to do Marikos's idea, the two teams of five and a spare man. He might not have anything to do but a spare man is a spare man."

"And if the spare man is Esclan," Damir said," he'd be fresh and ready to spend tomorrow fixing up the ship and less likely to fuck it up from not having had enough sleep."

"I agree, Ciorrin said. "That is the best plan."

"Me too," Ribas nodded.

"Me too," Narek nodded. "Good work today guys, I'm proud of you. Now who is on cooking duty tonight?"

"I am," Esclan said.

"Great," Narek nodded. "Okay, you go fix us a meal while half go take a shower. The rest keep watch until they get back, then go take a shower yourselves. I'm not prepared to spend however long cooped up in the ship with you lot stinking the place out. First thing in the morning, I'll be asking for volunteers to go find water."

"Some fresh meat would be nice too," Kaylak said and everyone grunted in agreement.

"Yes it would," Narek nodded. "That nutri vend will keep us alive but it's not exactly gourmet."

"We have plenty of ration packs," Vronil said, "so we won't starve for a good while yet"

"Curried Boghorn anyone?" Esclan said and everyone roared with laughter. This legendary substance is a staple in military ration packs and everyone hates it. Curried Boghorn is shrouded in mystery and although rumours abound, almost nothing is known about its actual origins. The only thing that is known is that it is actually edible. Beyond that is anyone's guess. It could be the finest meat available or rat's turds for all the soldiers know, but always it comes curried and everyone believes it is done to cover its real origins and taste.

After a meal and a shower, Narek and his men sat and talked for an hour before beginning the watch. He regaled them with funny stories from other survival exercises he had led and before too long they were all laughing. Ribas then asked him to tell him about Vendala and that led to each of the men giving the others their life story. When Narek and his four watch mates took up their positions in the quiet of the eerie yellow glow of the long burning flares, he felt they had all bonded very well as a unit, and knew that each of his men would go on to become excellent teammates when they were posted to active duty. He would miss them, he decided.

A.W.O.L

A few times during the six hour watch, the men heard creatures moving about beyond their field of vision and cries overhead told them large birds inhabited the sky. Each one hoped they were not predatory and none of them caused them any problems. As the hours wore on, Narek could not help but think of Risa and wonder what she was doing and how she might be feeling. He wondered if she was missing him as much as he ached for her. Then he remembered her letter and felt his heart reaching out through the cold cosmic void to some unknown and secret place where her own heart reached for his.

"Telariwa Risa, telariwa re chalosa," he whispered into the dark. "I love you Risa, I love you my darling."

The sun was burning off the morning mist as Narek heard a call. He turned to see Ablan standing in one of the gaps in the perimeter hedge with two of his men. He smiled and walked over.

"Ablan," he smiled. "Come in, come in. He beckoned them with gestures and they entered. Ablan smiled and indicated to his men, who stepped forward and offered Narek a large bundle they carried between them. Ablan spoke to Narek in his own tongue and when Narek's frown told him he did not understand, he touched Narek's laser rifle that hung from his shoulder, then pointed back towards the trees. Then he touched his hand to his heart and bowed his head, with another word.

"Makara."

Narek realised Ablan was thanking him for saving him from the creature and smiled, bowing his own head in response.

"You're welcome my friend." He accepted the large heavy bundle and set it on the ground before removing the leather covering to reveal the skin of the creature. It had been treated in some way so that the leather was pliable and soft, the fur luxurious and warm. There was also a necklace made from the fangs of the creature, threaded onto a leather thong.

"Wow," he said as he looked at Ablan. "Thank you." He picked up the necklace and put it over his head. Ablan and his friends smiled and nodded to each other, pleased that this stranger obviously approved of their gift. Narek picked up the fur and ran his hand over it. He looked at Ablan again and nodded, a smile telling the new friends that he was pleased. Ablan then turned and made the same high pitched whooping call Narek had heard the day before and before long, he saw forty men, women and children enter the enclosure, all carrying baskets laden with fruit, bread, dried fish and meats. Two women spread woven cloths on the ground and Ablan and his men sat and beckoned Narek and his men to do the same. He called his men from their work and told them to sit and all enjoyed the most wonderful breakfast any one of them could remember.

By the middle of the morning, Esclan appeared in the cockpit where Narek was making entries into the unit's training log.

"Sorry to interrupt Sarge," he said.

"That's okay, what's the problem?"

"I've discovered the reason for our engine problems."

"You have? Great. Now tell me you can fix it and I'll be a happy man."

"Oh I can fix it," Esclan nodded. "At least I can patch it up enough for us to reach civilisation for a proper repair."

"Fantastic. What is the damage?"

"It's the port fuel sequencer. One of Grilch's men was either very lucky or a crack shot. A laser bullet caught the sequencer and severed one of the heads. I can re-route power through the other six heads but we'll have to limit ourselves to two-thirds power when we take off. If we thrash her at top speed my repair probably won't take the punishment."

"How long will it take before we can leave?" Narek asked. "And what do you need?"

"Well, it'll be a day or two at a guess. I need to make a whole new section of power board to replace the bit that was blown out and I'll need to remove the starboard board to use as a template for the new bit. It'll take several hours to get the starboard board out, then at least all day tomorrow to make the new one. Then a few more hours to put them both back in again. At a guess, I'd say we should be on our way the day after tomorrow. Sorry I can't do it any quicker Sarge. If I hurry, I could knock an hour or two off but the sequencer has to be set just right or it won't work at all."

"That's fine, good work. You're seriously earning your keep here. Thank you. Do you need any guys to help?"

"A couple wouldn't hurt."

"Okay, no problem." Narek followed Esclan out of the ship and called his men together. "Guys, I need a couple of volunteers to help Esclan fix the ship." Ribas and Damir stepped forward. "Thanks. Now Esclan, I'm temporarily promoting you to Chief Engineer and as such, these guys here are under your command. You make the decisions about the repair and give them your orders. That means you also take the shit for any trouble but I know you're the best engineer I've seen in the last year of my service. I have faith in you."

"Thank you Sarge," Esclan replied.

"Ribas, Damir," Narek continued. "You take your orders from Esclan while fixing the ship."

"Yes Sir," they replied in unison.

"Okay, let's do this," Narek said and smiled as he watched them head back to the engine. He had no doubt that Esclan would go on to make a first class engineer, and had already decided to recommend him for further training. He sent a silent prayer of thanks for having Esclan on this mission, and knew that without him, they might very well be stranded here for a long time. He shuddered at the thought, but quickly pushed it from his mind and focussed on the immediate situation.

Halfway through the afternoon the sound of something crashing through the undergrowth brought Dodge and Kaylak to attention. Nearly a minute of breaking branches and cracking of undergrowth came to their ears before another of the huge creatures they had all seen the day before, broke cover and stumbled into the open. It sat down heavily and panted, slicks of drool tumbling from its jaws and every few seconds it shook its head. After a couple of minutes it dragged itself to its feet and headed left along the tree line, stopping at a bush with huge dark red leaves and bright orange flowers. With another shake of its head, it began to carefully pick off the leaves one by one and eat them, chewing with what both men could only describe as obvious pain.

"What the fuck is it doing?" Kaylak remarked.

"It's sick," Dodge replied.

"It must be. Surely a thing like that wouldn't eat leaves, it's a meat eater. You saw the teeth in that one last night."

"Yeah," Dodge nodded. "It's obviously got something wrong with it and knows those leaves contain something that might make it better. It's medicine. A lot of animals do it."

"I wonder what is wrong with it." Kaylak said.

"From the way it's drooling and the pained expression as it's chewing, I'd lay money on it having a rotten tooth."

"Ouch," Kaylak replied with a grimace. "Poor thing. Can't we do anything for it? Remove the tooth or something?"

"Yeah we could. We have our stun guns. If we stun it long enough for me to get some anaesthetic into it, I could take a look at least."

"Okay, keep watch on it and I'll go and ask Narek."

Ten minutes later, Narek and Kaylak took aim with their stun guns. It took three blasts to down the creature, but when it was down, Dodge approached cautiously and gave its hindquarters a gentle kick to make sure it was completely out. With a nod, he loaded his injector with enough anaesthetic to down three men and examined one of its legs. When he found a vein, he pressed the top of his injector and stepped back.

"Best we wait for five minutes to make sure the anaesthetic has worked. I don't want to be up to my armpits in its jaws when we find out it's not completely out."

The creature's jaws were huge and Dodge had difficulty opening them. He called for help and Marikos bravely stepped forward.

"Hold its jaws open would you?" Dodge asked.

"Umm, yeah sure," Marikos replied with a moment's hesitation. He took a deep breath and reached for the jaws, and had to use most of his strength to hold them open.

"Ahh, here it is," Dodge said as he peered inside. "One of its molars is totally rotten. Poor thing must be in agony." With the help of his dental extractor, and the combined strength of himself and Kaylak, the remains of the tooth came out with an audible squish that made Marikos grimace. After spreading the wound with a clotting agent, he laid the animal down and prepared to administer the anaesthetic antidote. Before he could use his injector, the animal showed signs of coming round on his own and Dodge yelled at everyone to get back.

"He's coming round on his own, get back guys, quickly." Everyone leapt away to the safety of the perimeter hedge and watched. "I was going to give him a large shot of antibiotic but he didn't give me enough time. Damn, he wasn't under long was he? With this rotten tooth out, he should recover on his own within a day or two."

"Good job guys, well done," Narek grinned as they watched the creature sit up and shake its head before trying, and failing, to get to its feet. He sat down with a thud and looked around, shaking his head and within a few minutes he was able to continue eating the large red leaves and after stripping the bush, he wandered back into the cover of the trees and out of sight.

"Let's hope he doesn't come back tomorrow and eat us," Kaylak said and everyone laughed.

The rest of the afternoon passed without incident and Domlin and Marikos were sent out to hunt for their evening meal. An hour later they returned with four furry creatures with cream coloured coats and black stripes down their hindquarters. Once skinned and cleaned, there was enough meat on them to feed the eleven men and with the addition of several vegetable ration packs, they had a substantial evening meal.

"This is wonderful Vronil," Narek said as he chewed. "Well done Manuk."

"That was a fantastic meal," Damir said.

"Who's up for first watch tonight?" Kaylak asked.

"Well my team watched first last night," Narek said, "so why don't we swap tonight? Your team take the first six hours and my team will take the rest of the night."

"Okay, that's fine by me," Kaylak nodded.

Just as it got dark enough to re-light the long burning flares around the perimeter hedge, a face appeared in one of the gaps and made Damir jump.

"Holy shit, you made me jump," he smiled at the pretty woman who stood at the entrance. He called to Narek. "Sarge? Sarge, we've got company."

Narek and Kaylak came running up. When he saw the female, he beckoned her inside with a smile. She nodded and stepped forwards, quickly followed by ten equally pretty girls. She said something to Narek, pointing to herself and her lady friends but Narek just frowned and shrugged. She stepped towards him and reached up to where her woven garment was tied at the shoulders and with a quick movement, she stood naked before him.

"Oh jeez," Ribas said.

"Wow," Marikos added. "Hey there pretty lady."

"I think our friend Ablan is offering us another gift for saving his life," Kaylak said.

"Well I for one would hate to disrespect him by refusing," Ciorrin smiled as he took a step forward.

"And I don't see a single flower," Ribas remarked.

"It might be a little awkward if we were to refuse," Kaylak said. "It could be seen as disrespectful and could conceivably make them hostile towards us."

"En pwiria," Narek whispered. "I cannot."

Kaylak stood before the woman, pointed to Narek and then shook his head at her, wagging his finger from side to side to emphasise the point. He then indicated to the other men and smiled.

"Okay guys, which three are on second watch with Narek and Vronil?" Ribas, Domlin and Ciorrin stepped forward. "Okay then you have six hours, enjoy yourselves. Save the one at the very end for me.

Narek lay down on his bunk, the giggles and grunts from the neighbouring bunks filling the ship and making him feel lonelier than ever. He would love to spend the night with a beautiful and willing woman and he was not lacking in desire. With Risa filling his mind and his heart however, he could not bring himself to touch another female; it would be as if he were cheating on her. Images of the many occasions he and Risa had spoken flooded his mind, and he felt the now familiar anger at himself for not having declared his feelings to her sooner. He remembered the first time he met her, when he lost his way looking for the communication building and asked her for directions. Her shy smile and the way she gazed up at him had melted his heart, and he had realised even then that he wanted her. Discreet enquiries amongst the base personnel revealed she was unattached and he allowed himself to believe that one day they might become a couple. The problem was his shyness, and every time an opportunity to reveal his feelings to her presented itself, he could not find the courage, afraid that she might reject him.

It quickly became apparent that Narek and his Vendalan friends were regarded as the best looking men on the base, and he never suffered for lack of female attention. Hardly a week went by without women flirting with him and making it obvious that they would like to have a relationship with him. There had even been a few very overt offers of sexual liaisons, which disgusted him, and he had turned them all down politely. Then there was Lorella Parks, Risa's older sister. She made it obvious she wanted Narek but he found her to be everything he would never want in a woman, and could not allow himself even to imagine accepting her offers. Just the thought almost made him vomit. She drank too much, flirted with every man on the base and had a bad reputation. A smile fluttered across his lips as he thought how his parents would react if he were to take Lorella home as his chosen woman. They would probably disown him, he decided.

The grunts and giggles from the neighbouring bunks filtered through to Narek, and his heart sank, heavy with grief at being separated from Risa. He was happy that his men were able to enjoy themselves, but their noisy sexual liaisons only served to make him feel lonelier than at any time in his life. Thoughts of Risa filled Narek's mind and he could not help but wonder what lovemaking with her would be like. Narek had always been popular with women, and had plenty of sexual experience. As a good looking young soldier with no ties, he never had a problem finding female company when he wanted it, and he regarded himself as a confident but tender lover. His body swiftly reacted as he whispered his love for Risa and imagined her soft but toned body against his own. With the physical release, the tears came and once again, he pledged to take the Tal ak Roi if he was not to be reunited with her.

He eventually drifted off to sleep and was unaware of the soft feet that padded into his room an hour later, and he did not stir as the soft hands caressed his neck and traced their way down his chest, ever lower.

Merita King

A.W.O.L

CHAPTER SEVEN

Narek's dream was filled with images of Risa but this time the feelings were overwhelming in their intensity. Again, he was running through the forest, hearing her desperate cries for help somewhere in the distance, but always just out of reach. Without warning, he tripped, fell, and immediately felt her soft warm body beside him as he lay in the grass. He smelled her golden hair and gave a deep sigh as he felt her fingers caress his body. They lay together under the stars and he told her over and over how much he loved her, begged for her forgiveness for not revealing his feelings to her sooner, and promised he would never leave her again. She smiled up at him; her head cradled in his arm and put a finger to his lips. Raising herself up onto one elbow, she licked his nipple as a finger traced its way down his chest to his lower belly, caressing the undulations of his abdominal muscles before finally reaching their target.

A groan of pleasure escaped him as her fingers found his penis and gently stroked and squeezed him to full hardness. His hand cupped her breast, teasing the nipple between his fingers as she continued stroking him. Desire soared through his body, the need to show her the intensity of his love in the most intimate of ways, irresistible. As if reading his thoughts, she straddled him, lowering herself onto him and taking his full length inside herself. Narek felt his whole being enveloped by her and gave himself up to his urgent physical need to show her the full extent of his physical desire. After waiting for so long, loving her secretly since the first day he arrived on the base, this moment was all he had dreamed of and he felt no desire to ignore it again. Holding her by the hips, he moved with her as she raised herself up, and then pulled her down onto him, timing his thrusts with hers. As he felt his orgasm approach, Narek looked into Risa's face, framed in her halo of golden hair and smiled, but as he gazed into her big green eyes, something changed. Something was wrong and at first, he could not make out what it was until he concentrated on her face. Her beautiful big green eyes did not seem quite so green after all, they were brown, and the unbridled zest for life he often saw within them was now a steely determination. He stopped thrusting as the strangeness of her overtook his focus and looked at her hair. He had always loved the way her golden hair shone in the afternoon sun back on Luzel 2, but now it had a brassy quality about it that he had never noticed before. As he continued looking, it started to change, and turned dark, hanging limp down to her shoulders. All thoughts of love were brushed aside as Narek snapped awake and found the woman astride him, grunting words he could not understand. When the realisation gripped his mind, he gasped first in shock and then revulsion, before grabbing her by the arms and thrusting her away.

"Get away," he screamed. "Get away from me."

The woman cowered against the wall, afraid of the sudden change in him. Narek was beside himself with anger, at both the woman, and how easily he had been duped. In the dream, he thought he was making love with Risa, his one and only love, but the dream had become a nightmare. His body was still affected by his sexual desire, despite his quick change of mood, and the lack of physical fulfilment only served to increase his anger. He lay back, breathing hard in an effort to calm his mind, and his body, and felt a hand gently caress his thigh. He reacted instantly and violently. Grabbing the woman by the wrist, he swung himself up onto his knees and dragged her beneath him. Taking hold of her by the hips, he swung her over onto all fours and entered her roughly from behind. She cried out as he thrust deep and hard, pulling her towards him by the hips as his own thrust forwards. He felt his orgasm approaching quickly and pulled himself out of her, not wanting her to bear the fruits of his desire. Grabbing her roughly by the hair, he yanked her head around and thrust himself into her mouth as she cried out in pain. With just a couple of deep thrusts that almost choked her, he felt his groin begin to convulse, and as she gagged and struggled against him, he came down her throat.

Narek was breathing hard and sat back as his body began to relax. It was not a state of loving euphoria that he experienced as he looked at the woman crying on his bunk, but disgust. He felt disgusted at the way this savage had managed to dupe him so easily, but he also felt anger at himself for being so easily influenced. He also realised at that moment, once his overwhelming physical desire was sated, that he felt guilty for having treated her so roughly. Common sense told him he should reach out to her, apologise or something, but his anger at having his bed invaded after he strictly forbade it, was greater than his guilt.

"Get out," he said, indicated towards the door. She leapt up from the bed, grabbing her garment from the floor and reached for the door. Before she could grasp the handle, it opened and in rushed Kaylak. The woman cried out and ran from the room.

"*Manuk, dushlariof teliari. Mwara do ko ishtiol?*" he asked, his face creased with worry. "Brother, I heard shouts. What is the problem?"

"*Matatch tioho. Illiomatch so Risa li lasmekuda filamaksi ko ilioysi poi re litash,*" Narek replied. "I said no. I dreamed of Risa and I awoke to find the woman in my bed."

"*Poshash,*" Kaylak cursed quietly. "*Situ do ko ilioysi teliashkia?*" "Shit. Why is the woman crying?"

"*Estrikuda manioy. Fibriale re litash, re dalimi li re kotara,*" Narek replied as a tear fell from his eye. "I was angry. She invaded my bed, my dream and my body."

Kaylak put a hand on Narek's shoulder. "*Enlarokriwa Manuk. Filamadri Risa li melashritoi palsol,*" he sighed. "I understand brother. We will find Risa and you will have peace."

Narek showered, dressed and went to the mess for a drink. His watch mates, Ribas, Domlin and Ciorrin were already there, having been woken by the commotion.

"Is everything okay Sarge?" Domlin asked.

"Sorry to disturb your fun guys," Narek said. "I guess some women don't know how to take no for an answer."

"Oh," Ciorrin remarked with raised eyebrows.

"I reacted badly and she learned the hard way not to disobey when a Vendalan man says no."

"Oh shit," Ribas hissed quietly.

"I umm, I hope my outburst doesn't cause any problems for us with the locals," Narek added.

"Hopefully we'll be away by the end of the day tomorrow anyway," Kaylak replied.

"How do I make amends for this with them?"

"I've no idea," Kaylak shrugged, "but do you wish for pelankway?"

"Yes," Narek nodded. "Yes please Manuk."

"What's pelankway?" Ribas asked.

"It means penance," Kaylak replied. "To repay for his misdeed so his soul will not be scarred."

"Is it painful?" Ciorrin asked.

"It would not be proper pelankway if it were not," Narek said.

"Come Manuk," Kaylak said. "I will raise Vronil and we can attend to it before the watch, we have a little time."

Kaylak and Vronil escorted Narek down to the very rear of the ship, away from the men's sleeping quarters and after removing his shirt, tied bindings to both his wrists. The bindings were tied to bulkheads and Narek dropped to his knees as Kaylak and Vronil removed their waist belts. The tough leather belts cracked as they struck Narek's back and left angry red welts on his light brown skin. With each blow, he arched his back as the sharp pains stung, screwing his eyes shut and biting his bottom lip. It took eighteen blows before he cried out, and in so doing, accepted his guilt and paid his penance for his misdeed. Kaylak and Vronil both had tears in their eyes as they put their waist belts back on and helped him to his feet.

"Kiyo sakri estri mayala ishwayi Manuk," Kaylak said. "Your soul is without stain brother."

"Swan kiahi," Narek replied as he wiped his eyes. "Thank you."

Vronil applied some salve that would stop the bleeding and Narek gingerly put on his shirt. After thanking Vronil again, Kaylak and Narek rejoined their watch mates and together, went out to relieve their colleagues, who were only too happy to end their watch and spend the rest of the night with the women who were keeping the bunks warm inside the ship.

The six hours dragged by without incident, apart from animal cries from the forest and intermittent sounds from the men and women inside the ship. As dawn broke, Narek saw the women leave the ship and head for the gap in the perimeter hedge. He was surprised to see the woman who had shared his bed was walking slightly apart from the others, and they appeared to be berating her, making gestures with their hands for her to keep away from them.

"That's odd Sarge," Ribas said as he appeared beside Narek and watched the procession heading away. "It's almost as if they don't want her near them, like they're telling her off or something."

"Kind of like she's committed a sin in their eyes," Ciorrin said, having joined them to watch the women.

"But how?" Narek replied. "She was doing as her people told her to do, so why should they be angry at her?"

"For displeasing you," Ribas said. Narek frowned and Ribas continued. "Well think about it. You save their leader's life, putting him in your debt in his eyes. He sends over his most beautiful young women to entertain us and she displeases you. In Ablan's eyes, she has made his guests angry, which will be an embarrassment to him."

"He's got a valid point there Sarge," Ciorrin said.

"I think that far from worrying about repercussions from them towards us, there are far more likely to be repercussions for her," Ribas continued. "We'll probably find Ablan comes over here soon with another gift in the hope of assuaging your wrath."

"I hope they don't do anything bad to her," Narek said. "I didn't want her but I wouldn't want her to be hurt, or worse."

"We cannot interfere with their way of life," Ciorrin said. "Whatever happens, we cannot, we must not interfere."

"I know," Narek nodded. "This is one of those situations you'll no doubt experience from time to time where you must stand back and remember your position. As visitors on someone else's world, we have no right to interfere in their laws or their culture. Sometimes things happen that we would never allow on our worlds or in our own cultures, but we are not here to tell people how to live their lives or run their communities. We are peace keepers, not saboteurs."

"All we can do is wait and see I guess," Ribas said.

"I'll go get the rest of the guys up so Esclan can get on with the engine repairs. He said we should be able to leave today sometime."

Narek went along the line of cubicles, banging on the doors as he walked the corridor.

"Okay boys wakey wakey, rise and shine," he yelled. "Up and out in fifteen minutes."

The six yawning but smiling men rose and joined their comrades on duty out in the chilly morning air. Narek sent Marikos and Noro to hunt for some game and sent Dodge and Damir to look for a fresh water supply to supplement their tanks. Two hours later Dodge and Damir returned, having found a stream, and after checking it with the water testing kit had found it to be safe.

"When we're ready to leave," Dodge suggested. "We can land right by the stream and use the hose to fill the tank. I'll go set the filtration to maximum now to save time later."

"Okay, thanks," Narek nodded.

"Wow," Kaylak exclaimed suddenly, looking over Narek's shoulder. Narek turned and saw Marikos and Noro returning, the carcass of some huge black creature strung over a pole between them.

"That's magnificent," Narek said as he examined the creature. Its long black fur was thick, shiny and luxurious to the touch. "Remove the skin with care if you can and we'll stretch it on a frame. We could give it to Ablan as a gift for his hospitality."

"That's a great idea," Vronil said. "I'll go rig up a frame now. Can I use some of the Unicord from the store?"

"Help yourself," Narek nodded. "Although the locals would probably use something more natural."

"And harder to produce," Marikos grinned as he and Noro dragged the creature away and began to skin and clean it. By the time they finished, the naked and now headless animal hung from a hastily rigged A-frame, the slit down its belly showing the now clean interior. The skin lay on the ground where Vronil was busy making holes around the edge through which to thread the Unicord. With Kaylak's help, they got the skin stretched across the frame tightly and stood back to admire their handiwork.

"Looks great," Marikos said.

"Bet that fur is warm," Noro added.

"Thanks guys, Kaylak said. "That was a great catch. We can joint it up and put it in the meat storage unit and it'll feed us all for more than a week."

"I hope it tastes nice then," Noro remarked.

"Hell, I didn't think of that," Marikos replied. "Suppose it's horrible."

"Meat is meat," Vronil said.

"And it's valuable protein," Kaylak said. "If you're stuck on some rock somewhere and fenced in by hostile forces, you take what you can get and be grateful for anything edible."

"Yes Corporal," Noro said, contrite.

"I'm sure it'll taste great," Vronil said. "Think positive huh?"

"Can we go wash up?" Marikos asked. "We're gonna stink of blood and guts."

"Sure, off you go," Kaylak nodded. "Take the carcass to the mess on your way and joint it up when you're showered and changed." He and Vronil watched the two head back to the ship, and then turned back to the task at hand.

"Right," Vronil said. "Let's get scraping." With their pocket knives in their hands, they set about scraping the inside of the hide clean. Kaylak was working out how much of each ingredient he would need to steal from the mess and stores in order to preserve it, when he heard voices approaching the perimeter hedge.

"It's Ablan," Kaylak said. "I recognise his voice."

The group, led by Ablan, approached one of the gaps in the hedge and waited. Narek smiled and beckoned them in, hoping this was not going to be a problematic meeting, given the fracas with the woman the night before, but was prepared in case events should turn violent. Ablan entered, followed by his people, everyone laden with baskets in the same fashion as the previous morning. They set out woven cloths and spread out the baskets of food and Ablan approached Narek. Kaylak and Vronil instantly appeared at his side, as much for moral support as anything else, and mentally readied themselves for a fight. Ablan put a hand over his heart and bowed his head to Narek, who gave the same gesture in return. Much to everyone's shock, he then turned and called over his shoulder and two women entered through the hedge with the woman Narek had found in his bed. The women dragged her roughly forwards, holding tightly to the bindings around her wrists and pushed her to her knees in front of him. Then, grabbing her by the hair, they yanked her head back.

"What's going on?" Narek hissed.

"It looks like they're trying to make reparation for her behaviour last night," Vronil hissed back.

"But I thought it was me that was going to be in trouble," Narek replied.

"I know," Kaylak said, "but they probably feel that she let them down by displeasing an important guest. They probably want you to punish her in some way."

"Oh I couldn't," Narek replied quickly. "I did that last night."

"You might have to, if you refuse you could very well end up in trouble."

Ablan indicated to a man standing next to him, who stepped forward and handed him a long spear with a sharpened tip. Ablan spoke to Narek, indicating to the woman a couple of times and ended by holding a hand to his heart and bowing his head, before offering the spear to Narek.

"Oh shit no," Narek said. "I can't do this. Think someone, quickly."

"Sarge?" Domlin called. Narek looked up. "See over there at the back of Ablan's group? There's an old blind guy being led by a child. Now that child probably doesn't get to go and play with the other kids, or learn how to hunt and be a man because he's busy looking after the old blind guy. Now if the old blind guy had someone to look after him, like a wife maybe, then the kid could do all the fun stuff that a kid should be doing."

"Domlin?" Narek said.

"Yes Sarge."

Remind me to kiss you later."

"Umm, yes Sarge. If you say so."

Narek took the spear, then bent down and took the leather straps from the two women. Trying to be as rough as he could, he dragged the woman to her feet. Ablan and his group watched, their eyes wide as Narek marched the woman over to the old blind man and gave him the ends of the leather straps that held her wrist bindings. He then took the man's other hand and placed it onto the woman's breast. Trying to look as angry as he could, he looked into the woman's frightened eyes, pointed to her and then to the man, before pushing her roughly to her knees in front of the old man.

"You belong to him now," he said, using gestures to illustrate his words. Hopeful he had done enough to spare himself the need to kill the woman, Narek then placed the spear into the man's hand and walked back to Ablan with a smile. As confidently as he could, he placed a hand on his heart, bowed his head and sent a silent prayer that this would defuse the situation and please Ablan. It did. Ablan smiled broadly and exchanged excited words with his fellows each side of him, then nodded at Narek and indicated for the breakfast feast to begin. Halfway through the meal, Narek showed Ablan the animal skin Vronil and Kaylak had stretched and started to scrape. Ablan's eyes widened, his jaw dropped and he uttered what Narek would swear until his dying day was something along the lines of 'shit.' He looked at Narek in surprise, ran his hand through the fur and muttered to his two companions.

"I think he's impressed," Kaylak remarked.

"It certainly looks that way," Vronil said.

"I believe you might be right," Narek replied.

Ablan looked at Narek and said something with a smile, then patted his shoulder, as if in congratulations. Narek smiled in response, then indicated the animal skin, and then pointed to Ablan.

A.W.O.L

"A gift for you," he said and bowed his head, before indicating to the feast laid out on the ground. "For your friendship," he added, putting a hand over Ablan's heart and then his own. "For the safety offered us by your world," he indicated the sky overhead and touched the earth beneath their feet. Ablan looked into Narek's eyes for several moments without speaking before nodding. He smiled and muttered something Narek guessed was a thank you and once again ran his hand through the luxurious black fur of the creature.

"Sarge, you're a diplomat," Esclan said as they continued their breakfast.

"As I said at the start of this exercise," Narek replied, "much of your job as a soldier will have nothing to do with firing your weapon, and will hopefully prevent you from having to do so. The more you can achieve with diplomacy and inter-personal skills, the less you will have to resort to violence and the fewer the deaths there will be on your conscience. We may be soldiers but our job is to try to prevent violence, not encourage it, and any soldier who tells you otherwise should not have joined the military in the first place."

Narek watched Ablan lead his people back towards the forest. Two women carried the stretched animal skin between them and the woman led the old blind man while the child ran with his friends. He was pleased at the way things had worked out and was proud of his men.

"I'm proud of you guys, all of you," he told them. "This could've been a very awkward situation here but your quick thinking and hard work has turned it into a successful visit. I'm confident if we were to return here, they would welcome us with open arms. Now, Esclan, how are you doing with the engine repair?"

"Just got to fit the new board and put everything back together Sarge. We should be on our way by mid-afternoon."

"Fantastic. Yell if you need anything."

Narek paced the perimeter hedge as the hours dragged by. He was desperately anxious that the Fa'ahlima were getting further and further away while they were stuck here, but he knew it would be wrong to pass on his impatience to his men. As he paced, he thought of Risa and prayed that she was not being harmed by the mysterious aliens that no one knew anything about. He also hoped that they would still be able to follow their exotran particle trail to catch up with them at their next destination. Kaylak calculated that since they had begun this last leg of the journey just minutes behind the Fa'ahlima, now they were just two days behind them. This would mean that by the time they had spent their normal two days at their next destination, they should catch them up and be right on their tail. This helped to calm his anguish a little and he sighed as he paced. He was so far inside of himself that when Esclan came running up behind him, he jumped.

"Finished Sarge," he puffed. "She's all ready to go but please, take it gently. She won't take a thrashing."

"Fantastic job," Narek replied and the two of them ran towards the ship. Once everything had been packed on board and everyone strapped in, Narek and Kaylak took the controls. Using the minimum power necessary, they gunned the engines and headed for the stream Dodge and Damir found that very morning to refill the water tanks. There was ample space to land the ship within easy reach of the stream and everyone jumped out to help with the water intake hose. Once the water was trickling into the tanks, the men sat down and relaxed. Narek lay on the bank of the stream and looked at the afternoon sky. In any other circumstances he would be happy to remain here for longer, the locale they had seen so far was beautiful and the indigenous people, easy enough to get along with. He wished very much that Risa were here to lay in his arms in the warm afternoon and suddenly felt very far away from her. As the warm sun bore down on him, he let his thoughts drift to his memories of her and again cursed himself for not declaring his feelings earlier. All this could have been avoided if he had only spoken up. Determined not to make such a mistake again, he decided he would never waste a moment, no matter how much the odds seemed against him. So much could be lost so quickly and if he never found her, the regret and guilt would be too much for him. This thought then took his mind to the question of how he would choose to take the Tal ak Roi if it came to it. In the old days, Vendalan men taking this traditional route would stab themselves through the heart with a Pantisal, a large ornate dagger, in front of their family and friends, who would all chant the ancient prayer to Shashowan, the receiver of souls, to plead with him to accept the half soul of this man. Nowadays though, a man who had chosen to take the Tal ak Roi could use any method he wanted to despatch his half soul into the god's waiting arms.

Narek knew one thing above everything else; not finding Risa or having her turn down his love would be too much pain for him to bear. He decided therefore that he should choose a method for his Tal ak Roi that was painful, in order to balance the guilt he carried at having caused this by not speaking up sooner. The more he thought about it, the more the old traditional way of doing things appealed to him. Although he had never declared himself a particularly traditional Vendalan and did not adhere to every old practice, he thought the Pantisal would be a fitting end for him. He turned to Kaylak and Vronil, who both sat nearby.

"*Manukichi? Palimaraksa ecashriel ko Pantisal shra re Tal ak Roi,*" he said. "Brothers? I have chosen to use the Pantisal for my Tal ak Roi."

"*Ko Pantisal?*" Vronil asked, shocked. "The Pantisal?"

"*Estrillie selashna manuk? Dosriloi am chiranichi lunwa kowow modirila ko Pantisal.*" Kaylak remarked. "Are you sure brother? There are ways less painful than the Pantisal."

"*Estriwa selashna,*" Narek replied quietly. "I am sure."

Kaylak looked at Vronil, raised his eyebrows in surprise and sighed. Vronil raised his own and shook his head in response.

"Hey look at this Sarge," a voice called. Narek raised his head and saw Noro, his pants rolled up to his knees as he stood in the stream. He got up and wandered over.

"What is it?" he asked. Noro handed him a small shell. It was conical in shape, about the size of Narek's thumbnail and its pearlescent surface flashed all different colours of the rainbow.

"Beautiful isn't it?" Noro asked and Narek nodded.

"It's gorgeous. Are there any more?"

"Yeah there are quite a few here," Noro nodded and put a hand into the icy water. "Want me to find some more and make em into a little bracelet for Risa?"

"That would be wonderful my friend," Narek smiled. "Thank you."

"My pleasure Sarge," Noro smiled as he bent down and thrust his hands into the water to search the sandy river bottom. Within a few minutes, he waded out with a dozen of the beautiful tiny shells and set them down while he dried his feet and put his socks and boots back on. He got up, gathered the precious haul and sauntered off towards the open hatch of the ship.

Narek was touched by the kindness his unit had shown to him during the past few days and wanted to do something to show them he was proud of them and valued their friendship. He let his mind rest and dozed.

Two hours later Kaylak shook Narek awake and reported that the water tanks were full and that they could leave. Everyone pitched in to help reload the water hose and with a last look around at the beautiful location, Narek and Kaylak lifted off and headed up into the late afternoon sky that was already turning red and gold with the impending sunset. Once safely out of the atmosphere, Kaylak tapped the scanner controls.

"There's still just enough of their exotran trail for us to follow," he announced.

"Wonderful," Narek sighed. "I'm so relieved I cannot tell you."

"I would recommend we stop in at the Deep Space Refuelling Station Zeta 12 Sarge, to get the repair properly checked," Esclan said and Narek nodded.

"Good idea, we'll head straight there. How long will it take to get there?"

"Just over twenty six hours at this speed," Kaylak replied. "We daren't push her any harder or we could end up becalmed and I for one don't fancy doing an engine repair in a suit."

"Me neither," Narek said. "Let's take it easy huh?"

The ship sped off into the cold vacuum of space towards the Deep Space Refuelling Station Zeta 12 where they could refuel the power cells and get the repair checked out. Narek thought perhaps the Fa'ahlima themselves may have stopped at the station to refuel, and maybe the staff will be able to tell him where they were headed. He wondered if he dared hope so. It was his turn to cook the evening meal and as he chopped, sliced and prepared the meat they caught on Kelmat 5, he thought of what would happen if he did find Risa and if she did come away with him. Thoughts of their reunion filled his mind and he felt emotion stinging behind his eyes. After his agonising chase across the cosmos to find her, and the seemingly endless worry and heartache that he might never see her again, he knew that if they were to be reunited, he would be an emotional wreck. In his mind, he saw himself embrace her as she fell into his arms crying his name repeatedly, and could almost feel her body against his. Smiling at the image, he watched himself kiss her for the first time, heard himself tell her how much he loved her and listened as she reciprocated his love, his tears splashing down onto the counter top as he prepared the meal for his men.

A.W.O.L

CHAPTER EIGHT

Narek looked at the enormous hulk of the deep space refuelling station as it came into view. He was pleased they had made it this far and felt great pride for Esclan and his engineering skills. They could have been stuck on Kelmat 5 for ages if it were not for his expertise, and he shuddered inwardly at the thought that they could have been stranded there and never found. He had already made a special note in his training log and recommended Esclan for further engineering training. A crackle from the intercom brought him out of his musings, so he flipped the switch and waited to be hailed.

"Unidentified ship, this is Deep Space Refuelling Station Zeta 12, please identify yourself and transmit your identification signal."

"Zeta 12, this is Sergeant Narek Jenn of the Inter-Galactic Military Force and this is military vessel LMB72. Sending our identification signal now. I have ten of my unit with me. We needed to make a hasty engine repair and request your engineering crew check it out for us. We also request a refuel and a fresh water top up."

"We have your signal now LMB72. Come around to dock eight. You will be directed to an engineering bay. Sending you the docking beacon now."

"I have it. Thank you Zeta 12. LMB72 out."

Narek expertly followed the landing crew's directions and touched the ship gently down onto a pad in the engineering bay. Several ships of all descriptions filled the area, all with panels open to reveal pipework, wiring and electronics. He hoped Esclan's repair would not need too much of an overhaul; he wanted them to be on their way quickly to catch up with the Fa'ahlima, and hopefully reunite with Risa. As the engine settled into silence, he got up from the pilot's seat and stretched himself before turning to his men.

"Okay guys, this isn't a military controlled base but it is run under the guidelines of the IGMF, so we may meet soldiers from other worlds. Kaylak?" Kaylak nodded and called the men to attention before Narek opened the hatch and stepped down into the deep space refuelling station. An engineer came up and smiled.

"Chief Engineer Dopwood. How can we help?" he said, extending his hand, which Narek shook.

"Sergeant Jenn, IGMF. We took some fire and our port fuel sequencer took a hit. One of my guys patched her up pretty nicely but we'd like you to take a look at it for us. We've kept her down to two thirds speed and she's behaved perfectly."

"No problem. We'll get some jets onto her and get her cooled down within a couple of hours, then we can take a proper look. I'll have you hailed when I have some news for you."

"That's great, thanks buddy."

"You'll have to leave all arms in the ship I'm afraid. As this is an inter-galactic station, we have to have strict rules about it and soldiers don't get preferential treatment. Sorry."

"No problem at all," Narek smiled and went back to join his unit, who were standing to attention at the side of the ship, awaiting his orders. "Okay guys relax. We have a couple of hours to kill so let's go get our papers checked and find a meal. We all get a night off from Dodge's cooking. We've got to leave all arms in the ship so unpack huh?" He approached the security guard and handed him his papers.

"Thank you Sergeant," the guard said as he handed back Narek's papers. "Welcome aboard Sir. Will you all be requiring rooms and meals?"

"We're not quite sure yet," Narek replied. "Your guys are checking the ship over now, so we won't know for two or three hours."

"No problem. Let us know as soon as you do and we'll fix you up with rooms. Would you like a meal? The restaurant is serving evening meals now."

"Yes please."

"Okay, follow the red line until you reach the accommodation section. The restaurant is on deck four. I'll call the desk and let him know you're here just for meals at the moment. Enjoy your stay Sir." It took a few minutes to have everyone's papers checked, then Narek led them down the corridor, following the red line. After several hundred yards of corridors, the mumble of voices came to their ears, and Narek caught the end of a conversation.

"Thank you again Mr Domenico. It's been a pleasure to meet you and thank you personally."

"Thanks buddy, take care of yourself huh?" a deep velvet voice replied. From around the corner came two huge men that Narek immediately recognised as Lileans. He once had a good friend from the planet Lilea and had mourned his loss for ages when he was killed in a shootout on Amtrelia 5. Another, shorter but solidly built man was with them and he looked official.

Narek guessed he was either military or law enforcement, but he was not in uniform so Narek plumped for law enforcement.   A woman was with them, holding hands with one of the Lileans, a huge bald man, so Narek guessed they were a couple. She was beautiful and he momentarily thought of Risa as a stab of pain leapt through his heart. The woman looked up into the Lilean man's face and smiled but her eyes looked red, as if she had been crying all night.

"I hope we find him soon Vincent," she said as they came towards Narek and his men in the corridor.

"We will baby, I promise," the deep velvet voice that Narek now knew belonged to Vincent, replied. They passed in the corridor and the man called Vincent met Narek's eyes and nodded, a worried smile on his face. Narek nodded back and turned to look as they carried on down the corridor away from them. Vincent, the woman had called him; a Lilean called Vincent. The other voice he heard had called him Mr Domenico.

"It can't be," he said aloud.

"What's up?" Kaylak asked, turning to look at the four people.

"Did you hear their conversation?"

"No, why?"

"The voice said Mr Domenico and that big bald guy is definitely a Lilean. The woman called him Vincent."

"So?" Kaylak frowned and then his eyes widened as he understood. "Oh, you don't think he's that guy do you?"

"I've no idea, but if he is, how cool is that huh?"

"Wow," Kaylak remarked.

Narek led his men around the corner and found a desk in front of him, a large man looking at them.

"Yes gentlemen.   You must be Sergeant Jenn?"   Narek nodded. "Welcome to Zeta 12. The restaurant is on deck four and is now serving evening meals. The elevator is just around that corner. If you find you need rooms, come and let me know. Would you like separate quarters for yourself Sir?"

"No, that won't be necessary," Narek replied. "I'm happy to share with any of these guys."

"Very well Sir."

"By the way," Narek asked.   Those people we just passed in the corridor. That wasn't Vincent Domenico of Lilea was it? You know, the guy who killed the Transmortals a couple of years ago?"

"It was indeed Sir," the man replied, "and a very friendly man he is too. I was honoured to be here on duty for him."

"Wow," Narek replied and looked at Kaylak, who nodded his agreement.

The meal was wonderful and everyone ate heartily for the first time in almost a week. It was good to be in safe and clean surroundings with people around them, but as always, Narek felt he was wasting time that he could be using to find Risa. As they ate, he looked around the restaurant at the other diners and wondered what their stories were, and if any were on a quest such as his own. A cheer from a table in the far corner made them all turn and look to see a group of men laughing and obviously celebrating something. It seemed somehow wrong to Narek that people should be laughing, joking and having fun when his situation was so perilous and he, so desperate with worry. All he could do was concentrate on the moment and get through the next days as best he could without losing his focus. However things were to pan out for him in the coming days, he knew that at least he was doing his best to make it right in the only way he knew how.

A voice came through the intercom and everyone stopped talking.

"Sergeant Narek Jenn to dock eight, repair bay twelve please."

Narek got up from the table. "Keep your fingers crossed guys," he said as he made his way from the restaurant and headed back down to dock eight.

"Ahh Sergeant Jenn," the same man Narek had spoken with earlier smiled. "I can tell you about your engine now we've had a look at her."

"Okay," Narek said. "How is she holding up?"

"Firstly, I have to compliment your guy on his engineering skills. He did a first class job of patching her up."

"Thank you," Narek nodded. "I'll pass that on to him."

"We can replace the entire port sequencer unit for you. Although your current repair will hold, you would be best to limit yourselves to two-thirds power, just in case. If anything else should happen when you're out in the middle of nowhere, you might not be able to fix it again. The choice is yours of course but I have to give you my advice, for your own safety and that of your men."

"Of course," Narek replied. "I understand. How long would it take to replace and would she be in fighting form again afterwards?"

"Oh yes," he replied. "She'll be on top form again. It'll take around twelve hours or so, give or take. You'd have to stay on board the station overnight, but you'll be able to leave sometime during the morning tomorrow."

"Okay, do it," Narek said. "Safety has to come first. These guys are on their first survival training exercise and although I want it to be realistic, I don't actually want them to risk dying."

"A sensible choice Sergeant," the man nodded. "I'll get my best men onto it right away and I'll hail you when she's done."

"I appreciate this," Narek said. "Thank you."

"No problem at all. I always wanted to join up but when I started taking firearms familiarisation, I found the prospect of killing another person terrified me so much I gave up my dream. I admire what you guys do though and it's a pleasure to help you out when I can."

Narek shook hands with him and retraced his steps along the long corridors. He stopped at the accommodation sector desk and rang the bell. The big burly man smiled.

"Sergeant, is everything okay?"

"Yes fine, thank you. I've just found out that we will be staying overnight after all, so there's eleven of us for beds and breakfast I'm afraid."

"No problem at all," the man said as he tapped on his digital console. "I made tentative bookings for you all anyway. Would you be happy to share with the two other Vendalans?"

"Absolutely," Narek nodded.

"That's fine then," he said as he handed Narek five key cards. "You and your two colleagues have room 1334 and I've put your men, two in each of the neighbouring four rooms. 1335 to 1338. Deck three Sir. Breakfast is served from six am. Call me if you need anything at all."

"Thank you, that's great," Narek said as he pocketed the key cards and went to catch the elevator to re-join his men in the restaurant.

"What's the verdict Sarge?" Ciorrin asked.

"He complimented you on your skills Esclan so well done, I'm proud of you."

"Thanks," Esclan said.

"He said that your repair would hold but we'd be safer to stick to two thirds power. He also said that if something else were to go wrong, we might not be able to fix it a second time."

"That's true," Esclan agreed.

"He said he could replace the whole unit just to be safe and I agreed that was the best idea so we're here overnight after all. I have your room keys here," he said as he deposited the four key cards on the table. "Two to a room so pair yourselves up. Kaylak and Vronil, you're with me in a triple, room 1334, and the guys here have the neighbouring four rooms. Deck three. Breakfast is served here in the restaurant from six in the morning, so how about we meet in here at say, eight?"

"Can I go visit the shops Sarge," Domlin asked. "I'd like to get a present for my wife and daughter."

"Of course," Narek nodded. You all deserve a night off. There's a map of the station just outside the restaurant and there's shops, bars, a vidicom theatre and even a whorehouse. Enjoy yourselves but behave and no getting drunk or you'll hear me swear at you in the morning. Remember you're representing the IGMF so be dignified huh?"

"We will Sarge," Damir said as he and the others got up from the table. "See you three in the morning."

"A drink or two would be nice," Kaylak remarked when the men had left them alone.

"Yes it would, how about it Manuk?" Vronil asked and Narek nodded.

"You're right. Come on then, we might as well at least try to relax since we're stuck here."

The three left the restaurant and headed down to one of the station's four bars. On the way, Kaylak drew Narek's attention to a sign above a door.

"Hey look at that?" he said pointing behind Narek.

"Library and data research," Narek read.

"We might be able to find out about the Fa'ahlima in there," Vronil suggested.

"Good idea, let's give it a try," Narek said as he approached the door and entered. A thin man sat at a desk and smiled as they approached.

"Good evening gentlemen," he said. "How can I help you?"

"Can we look up stuff in here?" Narek asked. "Y'know, research."

"That's the very reason for our existence Sir. It's ten credits per hour at the console. Just place your currency card in the slot on the side of the console and it will remind you when you're getting near to your hour so you can either print stuff off or pay for another hour."

"That's great, thanks," Narek replied.

"Are you familiar with library consoles?" the man asked.

"Umm, nope," the three Vendalans replied in unison.

"We're all grownups," Kaylak remarked. "We can fly spaceships across the galaxy. How hard can a library console be?"

"I'm here if you need any help," the man assured them and watched as they walked to a console and sat down. He retrieved his pad and pencil and continued with his drawing. Ten minutes later, a shadow fell across the paper and he looked up.

"Umm, how do we work the thing?" Narek blushed.

"Okay, let's see," the man said as he sat at the console and switched it on. "What is the subject of your research?"

"The Fa'ahlima," Kaylak replied.

"Okay," the man said and typed furiously. A page popped up with fourteen million, five hundred and two thousand, seven hundred and twenty five entries connected to the Fa'ahlima. "You see, the words you type into the search box at the top will govern what results you get, so it pays to be as specific as possible. Otherwise you find yourself with several million entries to trawl through."

"I get it," Vronil said. "Okay so try Fa'ahlima visiting schedule."

"Good one Manuk," Narek smiled. The man's fingers flew across the keys and resulted in just fourteen entries.

"That's more like it," Narek said.

"There you go," the man said as he rose from the seat. "Just tap the entry you want to read and the relevant page will come up. Tap that button there to return back one page if you wish to change your search criteria."

"Thank you very much," Kaylak said.

One by one, the three read each of the fourteen entries and found twenty planets that routinely recorded the dates of their visits by the Fa'ahlima. From those dates, they were able to work out where the Fa'ahlima go in three months of the year. The problem was, those three months were seven months away and Narek swore.

"Go back to the main search page and try searching on Fa'ahlima, planets visited," Vronil suggested. "Maybe we'll get more data to draw up a plan of their whole year's schedule."

Narek typed with two fingers and found several hundred entries. Kaylak and Vronil sat at separate consoles and, using the same search criteria, split up the research between them. Two hours later, they found many hundreds of planets having regular, almost yearly visits by the Fa'ahlima but one thing puzzled Narek.

"Guys, this is crazy. I've seen four planets in the last five minutes, all claiming to get a visit at the same time of year. That can't be right. Those guys may be mysterious but I'm damn sure they can't be in two places at once."

"Not unless they have several ships and each does a specific route," Kaylak offered. Narek sighed.

"Of course, that has to be it. Poshash," he cursed.

"How are you getting along?" the man asked, having crept up behind them. Narek jumped.

"What? Oh, you made me jump. We're trying to find out the schedule the Fa'ahlima use when they do their visits, and we've just found out that it looks like they have several different ships doing several different routes. We want to know where they'll be now, or in the very near future. The nearest place to where we are now. We know they visited Abdelia 3 just days ago, but when they took off from there, we got our engine problem and dropped behind and now we don't know where they went next."

"Okay," the man nodded. "So you have loads of data that needs to be split into groups, relevant to the probable route between them. That way you can tell where they're likely to be next. We need to cross reference these planets with star maps and work out routes between them on those specific dates." He tapped for a couple of minutes and then a screen popped up showing seventeen different star maps. On each one were highlighted the planets from the research data and each showed a specific route.

"Where's Abdelia 3?" Narek asked and the man continued tapping. One of the star maps came forward to full screen with Abdelia highlighted.

"Fantastic, thank you," Narek sighed with relief.

"Hey Manuk, look," Kaylak said and pointed to the screen. "Coroptima 8 is also on this map."

"So it should be," Vronil replied. "We followed them from there to Abdelia 3."

"Yes but don't you see what's missing?"

"Where's Luzel 2?" Narek asked as he searched the map. A few more taps and a different map popped up with Luzel 2 highlighted.

"Fuck it," Narek hissed. "It's on a different route. We've been chasing the wrong ship."

"Look," Kaylak said as he got up from his seat and paced up and down, scratching his head. "Yes, we've been following the wrong ship, but a Fa'ahlima ship is still a Fa'ahlima ship. We can't hope to get back to the right route now; we've no idea where on that route the ship will be by now. The sensible thing to do is to keep following the one nearest here and when we catch them up, hope they can contact the right ship and put us in touch with Risa."

"He's right Manuk," Vronil said and Narek nodded.

"Okay, so where are they going next?"

"I'll print out this map for you," the man said as he tapped again. "Then I'll ring those planets whose dates show that the Fa'ahlima must have already been and gone. You'll then have your next few destinations."

"Wonderful," Narek said. "Thank you so much for your help. I'm very grateful to you"

"My pleasure," the man smiled as he took the data chip and disappeared through a side door marked, Station Personnel Only. Two minutes later he returned with several large sheets of paper, which he handed to Narek.

"I've printed out all the star maps with the Fa'ahlima routes highlighted on each one," he said. "I've also printed out basic information about each of the worlds still left on your current route, just so you know a little of what to expect if you decide to go there. Best to have too much information than not enough I always say."

"This is really helpful," Narek said as he studied the map showing their current position. "Thank you."

The three sat in the quietest corner of the first bar they found and studied the map. From it they learned that the Fa'ahlima had seven further stops on this particular route, before ending up at their first port of call again.

"I guess they go back to their own planet when they've completed their route," Kaylak said.

"Look at the one with Luzel 2 on it," Vronil said. "This shows that Luzel 2 is their last stop on that route, so they would probably have gone back to their home world right after. No wonder we chased the wrong ship."

"And Coroptima 8 is the nearest stop on this route to Luzel 2," Narek said. "So we naturally assumed they went there from Luzel."

"Easy mistake to make," Kaylak said and the others nodded.

"Looking at the approximate dates of their visits," Narek said. "It looks as if we'll miss them if we head for the next stop on the route. Remember they're gonna be three or four days ahead of us now, so I vote we head for the stop after next and hope we can close the gap."

"Or even the one after that," Vronil suggested. "We have to add the difference in the capabilities of our ships into the equation don't forget. My personal view is that we stand more of a chance of closing the gap by jumping the next two stops and heading for the third."

"Good point Manuk," Kaylak said and Narek nodded. "What does it say about that planet?"

"Zelidol Prime," Vronil read. "An important location in a major shipping lane and the inhabitant's skills in producing state of the art robotics makes this planet one of the four major producers of robots, androids and synthetic humanoids for the manufacturing industry, service industry and non-combatant military applications. One of the co-signees of the Inter-Galactic Military Treaty, Zelidol no longer has its own independent military facility. It therefore surrenders all military independence to the combined forces of the IGMF."

"That's a relief," Narek said. "At least we won't have to keep looking over our shoulders down there."

"Since being given the designation of a Prime world," Vronil continued, "due to it being a major centre for trade, Zelidol has become a very cosmopolitan world since signing the Treaty. Politically stable, Zelidolians have enjoyed over six hundred years of peace since their civil war."

"So we should blend in without a problem," Kaylak remarked.

"What's the weather like?" Narek asked and Vronil scanned the rest of the page.

"Ahh, here it is," he said. "A generally temperate climate in the southern hemisphere, hot and dry around the equatorial region with a definite twice yearly wet season and cool in the northern hemisphere with colder winters."

"Sounds very much like most other places," Narek said. "Once we get there, our scanners will tell us where the highest density of populations are so we can decide where to land. Any guesses as to how long it will take us to get there?"

"Judging by this map, I'd say approximately three or four days, give or take a few hours," Kaylak replied and Narek nodded.

"I'd agree with that. Okay guys, we have a destination. I feel better now. Let's enjoy our drinks; you both more than deserve it."

The three drank and talked of the situation they were in, of their hopes for a successful outcome, and of their memories of Risa. They laughed as they recounted stories of when Narek first told them how he felt about her, of his obvious shyness around her and how Kaylak and Vronil teased him mercilessly about it. When Narek began to express his worries about how Risa might be suffering, his friends did their best to allay his fears. They reminded him constantly that no one knew much about the Fa'ahlima, and stories of their treatment of volunteers were only rumours, without proof or validity. Narek held on to his hope and decided to do his best to focus his attention on reaching the Fa'ahlima rather than falling into despair because of rumours and fireside tales. He pushed the dark thoughts from his mind and held on to the one thought that drove him; he must catch up with the Fa'ahlima and talk to them. Despair could come later if need be, once he knew the truth. Then, and only then, he would allow himself to think about how he was to proceed with his life. For now, he decided that hope would carry him through the next days far more efficiently.

An hour later the three left the bar and Narek felt more relaxed knowing he now had a definite route and plan of action to focus on, despite still feeling imprisoned by their current situation. Sometimes it seemed as if the universe was conspiring against him, punishing him for his shyness and at those moments, despair gripped his heart. He sent a silent prayer to Salifkan, the Vendalan god of triumph in adversity as they walked along the corridors, passing people of many races and worlds, hearing more languages than they had ever heard before. As they passed a brightly lit sign displaying a voluptuous female, her left eye winking provocatively, the door beneath it opened, a group of laughing men emerging and staggering away down the corridor. A tall dark haired woman with large almond shaped blue eyes stood in the doorway and smiled at Narek and his friends, her red lips parting slightly as her tongue emerged to moisten one corner. She spoke to them in a language none of the three could understand.

"Sorry," Narek replied, knowing what she meant without a translation. "Not tonight."

"How much?" Vronil asked.

"One hundred credits per hour," she replied in the common tongue adopted by all the worlds signed up to the Inter-Galactic Treaty. Her accent was perfect and the slight delay as she analysed which language was being spoken, telling Narek that this was a highly sophisticated robotic whore. The lack of life in her eyes as she gazed at them, confirmed it as Vronil nodded and handed over his currency card.

"Are all the girls the same as you?" Narek asked. The female looked at him with those almost perfect but lifeless eyes and after another slightly too long delay she replied.

"Like me?"

"Robots," Narek said.

"We are all guaranteed to give the greatest pleasure to our clients," she responded. "We are guaranteed infection free, self-cleaning and never say no."

"But are you all robots?" Narek pressed.

"We are."

"Okay," he nodded and handed over his currency card. "One hour for me." Kaylak looked at him in surprise. "She's a robot Manuk," Narek explained, "and I need to know that I'm not always going to be like I was on that planet with that woman the other day. I've never hurt a woman before and it worries me that I might've changed y'know? When I get to Risa, if I get to Risa, I need to know I can make her happy. I'm scared I've become something I don't like, a violent monster."

Kaylak and Vronil nodded. "We understand," Kaylak replied. "I know you are the same man I've always known you to be, but I understand your worry. You are the last person I would call a violent monster. You will please her, I know you will."

"And you cannot deny your own needs as a man all the time you are still without a permanent mate," Vronil said. "Your body needs to express itself and your soul needs you to be completely balanced. To deny one part of yourself is a quick way to imbalance."

They entered into a dimly lit reception area and waited while the appropriate amount was deleted from their currency cards. The woman then led them through into a larger room where around a dozen female robotic whores sat waiting for clients.

"You may choose gentlemen," the woman said, sweeping an arm around the room.

"That one," Narek said, indicating a blonde. The woman went over to the seated robot and pressed a finger to the back of her neck. Immediately she stood up and smiled. The woman beckoned Narek over and took a metallic bracelet from the blonde's wrist, placing it around Narek's own, before pressing a finger to the back of the blonde's neck again. The robot immediately looked at Narek and smiled, before taking his hand and leading him through a door in the far wall.

"Would you like to give me a name?" she asked him. Narek looked around the small bedroom and then down at her.

"Risa," he whispered. "For this hour, you are named Risa."

"Risa," she said. "That's pretty."

Narek reached for her and over the course of the next hour, learned that he was as gentle and tender a lover as he always believed himself to be. Thoughts of his angry assault on the tribal woman floated away alongside his worries that he might have become some sort of monster, capable only of violence and harm now that his heart was broken and his soul torn in two. He whispered her name repeatedly and as he reached his climax, he could almost have believed it was actually Risa's body entwined with his own. The sweet voice that cried out in pleasure could almost have been Risa's and as his emotions overflowed in time with his body's release, he allowed himself to believe that it was.

Merita King

CHAPTER NINE

Narek slept surprisingly well and awoke feeling more refreshed and focussed than he could remember since they left Luzel 2. Kaylak and Vronil joined him in an hour of silent prayer before sleeping, and beseeched Salifkan, the god of triumph in adversity for strength to see him through to whatever outcome this journey was to have. After a shower, the three collected their clothes from the station's laundry service and packed, ready for the next leg of their journey, one which Narek hoped would see them catching up with the Fa'ahlima. At eight o clock sharp, they entered the busy restaurant and looked around. Kaylak saw Ciorrin waving from the same table they used for dinner the night before and nodded in response. All three helped themselves to a large amount of food; knowing they were to be back on rations for goodness knows how long, they all agreed it would be sensible to make the most of what was on offer while they were able to. Much of the food was unknown to Narek, and some looked positively disgusting, but there was a large amount of which he felt happy to indulge.

"Morning Sarge," Domlin said as they sat down. "You sleep all right?"

"Yes thank you," Narek nodded. "Better than in a while actually. I hope you all enjoyed your night off."

"Yes Sarge," Marikos grinned and nudged Damir, who snickered and blushed. Kaylak looked at Narek and grinned.

"Okay what did you get up to?" Narek asked. "Tell me the truth now and I might let you off with double cleaning duties instead of triple."

"Oh nothing bad Sir," Marikos replied. "We didn't cause any trouble for anyone or anything like that."

"Then why is Damir blushing like a schoolboy?" Kaylak remarked.

"Because he's no longer a virgin." The men broke into spontaneous applause and Narek clapped him on the back.

"Welcome to adulthood my friend. Now all you have to do is avoid the clap, avoid becoming a father unexpectedly and avoid married women like the plague."

"I'll try to remember Sarge," Damir replied when everyone had stopped laughing.

Narek remembered the evening before and the group of men they all heard cheering and laughing, and how he felt an odd sense of them being disrespectful to his desperate situation. He then realised that the roles were now reversed, and he wondered how many of the other diners were in some terrible predicament that kept them awake all night. His smile faltered, and he took a quick look around but did not see anyone looking obviously worried or sad, so he sent out a silent wish that anyone suffering as he currently was, should find peace and closure soon.

"I wonder how much longer we'll be stuck here," Dodge said.

"Well the Chief Engineer said we should be away sometime during this morning," Narek said.

"How would everyone feel about chipping in to buy some additional food supplies?" Noro asked. "Just a few crates of fruits and vegetables and some more meat. I saw them for sale last night and the cost is surprisingly reasonable. Fifty credits apiece should stock us up nicely for another week."

"I'm happy with that," Esclan said, "but shouldn't we be relying on just rations and what we can glean from our environment?"

"Buying it when it's for sale is gleaning from our environment," Narek replied. "The stuff is available and we have the money. It would save our rations for such times as we have nothing else. I agree with your idea Noro, that's good planning."

"Great," Noro smiled. "Let's write a list. Is there anything anyone really doesn't like?"

"I hate Jolian berries," Ciorrin said. "I'm fine with most veg though."

"I'm allergic to Cantock roots," Domlin said.

"I'm not keen on Wulmats," Kaylak added and both Narek and Vronil nodded their agreement.

"Okay," Noro said as he scribbled. "No Jolian berries, Cantock roots or Wulmats."

"Once we've finished breakfast," Narek said, "we can each get fifty credits off our cards and give them to Noro. I noticed a currency dispenser down by the shopping area."

"Oh, by the way Sarge," Noro said as he dug into his pocket. "I have this for you." He brought out a small bundle wrapped in soft paper and handed it over. Inside was a bracelet of shiny Palentadium wire and a dozen tiny pearlescent shells. Narek gasped as he looked at it.

"Oh wow, it's beautiful. Thank you so much, Risa will love it."

A.W.O.L

"My god you're a craftsman Noro," Esclan remarked.

"Awesome work buddy," Marikos said.

"My father was a master jeweller back home on Prasnora 7," Noro explained, "and he started teaching me the basics when I was just a kid. You all know where to come for those presents for your wives. I'm afraid I had to cannibalise a few of our IGMF badges for the Palentadium wire though."

"I think we can overlook that on this occasion," Kaylak replied.

"Definitely," Narek nodded. "Thank you. I mean it, this is incredible work."

"My pleasure Sarge."

Narek looked at the delicate creation and smiled as he allowed himself to imagine giving it to Risa, and hoped very much that she would like it. Wrapping it carefully so as not to damage it, he dropped it into his pocket.

An hour later, having told everyone to meet at dock eight the moment they hear him being hailed, Narek wandered along corridors and found his way to the main observation deck and looked out at the stars. He could not help but wonder if Risa was looking at these same stars, somewhere on the Fa'ahlima home world and thinking about him. There was no way for him to know, but he hoped so. The thought of her so far away, and the circumstances that brought about her absence, seemed to be somehow exaggerated by the vastness of the cosmos that he now gazed at, and he ached to hold her close and tell her he loved her. Deep inside his gut, he felt a knot of pain as the gnawing loneliness gripped him, and he was so far inside of himself that he did not see the man come up beside him.

"Good morning Lashen," the voice said, startling Narek out of his musings. His concentration on his despair now broken, he turned to see an elderly man standing beside him. It was obvious at once that he was not Vendalan, and Narek wondered how he knew to use his military designation in his own language.

"Morning," he answered. "I'm sorry, I didn't see you there."

"No matter," the man replied. "I saw you were obviously deeply worried about something and thought you might like some conversation."

"Thank you."

"You're missing someone, yes?"

"Yes," Narek nodded. "I didn't realise it showed so obviously."

"Well perhaps not to everyone else but I can see it," the man replied. "I'm Xerosian. My name is Plaian."

"Xerosian?" Narek replied, raising his eyebrows in surprise. "I've never met any of your people before."

"Do the rumours of our psychic abilities worry you?" he asked.

"Not at all," Narek said. "I've nothing to hide really. Are the rumours true then?"

"Probably, at least the ones that say how accurately we can read thoughts and feelings. The ones that say we use our abilities for nefarious purposes however, are completely false."

"Okay," Narek laughed and wondered if he should ask him about Risa and whether his quest to reunite with her was to be successful. On the one hand, he was desperate to know, but on the other hand, if this journey were to fail, prior knowledge of the futility of it would probably break him. He spent a few seconds battling with the choice. Should he ask or should he keep quiet?

"Tell me my friend," Plaian asked suddenly. "If you knew what the ultimate outcome of your quest was to be, how would you proceed?"

"That depends upon the outcome itself," Narek replied, realising he had been reading his thoughts the whole time. "If it is to fail, then I would return with my men to our base immediately. If it were to be successful, then I would proceed with all haste. I guess anyone would do the same."

"And how do you intend to proceed, not having prior knowledge?" Plaian continued.

"I'm going on with it of course. Until I know for sure that I've failed, I must try to find her."

"Just supposing," Plaian said, "that the next stop on your journey is one where you will touch someone's life in such a way as to completely change the course of that life for the better. Supposing that without that moment, that person would die, or be destined to a life of misery, simply because they did not meet and talk with you for a few moments?"

"Well," Narek thought. "We touch each other's lives all the time, and I guess we don't know how those moments affect people. I can remember times when I've met and talked with someone and the moment has stayed with me and affected my choices, both positively and negatively. Just a few days ago, my unit and I had such an encounter, and three people's lives will now change for the better." Narek smiled as he remembered Jalien Talko who was, he hoped, feeling happy at her imminent reunion with her husband.

"Supposing that you knew your quest was doomed to fail," Plaian said as he looked Narek right in the eyes, "and you then decided not to continue but to return from whence you came. What then becomes of those people waiting for you to touch their lives, and those waiting to touch yours?"

"I guess those moments wouldn't happen and the people's lives would be different to some degree, as would my own," Narek replied, realising where this conversation was going. His heart fell.

"Vendalans believe in an afterlife yes?" Narek nodded.

"Yes. We believe we go to a spiritual plane of existence and that our actions in this life, affect the destinies of other Vendalans still in their physical lives. As we live, we know we are laying the foundations for the destinies of all future Vendalans who come after us."

"When you come to the end of your physical life," Plaian said. "When your actions are weighed and the effect they are deemed to have on all the other Vendalan energies is decided, will it make a difference if you had prior knowledge of the outcome? Would the fact that you gave up your quest, simply because you knew you were not to get what you sought, make a difference when your life is weighed?"

"Oh yes," Narek nodded, a tear escaping and running down his cheek. "It would make a great difference in a negative way."

"Then you know why I cannot tell you what you want to know," Plaian replied, placing a hand on Narek's shoulder. Narek could not speak for long moments, so he nodded his understanding as he tried to regain control of his emotions.

"My whole being aches to be with her," he explained. "Everything that is bad about this situation is my fault and I'm consumed with making it right, but I'm in despair that I may be too late. I won't be able to live if we never find her, my soul is now torn in half and it's my own fault. I will have no choice but to take up the Pantisal and face the Tal ak Roi with my guilt. That will end the suffering of my own half soul, but it won't help Risa, and she will spend the rest of her days believing a lie and not knowing I love her. She may be suffering at the hands of her captors, she may even be dead by now and blaming me for the torture of her last days. This is killing me and I don't mind admitting that it is becoming a hard burden to bear. A better man than I would struggle with it."

"Whatever the outcome of your quest is to be, you must go forward into it with focus and determination," Plaian explained gently. "You must experience every moment naturally and from your own will. Only then will your spirit grow in the proper way and both your destinies unfold as the universe dictates."

"I understand your wisdom," Narek sighed. "Thank you for listening. You must be forever burdened by people's demands for help."

"We do not see it as being burdened by pleas for help, but more as an opportunity to impart universal wisdom, which we hope will help them to live with more peace in their hearts. Now it is time for you to go," Plaian replied. "I bid you peace for your heart my friend." He took hold of Narek's hands and squeezed gently.

"Sergeant Narek Jenn to dock eight please," the intercom boomed through the observation deck.

"Thank you," Narek said as he turned and left. The ageing Xerosian watched him go and smiled.

"Fear not my new friend," he whispered to the empty room. "Fear not."

Narek entered dock eight to find Noro supervising the loading of the supplies into the ship. Kaylak and Vronil were already talking to the Chief Engineer and most of the men were standing about. Damir and Esclan came running in behind him.

"Ahh Sergeant Jenn," the Chief Engineer said. "She's all done and ready for you. If you could sign this invoice, we'll charge it direct to your base commander on Luzel 2."

"That's great, thanks," Narek said as he signed the mobile device and handed it back. "We really appreciate you doing this so quickly."

"No problem at all. I'll just move her onto the exit ramp and you can be away."

Narek took the controls and waited for the bay doors to open. The intercom crackled.

"LMB72 this is Deep Space Refuelling Station Zeta 12 confirming you are free to exit the docking bay. Thank you for your custom and safe journey."

"Thank you for your hospitality Zeta 12," Narek replied as he lifted the ship off the pad and headed towards the open bay door. "LMB72 out."

Once across the speed restriction zone that enveloped the station, Narek engaged the Trans Wave Flow Core and listened for the familiar hum as it began to spin. The ship leapt through space and Kaylak entered the co-ordinates for their next destination.

"Seventy six hours to Zelidol Prime," he announced.

"Okay," Narek nodded. "We should try to think of ways of keeping the guys amused over the next three days. Maybe you could come up with some oral tests on basic survival skills for them or something?"

"Sure, no problem. It wouldn't hurt to do some on military procedures and regulations either. Maybe even some questions on inter-galactic diplomacy."

"Great idea," Narek nodded.

"We could also set them some tasks," Vronil suggested. "Give them something to build maybe, or a make believe problem to overcome and get them working in pairs or groups of three to find a solution. We've plenty of stuff in the stores they can mess with and you never know, some of their ideas might be worth remembering. This bunch are very bright and work well together."

"That's fantastic Manuk," Kaylak said and Narek nodded. "Probably be a laugh too."

"They are a great bunch of guys, "Narek said. "One of the best groups I've had. They're all going to make first class soldiers. Make sure they get some down time each evening so they can relax and be guys."

The ship sped through the void towards Zelidol Prime and as the hours dragged by, Narek got more impatient. It seemed that the closer they got to their goal, the slower the time ticked by, and by the time Marikos called to say they were approaching the Zelidol system, Narek had not slept in twenty-seven hours.

"Four hours until we enter the Zelidol system Sarge," Marikos called through the intercom. Narek went up to the cockpit and checked the scanner.

"Thank fuck we're here at last," he said. "Give me another call when we're approaching Zelidol Prime."

"Yes Sir," Marikos replied.

Narek flipped on the intercom. "All hands, pack your bags. Remember this is an IGMF world so make sure you're dressed properly. The Governing Military Officer here is from Skanshass 2, so everyone refresh yourselves with the language so you can use the appropriate military designations." He went to his tiny room and packed his own bag before sitting down and cleaning his laser rifle and side arm for the tenth time since leaving Zeta 12. After putting his bag and rifle with the others by the exit hatchway, he sat with the men in the mess and had a drink.

"We have to talk about what might happen when we finally catch up with the Fa'ahlima," he said. "We already know that the ship that comes to Zelidol is not the one that came to Luzel 2, so Risa won't be on it. What I have to do is convince them to somehow communicate with the folks back on their home world, and see if they will let me talk to her or go visit to pick her up or something."

"They must have procedures for this kind of thing," Damir said. "I would assume that people sometimes volunteer on the spur of the moment, maybe due to family arguments or something, and their families must ask to get in touch. This can't be the only time this will have ever happened."

"I agree Sarge," Ciorrin said. "They must be used to angry relatives wanting to know what has happened to their loved ones. They must have a set procedure in place to deal with it."

"One that doesn't involve shooting us," Dodge remarked.

"Of course they must," Esclan said. "They're a very advanced race, so it stands to reason they will be diplomatic about this type of situation."

"Everything I've read about them," Narek said, "says how polite and friendly they are when spoken to. I didn't find one report about them being violent or aggressive. If I'm polite and just tell them the truth, I'm sure that even if they turn me down, they'll do so politely."

"What if they do turn you down?" Ribas asked.

"Then we go to their home world and turn up on their doorstep," Narek replied. "It's just a week's flying time from Zelidol, so there'd be plenty of time to put me down and get back home before you're overdue back on Luzel 2."

"Always assuming we'd be prepared to leave you," Esclan said and everyone nodded.

"I'm proud of you guys, every one of you," Narek said. "You've all been first class soldiers and I know you're all going to become men the IGMF will be proud to have representing them. I wouldn't allow people I care about to throw away their careers and maybe put their lives in danger, just for my own personal quest. If we do end up having to go there, you are all ordered to return to Luzel 2. Am I making myself clear?"

"Yes Sir," everyone chorused, each one silently vowing not to obey, should it come to it.

"As soon as we get into orbit," Narek said, "scan for the five largest populated areas and pick one that has some country nearby where we can set up base. The Zelidol authorities need to know we're here on a survival training exercise."

"No problem," Kaylak nodded. "That won't take long."

"Okay, Narek sighed. "Now we just sit and wait."

"We're approaching Zelidol Prime Sarge," Marikos called and Narek leapt up.

"Okay guys, this is it."

Kaylak was sitting in the co-pilot's seat scanning the planet. "I've found the five largest populated areas and this one seems the best candidate," he said, pointing it out to Narek. "There's open country all around and a mountain range over there. There's a couple of rivers and probably plenty of game too."

"Okay, put those co-ordinates into our identification signal."

The intercom crackled and Narek jumped.

"Unidentified vessel, this is Zelidol Prime Aerospace. Please identify yourself and state the reason for your visit."

"Zelidol Prime, this is," he hesitated. "This is Oshlok Narek Jenn of the Inter-Galactic Military Force and this is military vessel LMB72. I am here with ten of my men on a survival training exercise and respectfully request permission to land at the co-ordinates attached to our identification signal, which should be with you now." Turning to Vronil, he grinned and blushed. "I almost forgot what Skanshass for Sergeant was. Make sure everyone knows the full range of designations in the language."

"No problem," Vronil grinned back.

"LMB72 we have your signal. Your request is accepted. Two military fighters are on their way to escort you to the co-ordinates."

"Thank you Zelidol. Awaiting their arrival. LMB72 out."

Marikos followed the two fighters down through the upper atmosphere of Zelidol Prime towards their chosen landing co-ordinates. Narek looked out of the cockpit window and wondered if the Fa'ahlima were waiting down there, or if they were yet to arrive, or, Gods forbid, if they had already left, and he hoped with all of his being that they had not decided to change their schedule and not visit the planet at all. As the ship approached the surface, Narek shook his negative thoughts away and refocused his attention on the matter at hand. He knew this was probably his last chance to catch up with them and if he could not make contact with them here, it would mean a dangerous flight to Fa'ahla to demand attention. If not that, then he would have many months to wait it out back on Luzel 2 with Lorella a constant thorn in his side before the Fa'ahlima visited again next year.

The landing site was three miles from the boundary of the city, at the edge of a beautiful valley with the foothills of a mountain range to the south, the open expanse of the valley stretching out for several miles to the north before meandering around to the east between the mountains and out of sight. Stands of trees dotted the valley and a mile to the north, three rivers converged into one raging torrent that plunged southwards along the valley floor. It was beautiful and reminded Narek of the area around his home city on Vendala 4. The fighters landed beside them and he went to meet the pilots.

"Okay guys, get your papers ready, these guys will probably want to make sure we are who I said we are." He strolled towards the two men and smiled.

"Thanks for the escort guys. Oshlok Narek Jenn of the IGMF. Base 7, Luzel 2. Here are my papers."

"Welcome to Zelidol Oshlok, I'm Draille Talen Sebb and this is Draille Aslik Morda, the man on the left said as he examined Narek's papers. "This all seems to be in order. We will need to check everyone's papers I'm afraid. Security is a little tight just now."

"No problem," Narek said, mentally reminding himself that the Skanshass military designation Draille meant pilot. "Follow me, the guys are just unpacking. Has there been a problem?"

"No, not a problem as such," Aslik Morda said. "It's just that we're expecting the Fa'ahlima here tomorrow morning, and in previous years, their visit has attracted the wrong sort of attention."

"Oh?" Narek remarked. "We've never had problems with them on Luzel 2."

"They aren't the problem," Aslik said. "For the past few years, up until a few months ago, there was quite a bit of a problem with fanatical religious groups here on Zelidol. They tried to cause problems with the Fa'ahlima and almost caused an inter-galactic incident during last year's visit. Things are calm now but we're not taking any chances."

"That makes sense," Narek nodded.

"You're free to make use of the valley and mountains as much as you need to," Talen said, "but if you go two miles eastwards from here, you'll see a military presence. They won't cause you any problems; they're just guarding the area that's been put aside for the Fa'ahlima compound. It's probably best if you just stay out of that area. They will know of your presence here so you won't have any hostility should you run into them."

"Okay that's fine, thanks," Narek said. "Okay boys come get your papers checked, step to it guys," he yelled into the open hatchway of the ship.

Narek watched the fighters take off and head away to the east and smiled to himself. He was so relieved they had beaten the Fa'ahlima and was happy that Talen and Aslik had given him all the information he needed. Without even asking, he now knew when they were to arrive and where they would be camped. All he needed to do now was decide how he was to approach them. He sighed and felt a conflict within. On the one hand, he felt the end of his journey was near, but on the other, he sensed this was just the beginning of a new one, but he could not explain the reason for this conflict. All he knew for sure was that whatever was to transpire in the coming days, would not only decide whether he was to find Risa, but whether he was doomed to end the suffering of his half soul on the point of a Pantisal. His parents heartbroken wails would be ringing in his ears as he waited for Shashowan, the Receiver of Souls to decide whether he will receive him with open arms or order him to the Kon so Fahl, the Pit of Sorrow, for eternity. Although not a devoutly traditional Vendalan, Narek trusted Shashowan to do the right thing, and decided to accept whatever decision this most revered of his gods came to, with as much grace as he could muster.

Once the ship was unpacked, Narek decided to let everyone relax for the evening, rather than begin a training exercise right away. This was their first real survival experience so he did not want to push them too hard, especially as they were all being so loyal to him during this personal quest. There would be plenty of opportunities to push them to their limits later in their training, when they had more experience.

"Okay guys, tonight we relax for tomorrow, you will all be on a training exercise for a whole day and night. This will be your final examination of this exercise, and the points you get from this trip are very important for the rest of your training schedule. You're all going to be first rate soldiers but don't let my confidence in you encourage you to drop your standards. Always remember that at any moment, your own survival, and that of your company, could depend on what you learn here. Wars could be won or lost on what you're now learning; millions of lives are constantly at stake for any soldier on duty, so pay attention to your learning and use it well in your career. Okay lecture over, who's cooking tonight?"

"I am," Kaylak said. "Shall I use the ship's kitchen or do it survival style?"

"Use the ship's kitchen," Narek replied. "Let's take tonight to relax and take in this beautiful scenery." Kaylak nodded and headed into the ship.

Narek was up before dawn. He wanted to spend an hour in silent prayer to Alima, the god of love and bonding and beseech her to help him reach Risa and accept his love. By the time Vronil found him, he was on all fours, tears streaming down his cheeks as he silently mouthed the words of his prayer. He sat beside him and joined him in his prayer and when they were done, he reminded him that he and Kaylak had freely shared their souls with him and begged him to take strength from them.

"Reil estrima maiy Manuk, escashriel so potra sakrichi," he whispered. "We are with you brother, make use of our souls."

"Swan kiahi, niahaksa sakrichi," Narek replied. "Thank you, I feel your souls."

"Nitchayi, estri coyan lasmeriel ko cheyonichi," Vronil said as he looked at the rapidly brightening sky. "Come, it is time to wake the men."

Narek wiped his eyes and stood, looking at the sky. With a deep sigh, he turned and went into the ship to wake the men. Fifteen minutes later, eight yawning soldiers stood to attention.

"Okay boys today is the day you put everything you've learned in class into action. From now until this time tomorrow morning, you are the only eight survivors of a military troopship crash. The ship was a total loss and all you have is your full kit, a few bits of the ship's outer hull, your laser rifle and sidearm." He indicated a pile of scrap metal from the stores. "There is no working comms, all of the food on board the ship, along with all of the water, has been lost, as have I and your Corporal and Lance Corporal, but someone did manage to get a distress signal off just before the crash. You had the unfortunate luck to crash land onto an extremely hostile planet where you know from previous intel, several hostile factions operate. For the entirety of this exercise, you are on your own. You will pick a leader, investigate your immediate surroundings, find or build shelter, find food and water. You must dig in and make a camp you can defend, whilst trying to remain as invisible to the locals as possible, and waiting for rescue. We will be observing at all times but we will not be answering questions or helping you out in any way unless your life is threatened. Do you understand?"

"Sir yes Sir," the men yelled and Narek grinned.

"Get to it boys and good luck, he said and went to stand with Kaylak and Vronil to watch.

Merita King

A.W.O.L

CHAPTER TEN

Narek was impressed with the men. They quickly voted Noro as leader and all three of the observers agreed with the choice. As mid-day approached, they had secured a supply of water, hunted successfully for a meal, scouted the immediate area and selected a good spot a hundred yards up the side of the mountain to the south of the ship to dig in. A gigantic boulder stuck out from the mountainside and with the aid of several scrap metal sheets which they propped up on piles of stones, and a covering of stones to hide the metallic surface, they had a good hideout. As the men fed, Narek heard the familiar drone of a spaceship overhead and looked up. A very large shuttle was headed east of them and came into land a couple of miles away, just out of sight around the curve of the valley entrance.

"Ko Fa'ahlima metafoma," Vronil said and looked at Narek. "The Fa'ahlima have arrived."

Narek felt his insides flutter as he watched the ship until it was out of sight. His heart leapt up into his mouth and he breathed sharply in to stem the emotion. He knew Risa was not on that ship, but just the fact that it was here, in the same valley, brought his feelings bubbling to the surface and he fought to control them.

"Re humyi akwahash do ko cheyonichi. Reliopak matan maiy noya insius," he said quietly. "My first priority is the men. I will go and speak with them tomorrow."

Despite aching to go and talk with the Fa'ahlima, Narek was as good as his word and stayed with his men throughout the exercise. He watched them with Kaylak and Vronil, discussed their performance and made extensive entries into the training log. The only slight disappointment was when the men changed the watch halfway through the night. Not only were they sufficiently noisy clambering over the rocks so that any hostiles lurking in the immediate area would hear them, but he could clearly see Marikos and Dodge as they hunkered down at their respective watch positions. In the early hours of the morning, Kaylak suggested they give the men a little surprise. After carefully donning their laser bulletproof jackets, they crept up to the hideout. Kaylak lobbed a rock, which fell a few yards from Ciorrin as he sat at his watch. Ciorrin had been struggling to stay awake but he was instantly alert and flipping down his night sight goggles. He lifted his rifle in the direction of the sound. Vronil crept around to the side and broke a stick, just twenty yards from Ribas' watch position and had to force himself not to laugh as he almost dropped his rifle in surprise. After his initial fright, Ribas levelled his rifle in the direction of the noise and Vronil was very impressed to find the gun pointing right at him.

Narek heard the whispers of the two on watch as they notified their comrades and in less than a minute the three had eight rifles pointing at them. They crept away and waited for an hour until the watched team changed, before repeating the procedure. As dawn broke, Narek stretched himself and yawned. Despite taking it in turns with Kaylak and Vronil to get a couple of hours sleep, he was exhausted and realised that sitting on his ass and doing nothing is often more tiring than hours of hard labour. He fired the flare to signal the end of the exercise and waited while the men clambered out of their hideout and came down the mountainside yawning. Once they were all present, Kaylak brought them to attention.

"Well done guys, all of you. I'm proud of you. All three of us are very impressed with your performance during the exercise. Once you've dismantled the hideout and made sure you've left no trace to harm the environment, go get a shower and some breakfast. Those who want to catch up on sleep may do so; you have eight hours free time. Go."

Over breakfast, Narek decided on a plan of action.

"After breakfast, I'm going to go and see if I can speak with the Fa'ahlima," he said.

"What if you don't come back Sarge?" Noro said.

"I'll be back," Narek said. "They usually only take people when they sound that horn of theirs so unless they take me under guard for my cheek at approaching them, I'll be back."

"What will you say to them?" Esclan asked.

"The truth I guess," Narek replied. "I'll tell them Risa volunteered because she mistakenly believed something that wasn't true, that someone lied to her and she decided to leave because of that lie. I'll tell them I want her to know the truth and ask them if they will let me speak with her, or communicate with her, or even go with them to visit her."

"I hope they have some form of compassion," Ribas said and everyone nodded.

A.W.O.L

After a quick shower and change of uniform, Narek set out, the good wishes of his men ringing in his ears. He was unarmed, determined to show the Fa'ahlima that he was approaching them in peace and meant no harm. As he walked across the valley, he knew that a door was closing on part of his life and although he could not know what was to come, he knew that after this meeting, his life would never be the same again. The leaves were beginning to turn gold and Narek guessed it was autumn time on Zelidol and his heart sank a little. He had never liked this season and always thought of it as the time when everything begins to die. Even winter was better than autumn, at least you knew everything was waiting to spring back to life again once the cold weather disappeared.

When he got to within sight of the Fa'ahlima camp, Narek noticed that a large number of people were standing around, looking at these strange visitors. Groups of them sat with picnics spread out, cases of beer and he heard heated discussions in languages he did not understand. It seemed to him that the Fa'ahlima were quite a draw wherever they went. For once, he did not feel the odd one out, his spots not causing him to be self-conscious for the first time in a long while. As he got nearer to the Fa'ahlima compound, Narek saw IGMF soldiers patrolling the perimeter fence and nodded to a couple of them who happened to notice him. He saluted when he passed an officer, who nodded and returned the gesture and felt pleased that the military here were not bothering him.

The entrance to the Fa'ahlima compound came into view and Narek saw the two guards standing at the gate. He stopped, knowing that this was his moment and hoping with all of his being that they would receive him favourably. He took a deep breath and marched up to the guards.

"May I speak with someone please?" he asked. One of the guards looked at him, turning his head ever so slightly to the side as he did so. The prominent ridge down the centre of his face causing his eyes to be just a tiny bit side facing rather than front facing. The weapon he held looked fearsome to Narek and he guessed it was some sort of pulse energy weapon. If they shot him for his cheek, he would not stand a chance. He took another deep breath and smiled at the guards.

"What is your business with the Fa'ahlima?" the guard on the right asked in the common tongue adopted by all of the worlds in the Inter-Galactic Treaty. Narek was impressed with his accent.

"I mean no disrespect Sir," he said. "I'm unarmed and here peacefully. I want to speak with someone about a personal matter." People had started to notice and Narek blushed as he looked at the crowd beginning to gather behind him. The guard spoke into some sort of communication device attached to his wrist and Narek wished he could speak their language. He hoped the guard was not calling for someone to come and arrest him, or worse.

"The Kreelak will come," the guard said when he finished his communication. "Wait here."

"Kreelak?" Narek asked, thinking that by seeming to take an interest, they would be friendly to him.

"The one in charge of this vessel," the guard answered.

"Ahh, thank you," Narek replied with a smile. "I don't speak your language and didn't know what the word Kreelak meant."

"No one but the Fa'ahlima speaks the Fa'ahla tongue," the guard said. Narek was trying to think of something to say to continue the friendly conversation when a man appeared from the open hatchway of the huge shuttle and walked towards him. He wore a long blue robe with two wide bands from each shoulder that met in the centre of his chest with a large embroidered symbol. He said something to the guards and both stepped aside. He looked at Narek and then smiled.

"Welcome friend, you may enter," he said. "I will speak with you on your personal matter."

"Thank you Sir," Narek replied. "I'm very grateful for your time." He followed the man in through the open hatchway and along a corridor. Halfway along, the man waved his hand across a sensor plate and a portion of the wall slid back, revealing a small room with seating arranged around the walls. A small table in the centre held two glasses and a jug of bright yellow liquid.

"Sit please, and make yourself comfortable. It is hot on Zelidol, help yourself to a drink."

"Thank you very much," Narek replied as he poured himself a glass and took a tentative sip. "That's delicious," he replied.

"It is called Barit. It's a mixture of fruit juices and other extracts and has many health enhancing properties. Have as much as you want. When your body has received all the health enhancements it needs, you will find you no longer crave it."

"Thank you," Narek said, helping himself to a second glass.

"Now what is this personal matter that requires you to draw such a crowd by daring to approach the Fa'ahlima guards?"

"Oh I'm sorry," Narek said. "I didn't want to cause any problems. That's not why I'm here at all."

"Do not apologise my friend," the man laughed. "I was joking. No one has dared to approach us in such a manner for a long time, despite the fact that we are always open and friendly with everyone when engaging with them."

"You are a mysterious people," Narek remarked. "No one knows much about you and with all the rumours that go around, I guess people are afraid of what they don't know."

"But you are not afraid."

"No," Narek replied. "I believe that if strangers are approached with honesty and openness, they are more likely to respond in kind."

"Is that the man or the soldier talking?" the man asked.

"The man," Narek said. "As a soldier, I have to take a slightly different stance of course. I'm not here as a soldier Sir, just a man who is desperate to right a great wrong."

"Tell me of this great wrong, after you have introduced yourself properly. My name is Ka'abash and I always like a man's name when he has been brave enough to overcome his fear and approach me."

"Yes of course, forgive me my manners. My name is Narek. Narek Jenn."

"Well Narek, what do you have to tell me?"

Over the next hour, Narek told Ka'abash everything. He held nothing back and more than once, his emotions overcame him but he wanted him to know the whole story, and more importantly, how it had affected him. Ka'abash listened intently, not once did he interrupt Narek but gave him his full attention, for he believed that when someone has approached them in such a manner, the least he can do is listen. Narek explained about Risa, the lie woven by Lorella, the letter that Risa left for him and how it broke his heart to read it. He told him of his love for her and his hesitation in approaching her, and his deep regret for that hesitation. He explained about the desperate chase across the galaxy and his sadness at the prospect of never catching up with them to at least try to make things right. His voice shaking with emotion, he told him how his soul was broken and how, as a man with only half a soul, he is doomed to the Kon so Fahl. He told him of his obligation to take the Tal ak

Roi and put his half soul in the hands of Shashowan, the Receiver of Souls. Finally, he told him of his hope that the god takes pity on him and brings him to a peaceful afterlife so that he does not cause anguish for future Vendalans with his damaged soul. When he was finished, Narek was mentally and emotionally exhausted. He drank the yellow Barit and dried his eyes.

"That is my story Sir," he said. "You have the whole truth now. I beg you to allow me to speak with Risa, or at least get a message to her so that she can know the truth. She still believes the lie and it kills me to know that she will live her whole life believing it. Please, at least let me give her the truth. I'm begging you, I'll do anything, pay any price that is within my power to provide. I have money, not a lot but I have savings from my pay as a soldier. You can take it all, please."

"It is not within my power to grant such a wish," Ka'abash replied. "I am simply Kreelak of this vessel and it is not the Fa'ahlima way to expel volunteers once they have given themselves to our service."

"Please, I'm begging you Sir," Narek said as another tear escaped and traced its way down his cheek.

"As I said Narek," Ka'abash continued. "It is not within my power to grant your wish. What is within my power though, is to pass on your request to those who do have the authority to grant it, or not. I will communicate with those back on Fa'ahla who can decide this. I will come to you with their decision this evening. I will have guards escorting me; there has been some trouble here on Zelidol in past years during our visit and the local military have advised me to take a guard when I leave our compound. They will not cause you or your men any hostility, I give you my word."

"Thank you," Narek replied, the relief obvious in his voice. "Thank you so much. I would be happy to return here this evening, to save you the walk."

"That won't be necessary," Ka'abash said. "I will enjoy the evening air after being on the ship for so long. To see the sky and feel the breeze is something you don't realise you miss until it's too late to appreciate it. Until this evening Narek. I cannot promise you the governors will grant your wish, but I will make sure they hear you."

"Thank you Sir, I really appreciate your time."

"Come, I will escort you to the gate. Let's give the locals something to gossip about eh?"

A.W.O.L

The people stared as Narek walked back through the crowd and headed back to his ship. He felt self-conscious but in a good way this time. As he walked, he went over their conversation in his head and tried to decide whether Ka'abash was on his side or not, but he found the man almost impossible to read. He had been open and friendly and had listened to the story with what seemed at least to be his full attention and, Narek realised, it did feel good to tell someone else about the problem. As he saw the shuttle ahead, he knew he had done his best and all he could do now was to wait for their decision. He also knew that this afternoon was going to be one of the longest of his life.

"How did it go Sarge?" Ribas asked.

"I talked with a guy called Ka'abash," Narek replied. "He's the Kreelak of their ship, which I guess is their word for Captain."

"What was he like?" Noro asked.

"He was very friendly. I told him everything and asked for his help."

"And did he give it?" Esclan asked.

"Well sort of," Narek replied. "He said he doesn't have the authority to grant my request, which is understandable I guess. He promised to communicate with some folks back on their planet who can decide such things and let me know this evening what they've decided. He's coming here this evening to tell me by the way, so don't freak out when you see the guards with him. Everyone is to be unarmed."

"Yes Sir," everyone nodded.

"I warn you now though," Narek continued, "that this afternoon's waiting is going to kill me, so if I'm snappy with you, I apologise now."

"No problem Sarge," Damir nodded. "I've kept some lunch for you by the way."

"Thanks. Hey, is it possible to get hold of something called, oh what was it called? This bright yellow drink called umm, Barit. You ever heard of it guys?" Everyone shook their heads.

"We'll certainly look out for it though," Marikos said, making a note in his journal. "Is it nice then?"

"It's lovely," Narek replied.

Narek spent well over an hour in prayer with Kaylak and Vronil and together they beseeched their gods for help and strength, and Narek gave his word to Shashowan that he would honour the proper tradition and take the Tal ak Roi if necessary. As the afternoon dragged on, Narek became more and more stressed. He spent some time working out and sparring with the men to get rid of some of the emotional tension and it helped, a little. The sound of a shuttle landing nearby had Narek racing from the ship, expecting to see Ka'abash and his guards but the sight of an IGMF Captain almost made him swear aloud. He saluted and greeted the Captain, who returned his salute and smiled.

"Oshlok Jenn?" Narek nodded.

"Yes Coltona," he replied, thankful he had remembered the proper Skanshass military designation. "How can I be of service?"

"At ease soldier. I just wanted to ask a favour. I have a unit heading for Luzel 2 for survival training in a couple of days and I was hoping our ship could tag along with yours. We're using the trip to give some trainee pilots some field experience. They will have the relevant officers with them but they're going to try to be just observers and let them do the work. Another ship around with experienced pilots on board would make them all feel better."

"Of course Sir," Narek replied. "They're welcome to tag along."

"Thank you. Is your departure date flexible? They should be ready to go in two days' time, but there just might be a day's delay. I'm hoping not but there is a slim chance. Will that be a problem?"

"Not at all Sir, just tell us when you're ready and we'll fit in with you."

"Thank you very much. Someone will get back to you as soon as we've worked things out."

"Very well Sir," Narek said and saluted as the Captain turned to leave.

"Looks like we'll be having company on our return to Luzel guys," he said once the ship had left.

"Well if they're trainee pilots," Ribas said, "better they go in front."

"Now now," Narek said when they had all stopped laughing. "You were a trainee pilot once."

"Anyone fancy a few games of Tapshots?" Noro asked and several of the men nodded.

Narek was dozing in the cool of the early evening when a hand on his shoulder woke him.

"Sarge?" Narek awoke to see Ciorrin standing over him.

"What's up?"

"Over there," he said, indicating with a nod. "Look." Narek looked and saw Ka'abash approaching with four guards, two of whom carried a wooden box between them.

A.W.O.L

"Oh shit, they're here," Narek said as he jumped up. "Pray for the right answer guys." He went and greeted the Fa'ahlima party. "Welcome. Come and sit."

"Thank you Narek," Ka'abash replied with a warm smile. Narek led them around the ship to where several chairs were laid out, a small box in the middle serving as a makeshift table. The men stood and he introduced everyone.

"It's basic but please make yourselves comfortable," he said.

"I've brought a gift for you and your men," Ka'abash said, indicating to the two guards to bring the box forward. They opened it to reveal six large bottles of bright yellow liquid. "Some Barit for you all to enjoy."

"Wow, thank you," Narek said. "Guys? This is the drink I was telling you about. Try it, it's wonderful." When everyone had tried it and agreed it was indeed wonderful, Narek looked at the Fa'ahlima Kreelak and said one last silent prayer.

"Please tell me Sir," he said. "This waiting is killing me."

"I understand Narek," Ka'abash replied, "and I do have a solution for you that is not an outright refusal."

"Oh thank the gods," Narek sighed.

"The Governors back on Fa'ahla have deliberated this problem for the past few hours. Normally we would not consider letting go of someone who has willingly volunteered themselves to us without duress. In this case however, the woman Risa volunteered wholly due to her belief in what she had been told, which was a lie. The Governors decided therefore, that her decision to volunteer was flawed and that it must, somehow, be made right. It is not our way to keep people with us under any form of duress. We only accept those who come willingly. What has been decided is that if you should volunteer for one year, you will then be free to find Risa and if she wishes, you may both leave Fa'ahla with our blessing. If she should decide to stay, you may choose to leave or stay as you wish."

"A year?" Narek replied, his eyes wide with shock. "A whole year?"

"That is the Governors' decision, yes."

"I umm, I don't know what to say," Narek said, his mind racing to try to make sense of this offer.

"I know it is not what you were hoping for but think of it this way. The decision you have to make is whether you wish to let Risa know the truth or not. Now, you can decide either that even taking a year to get the truth to her is worth the effort, or that it is not. You must decide of your own free will."

"I want to be with her, more than anything else in my life. If it takes a year than that is how long I will work to bring her the truth."

"You don't have to decide now Narek," Ka'abash said. "You will hear the horn tomorrow and you have one hour to come to us and volunteer. If you don't turn up, we will assume you've decided not to come and leave as our schedule demands. If you are there when the horn sounds, you may come with us, finally knowing where she is and you will find the time goes quickly when you focus your mind to your work."

"Okay," Narek nodded.

"Until tomorrow. If I don't see you again Narek, know that it has been a pleasure to talk with a man who gives his truth so openly and with such sincerity. I bid you all goodnight."

"Thank you Sir, good night."

'Reliopashi maiy noya Manuk, kiana?'' Kaylak asked. "You'll go with them brother, yes?"

"Enshasta, enshasta filamaksi Risa," Narek nodded. "I have to, I have to find Risa."

"Enlarokrima, li reliopashi maiy potra teliam," Vronil said. "We understand, and you will go with our love."

"You're leaving us, aren't you Sarge," Damir said quietly and Narek nodded.

"Yes buddy."

"We'll miss you," Ribas said. "We'll all miss you but we know you gotta do this so we understand."

"Thank you."

"What'll we say about why you've gone?" Marikos asked.

"Tell everyone the truth," Narek said. "There is no need to lie or cover anything up. None of you guys has done anything wrong. You've done your survival exercise, Kaylak, Vronil and I have done your reports, and the training journal is all up to date with our observations and recommendations. The unit of Zelidol soldiers will be accompanying you back to Luzel, so you'll have at least another Sergeant with you. Just tell the truth, I'm the one who's going AWOL and it's my record that will carry the black mark for it."

"Okay," Marikos nodded.

"Well I vote we have dinner now," Dodge said, "and a couple of bottles of that yellow stuff the guy gave us. I for one want to celebrate having served under you Sarge and to bid you safe journey in the only way a good soldier knows how, with food and drink."

"That's an excellent idea," Kaylak nodded and everyone grunted their agreement.

Narek awoke early and after spending an hour in prayer with Kaylak and Vronil, he packed his backpack for his trip. He wondered what it was like on Fa'ahla and hoped the volunteers were treated well. There was no way for him to know what sort of work they were to do once they arrived, but whatever it turned out to be, he hoped it would fill his time sufficiently so the days and weeks would not drag too slowly. He kept one thing at the forefront of his mind; he was at least now guaranteed a chance to meet and speak with Risa to give her the truth. If her love died in the space of this coming year, at least he would know that he had given her the truth she deserved and then he would be free to leave and return to Vendala to take up the Pantisal and endure his Tal ak Roi. He went outside and found the men waiting for him.

"We're going to accompany you to see you off brother," Kaylak smiled. Narek smiled and nodded. Noro approached with something in his hands.

"The guys and I have a gift for you Sarge, to remember us by." He handed over a digital holographic viewer and he laughed at the crowd of men grinning at the camera, the sign held over their heads that read, 'see you in a year Sarge' written in large black letters.

"This is awesome as Marikos would say, thank you guys."

"That's great Sarge," Marikos replied. "You're speaking American at last."

"We can't let you go without a decent breakfast inside you, so get inside and get it down you while it's hot," Esclan said.

"Sir yes Sir," Narek replied and everyone laughed.

They set off across the valley to accompany Narek to volunteer with the Fa'ahlima. Each one was sad to see him go but each understood his reasons. No one tried to persuade him to stay and he was grateful for that. As they approached the compound, the horn sounded and the large crowd of people stopped chatting and stood, all looking towards the gate to see if anyone was going to volunteer.

"Time to go now guys," Narek said as he turned to the men. "Thank you for being friends. I'll remember each one of you, always." He went up to Kaylak and Vronil who both had tears in their eyes, and gave each the proper Vendalan greeting. Grasping their right hands together, they touched their right cheeks together in the traditional Vendalan parting embrace.

"*Enkiarae re teliam maiy reil Manuk,*" they said to each other. "You are taking my love with you brother."

Each of the men in the unit hugged Narek and bid him safe journey and a happy reunion with Risa, and as they watched him turn and walk towards the gate, each had tears on their cheeks. They had come to admire and respect Narek, both as a leader and as a man and they were genuinely sorry to see him leave, perhaps never to return. They watched the crowd stare in silence as he walked purposefully towards the gate of the Fa'ahlima compound and stand before the guards. They saw him speak to them and watched sadly as they stood aside and indicated for him to enter the open hatchway of the ship.

"*Liskanshoway Manuk,*" Kaylak and Vronil said. "Goodbye brother."

A.W.O.L

CHAPTER ELEVEN

Narek felt sad to be leaving his men; they had become as much friends to him as they were his students, and he swallowed hard to control the emotion that rose from his heart and pricked at his eyes. Leaving Kaylak and Vronil, his only Vendalan friends, made him feel suddenly alone and his insides fluttered as he bid them goodbye. Fear swelled in his breast, dark and cold as he wondered if he would ever get to see them again, or indeed anyone of his own race, and hoped that he might meet another Vendalan amongst the volunteers one day. He held on to that hope with everything he had, and it helped push his fear a little farther back. The stares from the crowd burned into his back as he approached the guards at the gate, and though he tried to prevent himself from blushing, he failed. The Zelidolian soldiers guarding the compound perimeter gaped at the sight of another IGMF soldier approaching the Fa'ahlima to volunteer. Never in all their years of service had they witnessed such an event, and this would be the talk of the IGMF for a long time to come.

"I've come to accept the offer given to me by your Kreelak," he told the guards. "I'm going with you for one year." The guards stepped aside and indicated towards the open hatchway of the huge shuttle.

"You may enter of your own free will," one of them said. Narek resisted the urge to look back at his men, despite the temptation to do so almost overwhelming him. This was his only chance to find Risa, and if he looked back at the sad faces of his men, his friends, the fear whose cold hand still gripped him might make him hesitate. No, he had to take this opportunity, whatever was to come from it. He strode forward and entered the hatchway to find two more guards waiting inside.

"You have volunteered to give service to the Fa'ahlima of your own free will?" One of them asked.

"I have," Narek nodded. "I accept the offer given to me by your own Kreelak and I give my service to your people for one year."

"Then you may pass," the other one said and stepped aside. "Follow the corridor to the end."

Away from the noise of the outside, the blood rushed in his ears as Narek walked the corridor and followed as it turned through ninety degrees, to find himself in what looked like a reception area. Seating was arranged around the walls and many small tables held jugs of the same bright yellow drink he had become fond of the day before. His hands shaking with adrenalin, he removed his backpack and sat down, and after helping himself to a drink, closed his eyes and sighed deeply. The horn droned on, its sonorous tone putting him on edge, and within minutes he realised he just wanted it to stop so they could leave and he could concentrate on working his year. After what seemed like hours, the sound of boot steps came to his ears and he looked up to see a middle-aged man enter.

"Hello there," he said, a nervous smile on his face as he extended a hand towards Narek. "I saw you volunteer. Very brave to be the first one. I've been wanting to volunteer for the past four years but never had the nerve until I saw you just now. Thank you for helping me find the courage."

"Hello," Narek replied as he shook the proffered hand. "My name is Narek."

"Soolian," the man responded. "Is that stuff drinkable?" he asked, pointing to the bright yellow liquid.

"It's probably the most delicious drink you'll ever taste," Narek replied. "Go ahead, it won't hurt you." Soolian poured himself a small glassful and took a hesitant sip. Raising his eyebrows appreciatively, he nodded, downed it in one go, and refilled the glass.

Narek felt better having someone to talk to and within a few minutes, he felt his anguish begin to calm a little. Soolian confessed to feeling the same and they both laughed nervously. Eventually the horn fell silent and they both leapt up to the window to watch the crowd disappear as the shuttle rose quickly into the sky. Narek glimpsed his friends and silently bid them farewell as a fresh surge of anguish rose from his heart at the sight of them and the familiarity they symbolised.

"Welcome gentlemen," a voice behind made both men jump. They turned and Narek recognised Ka'abash. "Hello again Narek. I knew you would come, I could see it in your eyes as you told me your story."

"It is just for one year, right?" Narek asked, hoping with all his heart that he had not been stiffed by this very alien stranger.

"Our word is our bond," Ka'abash said. "We have not deceived you. One year from now, you will be free to find your woman."

"Thank you."

"And you my new friend," Ka'abash said to Soolian. "At last you found the courage to step forwards. I've seen you every year for the past four years, waiting to find the strength to approach. Welcome. My name is Ka'abash and I am Kreelak of this vessel, the Captain if you like."

"You noticed me? And remembered me?" Soolian said and Ka'abash nodded. "I am Soolian and yes, I've wanted to come for four years now. It was only seeing Narek step forward today that helped me find the courage. I guess I'm happy to meet you Sir."

"Sit and relax while we journey to join with the Shi'maq," Ka'abash told them, "our inter-galactic ship that waits for us in orbit. Let me tell you what will happen over the course of the next day. Firstly, let me assure you that you are not prisoners of the Fa'ahlima. You give us your service willingly and you will be treated as guests. You will first be taken to have a meal, after which you will spend the afternoon getting to know all of the others who have volunteered from the other stops on our journey. You will then be able to choose three others with whom you are willing to share sleeping quarters."

"May I share with you Narek?" Soolian asked nervously.

"Of course," Narek nodded. "I'd be happy to share with you."

"After your evening meal," Ka'abash continued, "you will all be given a tour of the ship so you can familiarise yourself with the layout and begin to feel at home. After breakfast tomorrow, you will attend a meeting where I will begin to introduce you to Fa'ahla and explain why we seek help from people such as yourselves. By the time you have your mid-day meal tomorrow, you will no longer wonder what the mysterious Fa'ahlima are up to, and all the rumours you've heard over the years can fall away and be forgotten."

Narek and Soolian looked at each other and nodded. They were both nervous but both determined to meet this new experience with open minds.

"Ahh, we're about to dock with the Shi'maq," Ka'abash smiled and indicated towards the window. "See?" Narek and Soolian got up and went to look. The enormous ship hung in space like a fantastic tentacled sea creature and Narek understood immediately why it always remained in orbit.

"Wow," he said as he gazed at it and Ka'abash smiled.

"I thought you would be interested to see her. As a pilot yourself you will no doubt be wondering how she flies?"

"Well yes," Narek nodded. "And what are those long bits that hang down underneath?"

"They are part of the Helmat Energy Drive Core."

"You use Helmat Energy?" Narek asked. "But it's so unstable. How do you control it?"

"It is not actually unstable," Ka'abash explained, "but it does get very hot and as you are no doubt aware, all previous attempts to deal with the heat safely have ended in disaster. Those long trailing bits you see are part of the cooling system. The super-heated energy is filtered down into them and because of the material they are constructed from, the heat leeches out into space very quickly. The intense cold of space deals with the excess heat very efficiently, and once the energy is pumped back up into the core, it is cool again and ready for re-use. It has proved to be a very efficient system and has allowed us to make use of the unlimited energy available from the Helmat system for many years."

"That's incredible," Narek exclaimed.

"I will see to it that you get to visit the bridge, if you'd like to."

"I'd love to, thank you."

"What do you use to filter out the Crobium gas?" Soolian asked and both Narek and Ka'abash looked at him in surprise.

"You are an engineer my friend," Ka'abash said and Soolian nodded.

"Yes. I work in, I mean I worked for a company that does research and development for space ship drive cores, and we had an ongoing project to try to tame the Helmat Energy problem. We never did work out how to deal with the excess heat, but we did come up with a Nicrotanium filtering system that filtered out ninety seven percent of the Crobium Gas that makes raw Helmat so dirty as a fuel."

"Ahh yes, Nicrotanium," Ka'abash nodded. "We use that too, but we mix it with a small amount of Tronexiol. The resulting alloy makes the filtration run at one hundred percent."

"Tronexiol?" Soolian asked as he scratched his chin. "Now why didn't we think of that?"

"Would you like to see the engineering section?"

"Oh it would be an honour Sir," Soolian smiled.

"Then it will be done."

The shuttle docked with the Fa'ahlima mothership, the Shi'maq, and Ka'abash led Narek and Soolian back along the corridors. They stepped down into a huge docking bay and Narek noticed many other shuttles also disgorging passengers, most of whom looked about them nervously, as he supposed himself and Soolian must also be doing. After being issued with a tag that showed their name and a unique serial number, Ka'abash escorted them into an elevator.

"Keep those tags around your necks at all times gentlemen. They tell us who you are, when, and where you volunteered. If an accident occurs, we need to be able to identify you and with so many volunteers, it can be hard to keep track of everyone." Narek and Soolian put the tags around their necks and looked around the interior of the elevator. With a ping, it stopped and Ka'abash led them along shiny metallic corridors and into a large room where several hundred people all stood talking, introducing themselves to each other and swapping stories. Tables filled one end of the room and Fa'ahlima personnel were busily setting out for a meal.

"Here we are," Ka'abash smiled. "In here are all the other volunteers from our journey. You will all be given a meal soon and can spend the rest of the afternoon getting acquainted and making new friends. You need two more roommates remember. The four of you will be living and working together for the entire duration of your stay on Fa'ahla, so choose people you know you will get along with. You are free to choose whom you like, but you must choose males. We find that keeping the genders separated avoids so many problems. You may leave your bags in those lockers over there. The ones with key cards still in the locks are still available. I will bid you goodbye for a while and will be seeing you later this evening for a tour of the ship. Enjoy your meal." He smiled and placing a hand over his heart, he bowed his head slightly before turning and leaving the room. Narek and Soolian looked at each other.

"Well it all seems okay so far," Soolian said and Narek nodded.

"Yeah, nothing suspicious yet," Narek agreed. "Maybe they're good guys after all."

"Let's jump in then eh?"

After depositing their bags, the two friends wondered how to choose roommates amongst such a large crowd. Narek was just about to say hello to a huge man with a bald head when a voice behind made him spin around, his eyes wide and his mouth open.

"Prifirsa Manuk. Estriwa maitiliok ruliksi carimteyi so re manukichi." "Hello brother. I am overjoyed to see another of my brothers."

Narek spun around and gasped as he looked into the face of another Vendalan, a man of around his own age whose eyes brimmed with tears. He rushed to him and they embraced, sharing words of greeting, both relieved to find another of their own kind.

"I am Telkan Preel."

"Narek Jenn. I am so happy to see another Vendalan. Will you room with us Manuk?" Narek asked, indicating Soolian. "This is Soolian. He volunteered the same time as I did and we agreed to share."

"It would be an honour," Telkan nodded.

"Are you happy for Telkan to share with us Soolian?" Narek asked and Soolian nodded.

"Very happy. I had several Vendalan friends and I trust you people without a moment's hesitation."

"I am grateful Soolian," Telkan said as they shook hands.

The three mingled with the crowd and within an hour, had found their fourth roommate. Soolian got talking to a man from Earth, his dark brown skin making him stand out, even within this crowd of many different galactic races. Royden Johnson had been a builder on Earth and had made quite a good living by being one of a specialist crew trained to design and build the new floating villages that had begun to spring up on Earth's oceans. His speciality was constructing the unique deflectors that not only kept the largest waves from causing damage to the structures, but also collected the energy from those waves and channelled it to be used to power them. The company he worked for had been the subject of a massive lawsuit, and it was discovered that the Managing Director had been syphoning off large amounts of money over several years. It had only come to light when the company's suppliers suddenly refused to fulfil their orders due to non-payment of outstanding debts. Royden lost his job and after a year's fruitless search for another, he decided on a whim to volunteer when he happened across the Fa'ahlima compound in Central Park, New York. The three liked him immediately; his happy and optimistic disposition and permanent smile endearing him to them within minutes.

The meal was wonderful; everyone ate heartily and soon overcame their initial nervousness. Now they had friends, they all felt more secure and optimistic that whatever was to transpire, they would come through. They spent the afternoon swapping stories about what brought them to volunteer and all shared a common theme, desperation. Telkan told how his whole family was wiped out in a bomb blast that rocked the hotel on Stalinoka 7 where they were holidaying. With no surviving family, Telkan was too upset to return to Vendala alone with no support network and like Royden, happened across a Fa'ahlima vessel as he was waiting for a hover bus to take him to the spaceport and away from Stalinoka. Narek shed tears as Telken relayed his story, and realised that his was not the only desperate situation.

Soolian explained how, after his wife died five years previously, he had realised that his life held no more joy without her. He dragged himself through each day and so often wished he had the courage to end his life. Despite being well respected and well paid in his work as an engineer, life quickly became a grey void for him. He told them of the four years when he stood near the Fa'ahlima compound, a small bag of possessions in his hand, wishing he had the courage to step forwards. He again expressed his gratitude to Narek for helping him find the courage to move towards a new life, whatever it was to entail, and Narek told him he was glad to have made friends with him.

Finally, Narek told them of Risa and the lie told to her by Lorella. He told them of his desperate chase across the galaxy to catch up with the Fa'ahlima, and of his anguish when he realised they had been chasing the wrong ship. They gaped as he told them of his talk with Ka'abash, how he had marched up and asked to speak with someone, and the offer he made him. Lastly, he told them of his pain at walking away from his Vendalan friends and the unit of men who had been so loyal to him. Everyone knew they had a good team, and each one felt sure that their friendship would carry them through whatever was to happen in the future.

After the evening meal, Ka'abash called the room to silence.

"Welcome new friends. It pleases me to see you all making friends and to see so many smiles. I know you are all nervous and wondering what the mysterious Fa'ahlima want with you. I give you my word that all will be explained after breakfast in the morning. I want to assure you all that you are not our prisoners but honoured guests who have shown the courage to come to us without any foreknowledge of what is to come. We will now be taking groups of you on a tour of the ship so you can get your bearings and see what is available to you on board. We endeavour to provide for as many of your needs as we can, and we hope that you will find everything to your satisfaction. Once the tour is over, each of your groups of four will be allocated sleeping quarters and you will be free to spend the evening as you wish. Right, let's begin."

Narek and his group enjoyed the tour and were delighted to find not only a bar, but also a state of the art gymnasium that seemed to cater for the needs of more races than they each knew existed. Royden's eyes almost popped out of his head when he saw the gym.

"Oh my god I've died and gone to heaven," he sighed as they entered.

"If ever you can't find me guys," Narek said, "look here first."

"You like to work out too Narek?" Royden asked and Narek nodded. "Every day."

"Me too," Telkan said. "My parents built a gym onto our house and I spent many happy hours in there."

"Well then," Soolian said. "I guess I'm going to learn how to keep fit."

"Soolian old buddy," Royden grinned. "We'll have you fitter than you've ever been in no time."

Room 1620 proved to be very comfortable accommodations for the four men. They had a bathroom to themselves which contained two showers and basins. A separate cubicle provided two toilets and basins. The beds were comfortable and one wall had a window through which they could see the stars. Narek went to answer a knock on the door to find a Fa'ahlima man with a digital scanner in his hands.

"Good evening gentlemen. I hope the accommodation is adequate?"

"Yes indeed, thank you," Narek replied. "Come in, please."

"I have come to measure you all for garments. Most volunteers only bring a change or two of clothes, so we always provide suitable clothing. It won't take a minute to scan you all. If you could just strip down to your under garments." The men stripped and the Fa'ahlima man scanned them with his device and after entering the details from their tags, he thanked them and left.

"I've never worn a bespoke suit before," Royden laughed. "Seems a bit odd that I had to leave Earth in order to do something so ordinary."

"Just pray the garments aren't made of Modsal hair," Narek said and Telkan laughed loudly.

"What's that?" Soolian asked.

"An animal from Vendala. Its hair is very coarse and scratchy and usually used to make sacks."

"Well I vote we all go to the bar and have a drink," Soolian said when everyone had stopped laughing. "To celebrate our new team."

"Hell yeah," Royden nodded. "That's a great idea."

A.W.O.L

The four made their way to the bar and found it bustling and lively, many of the new volunteers taking advantage and trying to enjoy themselves. They inched their way to the bar and Royden called the bartender over.

"What can I get you gentlemen? We have alcoholic based and non alcoholic, fruit based and waters from many different worlds."

"Umm, how do we pay for it?" Royden asked.

"You do not pay," the bartender replied. "It is available to you without the need for payment."

"Well in that case, do you have a cold American beer?"

After an hour, the four made their way back to their quarters. It had been a day of sadness for each of them, an ending of a cycle that was familiar and comfortable, yet desperate. This day marked the beginning of a new chapter for each of them and each was hopeful that whatever was to come for them, it would be at least tolerable.

"Would anyone mind if I spent some time in prayer?" Narek said.

"I will join you Manuk," Telkan said.

"So will I," Royden declared. "My words will be different to yours but a prayer is the same in any language."

"And I will too," Soolian said. "I used to pray daily until my wife died. After that, I lost my faith somewhat. Maybe now is a good time to rediscover it."

The four sat in prayer; each beseeching their god in their own words and despite the differences of race, culture and creed, this simple act of faith bonded them.

Narek was just tying his boots when the intercom sounded, announcing breakfast was now being served.

"I hope the food is always this good," he said and the others nodded.

"Yeah," Royden agreed. "I haven't eaten this well in years."

"I hardly ate at all this past year," Soolian remarked. "Just couldn't raise the enthusiasm."

"Things are different now," Royden said, "and besides, you're gonna need your strength for your new workout regime."

"Oh dear lord," Soolian replied and the others laughed.

After breakfast was finished, everyone was shown into a huge room. A lectern stood facing them and a large vidicom screen hung from the ceiling. When everyone was seated, Ka'abash stood at the lectern and smiled.

"I hope everyone is rested after the first day among us. If anyone has problems with their accommodations, please let any of the Fa'ahlima crew know and we will do our utmost to sort it out quickly. Now I am here to finally tell you the reason for your being here, to dispel all those ugly rumours you've no doubt heard, and to assure you that none of them are true. Firstly, I want to give you a little history of our world." Ka'abash outlined the history that first brought about the need for volunteers, and the political struggles that made this the only solution.

"Fa'ahla is a beautiful world," he began. "Our people have lived in peace for many thousands of years; our ancient traditions binding the two Fa'ahla political parties together in relative harmony. Our way of life, our traditions and culture, are ruled by the Sha'yve Midal, the High Governors. There are twenty-two of them, eleven from each of the two political parties. They meet in the Sha'yve, the Governing Temple on Mount Tuliash, which is the location of our most sacred and symbolic icon, the Ta'ahli, which sits atop the sacred ottoman. Five hundred years ago, an acolyte of the Sha'yve Midal named Ma'imosh was denied a position amongst the twenty-two governors. It was felt that he was still too young and inexperienced to hold such a position and wield the considerable responsibilities in the appropriate manner, so the others denied him. His father was of one political party and his mother, the other but despite this, his family was a harmonious one."

"Politics," Royden whispered. "God I hate politics."

"Ma'imosh found it very difficult to cope with their decision, and in his anger at being denied the position," Ka'abash continued, "Ma'imosh broke into the Sha'yve one night and stole the Ta'ahli. Each political party immediately accused the other of stealing it, and when it was discovered that Ma'imosh was missing and had bragged to a friend of wanting to steal it, each side then accused the other of putting him up to it. His parents being from each of the two political parties suffered dreadfully, and consequently, it tore his family apart and both his parents died with terrible shame in their hearts. Everyone on Fa'ahla was united in one desperate aim, to find Ma'imosh and retrieve the Ta'ahli, but despite intensive searching, he was never found. Within months, the political row turned to rioting and within a further year, war. For two hundred years this terrible war raged over Fa'ahla and in our political anger, we almost wiped ourselves out."

"I'm beginning to hate it too," Soolian hissed as Ka'abash took a drink. Narek snickered.

A.W.O.L

"The Ta'ahli is a stone tablet made up of one thousand tiny stone squares, each bearing one of our sacred symbols of power. As the people searched for the stones, it quickly became clear that Ma'imosh had not simply disposed of them all together, but had scattered them across the whole of Fa'ahla. Whenever one party found a stone, the other side accused them of hiding it in the first place and soon, everyone was afraid even to look for them for fear of being murdered as accomplices to this heinous crime. The disappearance of the Ta'ahli was set to tear us apart as a race, but finding it was almost impossible to achieve without doing further damage. For a long time it seemed as if everything we had come to stand for was to end, and we wept with anguish. It was not until one governor realised that none of the Fa'ahlima could look for the stones without awful consequences ensuing should they find one, that it was decided to ask for volunteers from all other friendly worlds, where no one could be allied with either party, that the war ended and tense peace began. Here is what they look like."

The vidicom screen came to life and everyone looked at a photograph of the Ta'ahli, complete in all its glory on the central ottoman within the Sha'yve. Each of the tiny stones holding a particular position within the completed tablet, the whole showing a fabulously ornate and extremely intricate design that looked to Narek like the claw marks of some crazed beast. Despite not understanding the design, he thought it was beautiful and decided he would like to be able to see the real thing. Gasps from the crowd of volunteers as they gazed at the screen seemed to please Ka'abash, who smiled at their response to the sight of his people's most sacred of symbols.

"Each of these small stones carries a symbol, an ancient form of Fa'ahla writing that means something in its own right, despite being a small part of a greater whole. An idea, a moral attitude, a fear, a desire, a goal worth achieving and other things of that nature. Together, the tablet shows a representation of our creator, Fa'ahloma in his energy body as he surrounds our world and keeps it safe. It symbolises those qualities each of us strives to achieve within ourselves as we further strive to reach toward our deity and in so doing, be at one with him. Although merely symbolic, without the Ta'ahli, we feel we cannot, as a race, continue to strive for this godly quality and many believe that it was Fa'ahloma's anger towards us that brought about this situation. Therefore, for the past three hundred years, volunteers like yourselves have come to live and work among us and search for these stones, in the hope that one day we can finally reunite them on the central ottoman. So far seven hundred and ninety one stones have been found and we are hopeful that within the next two years, the Ta'ahli will be complete again."

"So that's what all this is about? Stones?" Telkan asked and Royden raised his eyebrows.

"You will each be given housing to live in, money in recompense for your work, and food and clothing will be provided without cost to yourselves. Each of your groups of four will be given a specific location to search each day. Every inch of Fa'ahla must be searched, every building must be taken down stone by stone, the ground dug and searched, the building rebuilt. The ocean floors are being searched inch by inch by specially trained volunteers, the snow dug from our mountain peaks, the sand sifted from the desert. Every hole in the ground must be examined, nothing must be left unsearched. However long it takes, we will reunite the Ta'ahli."

"So we're not prisoners here but we're hauling rocks anyway," Royden exclaimed and Soolian nodded.

"Now you know why you are here," Ka'abash said. "We are not proud of this part of our history, and the way our forebears conducted themselves shames us, but we have learned from this terrible experience and it will never happen again. Each one of you, like all those who volunteered before you, and all those to come, are saving Fa'ahla, saving us from wiping ourselves out through our political short sightedness, anger and mistrust. That is why we have sought your help, that is why you are here my friends," Ka'abash finished. "That is your quest. The quest for the Ta'ahli."

CHAPTER TWELVE

The journey to Fa'ahla took eight days and by the time they saw the planet below them, Narek and his companions had come to feel a lot more at ease, both with each other and the Fa'ahlima personnel. The four spent a couple of hours each day in the ship's gymnasium and another couple in the bar each evening, bonding in the best way men from all over the universe know how. The group was pleased to find that they were excused lessons in the common tongue, as each of them already spoke the language that had been adopted by all worlds adhering to the Inter-Galactic Treaty in an effort to further communication between neighbours. Apart from their morning and evening commitments, they found the days dragged a little, so within three days, Narek, Telkan and Royden set up their own body building class and taught groups of volunteers the basics of keep fit and martial arts. Soolian was a good student and by the time they reached Fa'ahla, all four agreed between them to continue working out together every day whenever possible. On the last day of their journey to what was to be their new home, at least for the foreseeable future, Narek looked out the window at the planet below, and thought immediately of Risa.

"Estriwa allimala re teliam," he whispered. "I am here my love."

After disembarking and saying goodbye to Ka'abash, the groups of four were corralled into bigger groups, and Narek found himself on another shuttle along with one hundred and ninety nine other volunteers for the long journey to the northernmost continent. It was early morning when the shuttle took off and everyone got their first look at the Fa'ahla landscape. The city was large and looked just like all the other large cities Narek had visited, hot, noisy and no doubt smelly. Someone commented that there was no evidence of searching taking place below, and the Fa'ahlima man who was in charge of this group's transit told them the city below had already been searched and since rebuilt.

"Two of the Ta'ahli were found in this city alone," he told them. "Numbers forty seven and three hundred and eight."

"The stones have numbers?" someone asked.

"Yes," the man replied. "Each has a particular place within the tablet."

The shuttle rose into the sky, the skyscrapers passing underneath so close that one or two of the passengers gasped as they flew over them. Many had shuttle landing pads and Narek saw many craft parked, of all shapes and sizes. People, as tiny as insects, walked the streets far below them, and Royden suddenly voiced what everyone else was thinking.

"I suddenly feel a long way from home," he whispered.

"We all do," Telkan replied.

"We have each other though," Soolian said, "and that will help us all to settle in."

"I've travelled to many worlds with the military," Narek said, "but just knowing I'm to stay here for a whole year does make me feel a little lost. I can't imagine how you three feel, not knowing if you'll ever leave."

"No doubt by the time you come to leave us Narek," Soolian said, "we will all be feeling thoroughly at home. Let's try to look upon this as a positive opportunity eh? Just remember why we all volunteered in the first place, and keep that truth with you. It will help keep things in perspective."

"Look at you being so optimistic," Royden grinned at Soolian. "Just days ago life held no joy for you and you just wanted it to end. Now here you are looking forward to a new adventure and keeping the rest of us from getting depressed." Soolian blushed and looked down at his feet.

"Knowing that Risa is here on this same planet does make me feel a little better," Narek agreed, "even though not being able to see her for a year is painful. At least I know she's seeing the same sky, breathing the same air and feeling the same earth beneath her feet. It's a connection y'know? One I thought I'd lost a few days ago."

"Well this is a whole new life for me," Telken said with a sigh. "After my family were killed I felt lost, rootless, and had no idea what to do. All I knew was that I couldn't face returning to Vendala and being reminded daily of what I'd lost. This is an opportunity for me to make new friends, find a new purpose and discover myself again."

"It's the same for me," Royden nodded. "When my life fell apart so quickly back on Earth, I felt so betrayed that I didn't know how to express it. After working so hard for what I thought was a better life, giving everything I had to make my people and my world better, I felt like they kicked me in the face. I for one won't miss Earth, and in fact, I'm happy to take Fa'ahla as my new home world. The people have been open and honest with me since the moment I volunteered, and it took me just days to feel more at ease with them than I ever could back on Earth. This is my new life now, my new home and whatever it entails, it will be better than the old one."

The city gave way to countryside and the shuttle descended a little so the passengers could see the landscape. The Fa'ahlima man gave them a commentary as they flew over the land, telling them snippets of its history and other interesting information, much of it indeed very interesting. It was not until they reached the ocean and flew along the coastline that they got their first view of active searching going on below.

"That ship you can see on the ocean," the Fa'ahlima man said, "is a search vessel. Twenty groups of four live on board for a month at a time and search the ocean floor in a grid pattern. Those volunteers are trained especially for under water search. Your groups can volunteer for such work if you wish but there is something of a waiting list. The work is dangerous but they get more time to themselves away from the work as recompense."

"I'm not a good swimmer at all," Soolian remarked.

"I can swim fine," Royden said, "but I don't fancy it. I'd prefer to do anything else than go underwater."

"Me too," Narek replied and Telkan nodded.

As they flew, they saw many more search ships inching their way across the ocean, like enormous sea creatures sunbathing on the surface, gently rocking in the swell, the calm scene belying their purpose. Soon, ocean gave way to desert and all the passengers silently prayed that this was not their destination. They saw the volunteers below, lines of people a mile long that followed massive digging machines and carefully sifted through the sand as it belched out from long funnels at the rear. Although it was obviously hot down there, the people were clad in what looked like a one-piece garment that covered them from head to toe. Each person sported a large brimmed hat on their heads and big dark goggles.

"Those garments are specially designed to keep the wearer cool," the Fa'ahlima man said. "The outer fabric reflects the sun's rays, while the lining has a cooling gel mesh that sits next to the skin and keeps it at its optimum healthy temperature. The hats and goggles protect the face and eyes from both the sunlight, and the sand, which is rather caustic."

"I was thinking they must be boiling alive in those suits," Soolian remarked.

"I can assure you my friend, they are very probably more comfortable than you are right now."

After a three hour journey, the shuttle came into land at what looked to Narek like a refugee receiving station like the ones he saw on Palisar 6 during his active duty as a soldier. The landscape was rocky, with a huge bluff that ran for miles southwards, whereupon its course was abruptly halted by a mountain range. Another couple of hours of red tape ensued, during which Narek and his group were allocated living accommodations. Each was handed a key card on a chain, 'building 16, dwelling 7' inscribed upon it, before being ushered to a waiting hover bus. A twenty minute ride later, the group stood looking up at building sixteen. It was a modern structure and reminded Narek of the swanky apartment blocks back on Vendala that graced the nicer areas of the inner cities. He counted twenty storeys, each storey being made up of two four-man apartments.

"Follow me please gentlemen," a young Fa'ahlima man urged them with a smile. "You are in dwelling seven on the fourth floor." He showed them in through the main door and they all noticed the drop in temperature immediately.

"On this ground level, you will find facilities for laundry. All of your working garments will be laundered and repaired for you, but many volunteers like to wear their own garments on their time away from work, so you have the facilities here for laundering, drying and taking care of them. In that room there is all the equipment you should need for cleaning your dwellings." He knocked on a door and an elderly woman answered with a smile.

"Hello there new friends, welcome to building sixteen. I am Ja'ehla, your housekeeper. I can run errands, arrange deliveries of food and supplies, look after your garments and liaise with other authorities with any other problems or concerns you may have."

"I'm happy to meet you Ma'am," Royden smiled.

"Hello," Soolian blushed.

"It is a pleasure to know you Ja'ehla," Narek said.

"A pleasure to meet you," Telkan added.

The Fa'ahlima man, who told them he was named Si'anthil, showed them how to use the elevator and showed them were the stairs were, should they prefer to use them. On the fourth floor, the elevator opened and they found themselves in a short open ended corridor that separated dwelling seven on the right, from dwelling eight on the left. At the end was a metal grille through which they could see many other buildings like their own and many smaller buildings in between the blocks of dwellings. The buildings were arranged in a square, with a large green space in the middle. Narek saw trees, flowering plants and a small lake in which he could just make out people swimming.

The apartment was large and the rooms, airy and comfortably furnished. Just like on board the Shi'maq, the bathroom had two showers and basins and a separate cubicle held two toilets and basins. There were four small bedrooms, a kitchen and a central living area.

"If you wish," Si'anthil said, "you may have the bedroom walls changed to rearrange your sleeping areas. Some volunteers like to remain together as a four, some prefer pairs and others like individual rooms. Just let Ja'ehla know and she will arrange for it to be done."

"I think I'd prefer to remain with you guys like we did on the ship. I've got to like the company," Royden said and everyone quickly agreed.

"Very well, Si'anthil replied. "I will arrange for it to be done within the hour. Your kitchen has been stocked with foodstuffs from Earth, Zelidol and Vendala, and Ja'ehla will take your orders for more foodstuffs from your home world as you require them. It may take a time to get hold of some things but we always endeavour to get what you want. Over time, Ja'ehla will introduce you to many equivalent foodstuffs from Fa'ahla."

"Meat, vegetables and fruit are pretty much the same wherever you are," Narek remarked and everyone nodded."

"The only thing I'm gonna miss is coffee and ice cream," Royden said.

"Oh yes, coffee would be wonderful," Narek agreed.

"You know coffee?"

"Yes, there are many from Earth on Luzel and wherever Earth people go, coffee goes too."

"There is a large bag of coffee in the kitchen gentlemen," Si'anthil smiled. "As you say, wherever Earth people go, coffee must go also. We learned that very quickly. We have also learned about ice cream and have developed our own version which the other volunteers from Earth all seem to enjoy very much. We can also supply chocolate, which we learned was another necessity for all Earth people."

"Chocolate?" Royden exclaimed with wide eyes. "Oh man, chocolate."

"I got to rather like the white version," Narek said and Royden made a face.

"Oh yuck. The dark version is the best. Just like a man, darker means better," he grinned and everyone laughed.

"We can supply many kinds," Si'anthil assured them. "Now, let me take you up to the roof space." The four followed him out of the apartment and back into the elevator. A few seconds and the door opened to reveal a huge swimming pool that covered the entire roof space. Sun loungers sat around the edge, under a sun awning.

"Wow, a pool," Royden hissed.

"We try to provide everything you might require to make your stay comfortable and enjoyable," Si'anthil smiled. "Those smaller buildings you can see amongst the other dwelling blocks are shops, stores, bars and restaurants. There are two vidicom theatres, a gymnasium and a hospital. Everything is available to you at minimal cost, we don't like to charge at all but Fa'ahla is not as rich a world as it used to be, and the costs of supplying all the many races with their needs is high. All of your basic food supplies will be delivered weekly at no cost to yourselves, but anything extra you would like to order, or buy from the stores, does have a small cost, just to help us keep supplying them. The many years of war almost ruined us financially as well as in other ways."

"We're happy to pay," Narek said and the others nodded.

"I shall leave you now to settle in," Si'anthil said. "At eight o clock in the mornings, the hover bus will pick you up outside this building, by the number sixteen marker post. Your mid-day meal will be provided and you work for twenty days and then have ten days without work. The working day ends at four. If you have any problems or questions, Ja'ehla will be happy to help you."

"So we just come as we are?" Soolian asked.

"I almost forgot, my apologies," Si'anthil blushed. "Your garments were manufactured during your journey to Fa'ahla and have been placed within the storage compartments in your bedrooms. Each garment has your name and number on, so you will know whose is whose."

"Okay, thanks man," Royden said.

Between the four of them, they managed to provide a relatively acceptable meal from the supplies they found in the kitchen of their apartment. Meats, vegetables, fruits, bottles of juice of varying colours, and desserts all filled the cupboards and stasis units. Royden found the bag of coffee and several large slabs of chocolate and decided to eat a whole slab at once. He had been without chocolate for a few months now and although he was strict with it when it was available, he decided to drop his regime just this once. During the late afternoon, three Fa'ahlima men turned up and spent an hour removing the walls that separated the bedrooms from one another, and once they were done, the four arranged their beds and set out their few possessions.

Narek placed the photo of Kaylak, Vronil and his soldiers on the shelf by his bed and smiled. He missed them but he was comforted by the presence of another Vendalan. He reached into his backpack and pulled out his change of clothes, spare underwear, his razor and the little bundle containing the bracelet Noro made from the shells they discovered on Kelmat 5. He put his hand into the backpack to check it was empty, touched paper and drew it out with a frown. His heart fell as he looked at the folded letter Risa had left for him. Despite knowing it was a bad idea, he opened it and started to read. He got halfway before his emotions overcame him, and dropped his head into his hands. The others rushed over and sat with him.

"Hey Narek, we're with you y'know," Royden said. "You made it all the way here after your long chase and you know she's here somewhere. You know she's looking at the same sky and feeling the same sun on her skin as you are. That's gotta help huh? You said so on the shuttle over here."

"Yeah," Narek nodded. "It does but in a way it makes it worse. Knowing she's here somewhere but I can't get to her for a whole year is somehow worse than being half a galaxy away. She might be in the next building for all I know; I could pass by and miss meeting her by a minute."

"The year will go by Manuk," Telkan said. "We will endeavour to prevent you from having too much time to sit and brood okay? Even doing something boring is better than sitting and waiting for the hours to drag by, isn't it?"

"Yes, much better," Narek said. "I'm sorry guys for being such a wet blanket."

"Hey now young man just you take that back," Soolian said, giving him a grave stare. "I met and fell in love with my wife when I was fourteen years old and when she died, I'd loved her for forty years. I cried for months when she died and spent hours looking at pictures of her smile. Loving and missing her doesn't make me a wet blanket and missing the woman you love doesn't make you one either. Men who haven't loved aren't really men and I'll thank you to remember that."

"I'll remember, thank you," Narek said and Soolian nodded.

"After my wife died, I missed talking to her so much that I began writing her letters. I'd write every day at first, but as I got used to being without her, I found that once a week or so was enough. I wrote her the last letter the morning I finally found the courage to volunteer and haven't felt the need since. I send her my thoughts now and that's enough. I think this new start is really helping me to get over the grief. Why don't you write to Risa? Keep the letters and when you find her, share them with her so she'll know just how much you missed her every moment. It would be a way of sharing this time with her."

"That's a wonderful idea," Telkan nodded.

"Hell yeah," Royden agreed. "Do it."

"Yes," Narek said. "Thank you, I'll do that."

After spending an hour in silent prayer with his new friends, all of whom had kept to their habit of sitting in prayer together despite their differences in beliefs, the four got a surprisingly good night's sleep and after a big breakfast, set out to begin their work. Narek was pleased that his year's work was beginning and set out determined to focus on whatever lay ahead. They found that they were to search a series of Norlode mines and spent their days searching the tunnels and chambers, feeling every nook and cranny with delicate fingers. The huge piles of stone were dug and searched and the four found the work strangely satisfying. It was not hard work inside the mines, the cool moist air making the work decidedly chilly, but it was a relief from the hot sun outside.

Narek and his companions settled into a routine and it was not until six weeks had passed that something new happened. As everyone was making their way back to work after their mid-day meal, a siren went off and everyone started cheering.

"What's happened?" Narek asked the man next to him.

"Someone found a stone," he replied. "Every time another of the Ta'ahli is found, sirens go off all around the planet where workers are."

"That's great," Narek said.

"The person who found it gets taken to the Sha'yve Midal and they make a statue of them to put in the gallery of discovery. They get to stop working if they want to and can choose to leave Fa'ahla if they want."

"Wow, that's good to know," Narek replied, hoping that if he could find one, his year of work might not have to be a year after all.

152

A.W.O.L

Four months into his year, Narek and his friends were relaxing at the end of the day when there was a knock at the door of the apartment. Royden got up to answer it and found Simeon, one of the group from dwelling eight.

"Hey, come on in."

"Hi guys," Simeon said. "Your ten days off start tomorrow don't they?"

"Yeah."

"Everyone with time off tomorrow has been invited over to a neighbouring town for a party. Do you guys wanna come? There's gonna be women there from a female search community."

"You mean they're allowing us to mix with women? Telkan asked.

"Yeah," Simeon nodded. "Although we won't be allowed any umm, private time if you know what I mean, but hey, a whole afternoon and evening with loads of women."

"I'm in," Royden nodded.

"Me too," Telkan agreed.

"I think I'd like that too," Soolian added, "although a few months ago I'd never have believed I'd ever find myself saying so."

"No thanks," Narek said. "I couldn't spend time partying with women when I miss Risa so much. It would feel like I was betraying her or something."

"You know Narek," Royden said as he wandered over and sat down, "it's not beyond the realms of possibility that Risa has umm, you know, met someone here."

Narek's head snapped around and he glared at Royden, the anger flashing in his eyes as he balled his fists. Telkan came running over and put a hand on his shoulder.

"He is right Manuk. You must prepare yourself for this possibility. Do not be angry when a brother has given you such a profound truth." Narek let out an anguished sob and nodded to Telkan.

"She couldn't, she can't do that. Please let that not be so. If she has, I will take the Tal ak Roi right there and then, even without a Pantisal."

"Let's be sensible here," Simeon said. "They keep us pretty tightly segregated; they don't want unexpected children being born and having to be cared for. We don't get much chance to mix with women, so it stands to reason the women don't get to mix much either. I doubt she's had much of a chance to meet any men, let alone fall in love with one, especially as she declared such deep feelings for Narek. You can't wipe away such feelings so quickly."

"He's right," Soolian nodded. "This whole town is just men and you can't tell me that it's the only one like it on Fa'ahla. The women's search groups will have their own women's towns just like the men do."

"Yeah, that makes total sense," Royden agreed. "I'm sorry, forgive me for being insensitive."

"Of course," Narek said. "You were right to say it. Although unlikely, it could happen and I must be aware of the possibility. Thank you."

Narek spent the afternoon working out in the town's gymnasium, and then went for a run around the perimeter of the lake. As he ran, he thought of his daily runs around the perimeter wall of Base 7 on Luzel 2. It seemed like a lifetime ago that he was there and he realised he had not even thought of the place in weeks. Fa'ahla was becoming more like home every day and he was not sure whether he was glad about that or not. After a shower and a change of clothes, he went out to one of the town's vidicom theatres and watched a couple of terrible movies, before heading to a restaurant for his evening meal. After enjoying his meal, he spent an hour in a bar and had a couple of games of Tapshots with some other men before heading back to the apartment.

He found his three friends already there and all stood as he entered. The looks on their faces told him something was wrong, and that he was not going to like what they had to tell him. He took a deep breath and sighed before asking.

"What's happened?"

"Manuk," Telkan gasped as he stepped towards Narek. "Oh Manuk you should've come with us."

"Why? What's happened?" he demanded.

"We met a woman who knows Risa," Royden said. The breath left Narek's lungs as his eyes widened in shock and his knees gave way. Telkan and Royden rushed to his side and helped him into a chair.

"She knows her? Was Risa there? Did she say she's okay? Tell me everything, please."

"I overheard a conversation between a couple of women," Soolian explained, "and I heard one of them mention someone called Risa. I asked them about it and one of them said Risa was part of her search community but not her group of four. I asked about Risa and she said she was healthy and strong but never mixed much. She said Risa is always helpful and kind and works hard but always looks sad because she loved someone who was stolen from her."

"She's alive and healthy," Telkan said, "and obviously still loves and misses you. Let that strengthen your heart."

Narek's scream rang through the apartment and was heard by several of the neighbouring apartments, all of whom came running to see what was wrong. Royden, Telkan and Soolian sat with him as he cried out his anguish and relief, and then sat with him in silent prayer, the tears streaming down his cheeks as he beseeched Alima, the god of love and bonding to send strength to Risa's heart.

Narek found concentrating on his work harder than ever before during the following days. His mind was filled with anguish after having missed the opportunity to meet and talk with someone connected to Risa.

"It's like the gods are punishing me," he wailed. "I don't know how I'm going to get through the rest of this year. Just because I hesitated too long and didn't declare my feelings to her, I am being kept away from every chance to find out how she is." He cursed himself, his gods, his life and everyone with whom he came into contact during those days immediately after the party, worried for him. Finally, Royden could take it no more, and grabbed Narek by the shoulders and shook him.

"Listen Narek, for just a goddam minute," he hissed. "Would you honestly be feeling better had you gone to the party and spoken with the woman yourself? Would you? Would getting the information from her instead of us, make you feel easier today, cos I can assure you we got all the information out of her that she had to give." Narek glared into his eyes, fighting with his emotions.

"I umm," he began. "I just feel so," he faltered as a tear traced its way down his cheek.

"I know you do," Royden replied, "but you wouldn't have gotten any more out of her than we did, and believe me, we tried. What would you have done differently than we did anyway? Oh, I know, you'd have yelled at her, demanded to know where Risa is, maybe accused her of lying to keep you apart? Maybe you think the three of us didn't take enough care to find out as much information as we could huh? Is that what your problem is?"

"I'm sorry," Narek said as he wiped his eyes. "I didn't mean to mistrust you or anything. You're right, forgive me."

"It's okay," Telkan said, "we're with you in this." Narek nodded.

"Concentrate your mind on the positive Narek," Soolian said. "You now know she is alive and healthy and still loves you. Isn't that the most important thing? Of course you feel bad, anyone would, but you must hold strong to the positive."

"But I could've asked her to give Risa a message," Narek said.

"I tried, but just before I could ask her, the siren went off and everyone was herded out," Telkan replied.

"You never know," Royden said. "She may decide to tell Risa she met us anyway. Risa may be happy and thinking of you right now, knowing you're here and waiting to meet her again. Hold on to that huh?"

"That's true," Telkan nodded. "She may have told her."

"It would make sense wouldn't it?" Soolian asked. "I would, if I were in her situation."

"So would I," Royden agreed.

"Of course, we all would," Telkan added.

"Yeah, you're right," Narek said, brightening immediately, "she may have. I never thought of that. I'm sorry for being a burden to you guys. Thank you for this wake up call, I needed it."

"Oh anytime my friend," Royden said. "Believe me, anytime."

This change in Narek's demeanour was obvious to everyone, and those who knew and associated with him, were relieved to see him back to what they had come to know as his usual self. Life in the Norlode mine got back to normal, and the group spent their days groping along the tunnels and shafts, delving fingers into crevices with practiced care, feeling for the precious Ta'ahli. Royden's birthday was celebrated in style, and he shared a party with three other men who all had the same birthday, each bringing their own form of celebration according to their racial culture, to this combined event. A cake was produced by the Fa'ahlima, who had researched Earth customs and knew the importance of this ritual, and everyone laughed to see him, his face smothered in chocolate cream as he stuffed a huge slice into his mouth.

"This is one Earth custom I think I'd like to adopt," Narek laughed as he helped himself, and Telkan nodded his agreement.

CHAPTER THIRTEEN

Summer gave way to autumn on Fa'ahla and the trees that lined the top of the bluff overlooking the Norlode mine, turned to fire as green transformed into golds, yellows and oranges. This was the first obvious physical sign of the passage of time and Narek sighed as he gazed up at them. He remembered the days he spent back on Zelidol Prime, and how the autumn made him sad as he journeyed to the Fa'ahlima compound. Memories of Zelidol then brought memories of the men he had left behind, his Vendalan friends, Kaylak and Vronil, and felt a flutter of emotion rush through him as he remembered the binding ceremony that linked them. If he should not be successful in reuniting with Risa, or if she turned away from his love, Narek realised that he would be condemning his two friends to a life with half a soul. The weight of this responsibility bore down upon him, and the only consolation was the knowledge that by taking the Tal ak Roi, he would release his brothers from their bond and restore them both to wholeness. Comforted by this truth, Narek allowed his thoughts to wander to his men, and he smiled as the memories flowed back.

"You okay Narek?" the voice made him jump, and he turned to see Royden.

"Huh? Oh yeah. I was just thinking of the soldiers I left behind on Zelidol when I volunteered. I was wondering how there were getting along with their training."

"I can't imagine you yelling at raw recruits and making them shake in their boots with fear," Royden remarked and Narek laughed.

"I'm delighted to hear that," he said. "I didn't yell at them, and I hope they were never afraid of me."

"But isn't that what Army guys do? Aren't you supposed to shout at them all the time and call them names and stuff?"

"What? No, of course not. Wherever did you get that idea?"

"Well it's always like that in the movies."

"I might have known," Narek said and laughed aloud. "Life isn't like the movies, at least my life isn't. We don't all go around shooting everything in sight, and we don't always come out on top. I'm just a teacher really. I haven't had to fire on anyone in a long time, and I hope I never have to again."

"But you must get guys who join up because they want a licence to be a bully. How do you handle them?"

"Ninety nine percent of them are weeded out during the psyche evaluation before they ever get to me," Narek explained. "The IGMF have some pretty infallible ways of finding out a person's true nature. Not many get through without being found out. The odd one that does remain long enough to get to me soon learns his lesson."

"Oh," Royden grinned. "You're not admitting to being a tough guy at last are you?"

"I have my moments," Narek replied. "Besides, my report carries a lot of weight, and I can end a guy's military career with a stroke of the pen, if I haven't been able to educate them in other ways."

"We don't see that side of you," Royden said quietly, looking at Narek with concentration. "We don't see the confident soldier who knows what to do, how to tackle every situation and how to inspire everyone. If you hadn't told us you were in the military, I'd never have guessed."

"Really?"

"Yeah. The Narek we know is quiet, shy even, and a little insecure. He worries too much, cares far more for others than he does for himself, doesn't feel he deserves to have a good time. I've never seen you in a fight. I've never seen you get angry with anyone in fact. I can't imagine you quietly beating the shit out of some asshole military wannabe. I would love to see that happen."

"Well I'm not a soldier here, so there's no need for me to be like I am when I'm working. It's actually a relief to be able to just be me without having to be seen to inspire and lead all the time. When I'm working with the men in my unit, I can't get angry or upset in front of them, and sometimes it's very uncomfortable holding it inside."

"I can understand that," Royden nodded, "and it's something good you can hold on to from this time. The chance to get all that shit out that you've not been able to let go before. By the time you leave here to find Risa, you'll be in balance again and ready to take on the universe."

"Yeah," Narek nodded. "Although this time is agony for me in many ways, I also feel calmer now than I have in a long time. When I get the chance to leave here, if everything goes well that is, I know my work will benefit."

"Hey you two, stop nattering like a pair of old women and come take your turn." Narek and Royden turned and laughed at Soolian as he climbed out of the pool, ball in hand. "Telkan and I are thrashing you guys, come and take your punishment like real men."

Royden laughed and leapt into the pool, closely followed by Narek and an hour later, emerged victorious, having beaten Soolian and Telkan by seven goals to four.

The days rolled by, one very much like another, but Narek found the routine helped prevent him dwelling on his internal anguish. He ached for Risa every moment, and although he found it painful to not be able to go and find her for several more months, the routine of the days gave him visible confirmation that the time was indeed passing. Royden loved the work and declared often that he felt quite at home, and everyone agreed that the work was easy, the pay was good, and the time off was plentiful. Soolian told everyone within the first month that he was happy to remain on Fa'ahla for the rest of his life, and even asked some of the Fa'ahlima about the possibility of becoming a citizen. It was only Telkan who had feelings that matched Narek's own, and the two of them agreed that while life and work on Fa'ahla was good, it was not home, and never would be. When Narek asked Telkan what he would do when all the Ta'ahli were found, Telkan sighed and shook his head.

"I've no idea Manuk. I suppose I should return to Vendala, but at this moment, today, I don't feel that I want to. Maybe I'll feel different in the future. The passing of time may change my feelings."

"What if your feelings don't change," Narek asked. "What will you do then?"

"I don't know. I have thought about it, and I hope that when the time comes, I will know what I want to do."

"You could always come to Luzel 2. There are two other Vendalans working there, and even if I'm not there, if I've taken the Tal ak Roi, you will have friends who will welcome you. Everyone is good there, they're nice people and you will find work easily."

"I had considered asking you actually," Telkan replied. "From the way you talk of it, I feel confident I could make a nice life there."

"You could have a great life there, I give you my word."

"Then that is what I will do Manuk. Tell me though, will you really take the Tal ak Roi?"

"Yes," Narek sighed and looked down at his boots. "Yes, I will."

"Everyone who knows you will grieve deeply, including me."

"Thank you Manuk."

Shouts from above made them both turn and look up. They were sitting on some rocks at the foot of the bluff, enjoying the warm autumn sun as they took their mid-day break, and as they craned their necks to see up the face of the cliff, they saw the body hurtling towards them. The man landed with a sickening crunch, a few feet to Telkan's left, and both he and Narek leapt away instinctively.

"Oh fuck," Narek yelled as he ran towards the body, followed closely behind by Telkan who was shouting for some Fa'ahlima personnel. Narek crouched by the body and felt for a pulse, and was amazed to find one.

"He's alive, someone get help quickly," he yelled as the Fa'ahlima came running. Within minutes the unconscious man was on his way to the community's hospital, the wide and unbelieving eyes of everyone following as the hover cart rushed away.

"How did he survive a fall like that?" Telkan asked.

"That is the most miraculous thing I've seen in years," Narek sighed.

"He didn't tie off his safety harness properly," a Fa'ahlima man said. "He's a fairly new volunteer, and forgot how to work the magnetic strip locks that keep him secured to the safety wire. When he fell, the unsecured safety wire wasn't able to run through the harness bolts quickly enough, so it slowed his descent a little, enough to make a difference."

"Shit," Narek hissed. "I bet he won't make that mistake again."

"If he recovers enough to return to work, he will receive some extra familiarisation with the harness. We don't want to lose any of you Peace Bringers. You give up the lives that are familiar to you, your families and everything you know, to come here and help us, and we want you to be safe here. It is our mistake that he was allowed to climb the rock face before he was ready."

"It was one of those unfortunate circumstances," Narek said. "No one could've predicted this or planned for it. Don't beat yourself up about it. He's alive and that's the main thing." The Fa'ahlima man nodded, gave a brief smile and went to speak with the rest of the climbing teams.

Accidents did occur from time to time, and several times, Narek and his friends helped get injured volunteers to the hospital. A Norlode mine is a dangerous environment, and there were any number of twisted ankles, broken wrists and banged heads for the Fa'ahlima to deal with. During the late autumn, a virulent sickness bug flew around the community and every single person, both volunteer and Fa'ahlima alike, went down with it. Narek was the first of his group to display symptoms, and within a further two days, all four were in bed with it. Luckily for everyone, the bug was very short lived, although severe, and once symptoms were displayed, they were gone within two days. The medical experts worked around the clock to identify the particular bug, but it was gone before they got close to knowing what it was or where it came from. One particular day, the entire community was down with it, including every one of the Fa'ahlima personnel. As the days passed and the community returned to relative normality, the word reached the mine that the sickness was going around the whole of Fa'ahla but only within volunteer communities.

"So a volunteer brought it here," Royden said.

"It's to be expected," Soolian replied. "Every world has its own pathogens, and when you grow up in a place, your body gets used to them. People from a different world won't have any resistance to the pathogens that you're used to, and which you will be carrying around on and within your body. Cough, sneeze or shake hands after taking a shit and not washing your hands and you pass it on. I'm surprised it doesn't happen more often actually."

"You're right," Narek nodded. "I guess we've been lucky up to now."

"Very," Royden said. "And I for one lost several pounds in weight, so I vote we blow the budget on dinner tonight and have ourselves a feast." Everyone agreed that was a marvellous idea, and they all went to bed that night feeling uncomfortably bloated.

Narek had taken Soolian's suggestion to heart, and wrote letters to Risa every night. He poured out his heart to her, begged for her forgiveness, and promised her the universe. Most nights the letters would be stained with his tears, and dreams of her troubled his sleep. Over time, the dreams had changed slightly, and although he could still hear her anguished cries somewhere just out of sight, he was aware of an inner knowing that he was getting nearer to her. The four continued to pray daily, each beseeching their own gods in their own way, and Narek took great comfort from the bond he had with his friends. For quite a time now, he and Telkan had been referring to both Soolian and Royden as Manuk, – brother, and everyone admitted that they truly felt as close as any brothers sharing blood would feel. Narek asked the Fa'ahlima if he could purchase a couple of holographic photo viewers, and once the precious items were acquired, all four took many photographs. No one wanted their time together to pass without a memento.

Autumn gave way to the icy chill of winter and with it, the halfway point of Narek's year passed and the four celebrated with him. Now he knew he had less time to do than he had already done, and he felt renewed by this knowledge. His mood lightened greatly, and the change in him was obvious to everyone. The winters on Fa'ahla are very cold, and the men were given extra clothing to help keep out the chill while they fumbled their way along the tunnels and shafts. For the first time since their arrival, they did not enjoy the ever present, and now icy drips that fell from the roof and found their way down their necks. One day in mid-Winter, Telkan complained of pain in his hands and fingers, and admitted to having been suffering for over a week before mentioning it. The Fa'ahlima gave him an extra pair of gloves, but within another two days, his fingers were dark blue and Narek gasped when he saw them.

"Oh Manuk, your fingers. Look at them. You cannot go on like this; you must ask to see a doctor."

"I don't want to make a fuss or be a bother."

"A bother? For fuck's sake you're in agony. If you don't ask for a doctor, then I will." Narek turned away and called for one of the Fa'ahlima personnel, who came running at his anguished call.

"Is there a problem my friend?"

"Yes, my friend has a problem with his hands, look at them." The man looked and frowned.

"Why did you not say this had happened?" he asked, looking at Telkan. "Come, I will take you to the hospital right away."

"I didn't want to make a fuss," Telkan said.

"You make all the fuss you want, Peace Bringer," the man replied. "You did not volunteer to suffer in pain, and we will not allow it to continue. Come." He led Telkan out of the mine and yelled for a hover cart. Narek sighed and shook his head at Telkan's behaviour.

"Why didn't he say anything? He must be in agony," Royden asked as they watched the hover cart disappear.

"It is the traditional Vendalan way," Narek replied. "I didn't realise he was so firm in his adherence to our old customs."

"You have a custom that says a man cannot get his health sorted out when he's in pain?" Soolian asked.

"Not exactly, but in the old days, a man bore his pain without complaint as a way of showing that he was a strong and able provider for his family, and that he would work to keep them even when suffering pain. With advances in medicine, there is no longer any need for that old way of thinking, but Telkan was obviously brought up by a very traditional father."

"Or he has decided to adopt that old tradition," Soolian said. Narek and Royden looked at him and frowned. "Well think about it," Soolian continued. "He loses his entire family at a time when, as a young man just reaching the prime of his life, he needed their guidance and support the most. Feeling lost, abandoned, and too frightened to return to his homeland alone, his confidence in himself as a man must have been almost totally destroyed. He probably regards himself as worthless, weak, and of no interest to anyone. In trying to appear strong and able to endure pain and injury, he was probably hoping to regain some of his self-respect."

"Shit," Royden sighed as he nodded. "That never even occurred to me. I've been alone for years, and am used to making my life on my own. I know about his family because he told us, but I guess I underestimated the effect it had on him."

"So did I," Narek said, his face ashen. "I feel terrible at having failed him so."

"You didn't fail him," Soolian said. "None of us did."

"How can you say that?" Narek snapped. "He has been in pain all this time and none of us took care to share his anguish. You two aren't Vendalan, so you cannot be expected to understand, but I have failed him by not recognising that he was in need."

"Calm down Narek, and listen please," Soolian replied, hands raised in a placating gesture. "Just think about it. Telkan adopted this old tradition because he wanted to appear strong, capable, and worthy of admiration, yes?" Narek and Royden nodded. "Not one of us ever had occasion to wonder whether he was okay or not. We never saw through the facade to the pain within until now, when the physical pain was too much to bear. I'd say that means he succeeded in his effort to follow the old tradition. It tells me that he is indeed strong, capable and worthy of admiration because I can tell you with complete authority, that I wouldn't be able to stand it for so long. He's to be congratulated, not pitied. He accomplished what he wanted, and we reacted as he wished us to react. We didn't fail him; we gave him what he wanted."

"He's right Manuk," Royden said, looking at Narek. "You know he's right."

Narek sighed and ran a hand through his hair. "Yes, you're right of course, forgive me for yelling." Soolian waved away the apology. "So how do we proceed?"

"We make sure we take every opportunity to bolster his confidence," Soolian said. "Go to him for guidance from time to time perhaps."

"Oh yes, that's a good idea," Royden remarked.

Narek nodded. "And try to encourage him to open up about how he's feeling."

"Right," Soolian said. "Now come on, it's time for our mid-day meal and I want some hot food."

Telkan spent the afternoon being tested at the hospital, and when Narek, Royden and Soolian arrived after work to see him, he was smiling.

"How's it going Manuk?" Narek asked.

"You okay?" Royden said.

"How are you doing?" Soolian added.

"I'm okay, thanks. I'm just waiting for some test results."

"Does it still hurt?" Royden asked, looking at Telkan's hands at his still slightly blue fingers.

"A little, but not as much. It seems that the severe cold makes it worse. Since I've been here at the hospital and in the warm, it's got a bit better."

"Right then Telkan, would you like to follow me. We have the results now. Your friends can come with you if you want." Telkan got up.

"You want us to stay here?" Narek asked, making sure no one followed without Telkan's consent. Telkan shook his head.

"What? No way, come with me guys."

"Sorry to keep you waiting," the doctor said as everyone sat down. "We had to research our Vendalan medical records before we could begin to search for the problem. It seems that you have Mina Lastrel syndrome."

"Huh?" Telkan asked and looked at Narek, who shook his head.

"Never heard of it."

"It's an inherited condition," the doctor continued, "passed down by the mother. It's a defective gene in your seventh chromosome, which means that in icy temperatures, the blood vessels in your extremities constrict. If left untreated, the loss of blood flow inevitably leads to amputation." The four friends gaped at this news. "You might also be experiencing a similar problem with your feet?"

"Not really," Telkan shook his head. "Just my hands."

"That's probably because the special inserts we issued everyone with at the onset of winter, keep your feet comfortably warm. You will be issued with several more pairs, just to make sure you never go without them until winter passes."

"Thank you."

"As for your hands, on Vendala, they can easily repair the faulty gene for you, but we are not able to perform such a procedure here on Fa'ahla. I've been in contact with representatives of the High Governors, and it has been decided that you can leave and return to Vendala for treatment."

"Oh no, I don't want to leave here," Telkan said, horror stricken at the thought. "I'll put a pair of the boot inserts into my gloves, that'll keep my hands warm. Anything but make me leave, please."

"Don't worry Telkan," the doctor soothed, "you are not being banished. If you wish to refuse the offer, you can. We will issue you with a pair of the special gloves we make for the Sarramatan volunteers. Their world is very hot, and cold weather is unknown to them, and lethal. They die very quickly once the temperature gets too low, so we produce specially heated clothing for them, and they thrive here."

"Oh, thank you," Telkan sighed with relief. "That will be wonderful."

"Now here is a painkiller for you to take now," he handed over a small yellow tablet, which Telkan swallowed. "It will allow you to be pain free until your blood vessels relax again. Someone will call on you during this evening with some gloves. If no one arrives by the morning with them, stay off work until you have them. Remain inside your dwelling in the warm until you have them."

"Okay, I will."

"I've made a note into our database about this, so you will always be issued with new gloves each winter."

"Thank you so much Doctor."

"It is our pleasure to help you Peace Bringer."

"I've never heard of Mina Lastrel Syndrome," Narek said as they walked back to their apartment.

"Neither have I," Telkan said, "but I do vaguely remember my grandmother always having to take care to keep warm in the winter. Everyone was always fussing around her with blankets. She died when I was four, so my memory is hazy. She was my mother's mother, so that would fit with it passing down the mother's line. She might've had it."

"Seems likely," Narek nodded. "At least we know what the problem is now, and you don't have to suffer the pain anymore."

"Or lose your fingers," Soolian remarked. Narek went grey at the thought.

"Shit, you must take care in future Manuk."

Telkan felt much better by the time they had eaten dinner, and was relieved when a Fa'ahlima man delivered three pairs of the special gloves later that evening. He spent the rest of the winter in a lot more comfort as the group worked their way through the chilly tunnels of the Norlode mine's easternmost shaft.

Seven months into Narek's year, when spring had seen the last of the winter chill away, he and his group were deep inside one of the lowest tunnels when events quickly took an unexpected and tragic turn. The four were working their way along a downward sloping section of the tunnel, probing with practiced delicacy into every crack in the rock surface. Water seeped through natural cracks in the bedrock, melted runoff from the winter's ice, dripped onto their heads and pooled in natural undulations on the tunnel floor. It was once again, hot and humid work and they did not mind the wet drips that ran down their necks, it helped to keep them cool. Without warning, Soolian slipped on a patch of wet rock and his foot went from under him. He cried out in shock, arms flailing to find a purchase in the dark. Royden went to grab him but his fingers clutched empty air as a sickening thud silenced Soolian's astonished cry.

The Fa'ahlima came running, the shouts from Narek and his friends rousing them into action. The crack in his skull told everyone Soolian had died almost instantly and despite the Fa'ahlima's best efforts, he could not be brought back. Narek, Telkan and Royden cried for the loss of their friend and spent many minutes with him, saying their goodbyes and thanking him for his love and friendship. All around, a crowd of men from the other tunnels stood, silent and sombre. Narek and Telkan said a prayer for his soul and beseeched Shashowan, the Receiver of Souls to welcome their brave friend and reunite him with his wife. The three were given ten days away from work, to attend Soolian's funeral and to mourn him in whatever way they wished.

A.W.O.L

They journeyed to Mount Tuliash for Soolian's funeral and were allowed to travel with Soolian's body. Narek had insisted, they did everything together as a group and there was no way Soolian was going to be alone on his last journey. All three were surprised but pleased to see many thousands of Fa'ahlima crowded around the Sha'yve, the temple of the High Governors, where the ashes of all Peace Bringers as the Fa'ahlima called the volunteers, were interred. A huge pyre had been built on the approach to the Sha'yve and the three friends helped carry Soolian and lay him on the top. From the top of the Sha'yve, a horn sounded and everyone fell silent. Narek looked up, to see a Fa'ahlima man dressed in just a small cloth around his middle, a fantastical and frightening mask over his head, blowing into a horn that curved up and twisted around on itself. As the sound stopped, he lowered the horn and took up the bow that hung from his shoulder and aimed an arrow, its tip ablaze. The sun glinted and shone as it reflected from the metallic bow, the man aiming it high into the sky before letting the flaming arrow fly. The arrow flew up in a graceful arc, before coming down and hitting the pyre at Soolian's feet. Immediately the flames spread, and Narek guessed that something extremely flammable lay at the pyre's heart, for in less than a minute the whole pyre was ablaze. Narek and his friends cried for their friend and everyone remained for a whole day and night until Soolian's body was ash. Women wailed in their hundreds, brought gifts of flowers, fruits, woven baskets and all manner of other things, and laid them out along the walls of the great building, whose statues looked down mournfully upon the proceedings. At Dawn, Fa'ahlima workers dressed in long robes of red, collected his ashes, placed them within an intricately carved stone box and processed around the Sha'yve seven times, once for each month of his volunteering. The procession finally entered the Sha'yve itself, through the huge stone doors on which were carved all manner of symbols and sigils, and crossed the massive meeting room where the High Governors hold their meetings and where public events are held. The robed men placed the casket containing the ashes beside the Great Ottoman and everyone fell silent as a Fa'ahlima man dressed in bright yellow robes stood.

"Another peace bringer has been taken to join the throng who dwell beside our creator. We mourn his loss and will keep his memory alive in our hearts for as long as we remain here in this physical form. We look forward to the day when we too, can reunite with him in the sacred halls of Me'atash. He gave up everything he knew to come to us and every day that he was amongst us, peace drew ever nearer. He will forever have rest in peace within the Hall of the Peace Bringers."

Trumpets sounded throughout the Sha'yve and everyone rose their voice in song. The soulful, mourning words touched Narek and his friends deeply and rang throughout the Sha'yve and around Mount Tuliash for many minutes. The sound of thousands of voices all joined in song for the soul of their friend, was something Narek and his friends would remember for the rest of their lives. More than once, he wondered how often this ceremony needed to be performed, and hoped that the Ta'ahli were all found soon, so that no one else need be lost.

Once the song was finished, the casket, borne by four Fa'ahlima bearers, led the way through another door at the other end of this huge room. This second room was ten times as big as the first, but its huge windows held no glass and the far end was open, giving the most incredible view over the Fa'ahla countryside. Hundreds of thousands of small stone caskets stood, side by side, row on row from floor to ceiling around three sides of the room. The bearers strode to the end of the ranks of dead, and the man with yellow robes gently placed Soolian in his place amongst the throng. He then turned and indicated to Narek, who stepped forward and placed the tag that hung around Soolian's neck, beside the casket. Royden stepped up and placed his bracelet of stone beads beside the tag, and Telkan brought the photograph Soolian always kept beside his bed. It showed himself and his wife in their younger years, smiling and obviously deeply in love. A plaque beneath showed Soolian's name, his date of volunteering and the date of his death. There was also an inscription in Fa'ahla beneath the details and the man in the yellow robe pointed it out.

"It says our friend has left us for a new quest. We mourn him and we bid him safe passage."

CHAPTER FOURTEEN

Narek and his friends returned to the Norlode mine and spent some days just sitting around and talking of Soolian. The entire crew of volunteers threw a party in his honour, and for the first time in months, Narek and his friends had a hangover that they dedicated to Soolian's memory. One of the Fa'ahlima men, a counsellor as he introduced himself, asked them if they wanted another volunteer to take Soolian's place within their group.

"It is not required of you to replace him," he told the three friends. "Many groups who lose a member choose to continue as three and you may do so if you wish. If another should be lost, we will offer to combine the remaining pair with another pair who have lost two of their group, and many then choose to accept this arrangement. One new person with three friends often finds it hard to fit in, whereas two pairs don't seem to have the same difficulty."

"We'd rather just stay as we are," Narek said and the others nodded.

"As you wish," the man replied. "Now, you still have several days off from your work, so if you need anything, just let Ja'ehla know and she will arrange it."

"Actually, we've been talking about that," Royden said, "and we all agree that we'd like to return to work if that's allowed. Soolian enjoyed the work. He said it gave his life purpose again after so many years of feeling he was drifting, and we'd like to honour him that way."

"Well of course, if that's what you wish to do," the man said. "You may return in the morning and carry on. Would you like to be relocated to a different part of the mine? Some groups prefer not to return to the location where their friend was lost."

"No, we want to carry on in the same place," Narek said.

"It was the last place we saw him alive," Telkan said with tears in his eyes. "The last place he spoke to us, laughed with us. We want to go there."

"Then you may do so," the man said. "Return there in the morning as you normally would."

"Thank you," Narek said.

Merita King

In the last five months of Narek's year, the crew of volunteers at the Norlode mine found three more of the Ta'ahli and by the time he finished work at the end of his last day, there were just forty-one more to be found to complete the tablet. The friends had been talking about his imminent departure for several days leading up to this, but still both Royden and Telkan were visibly upset at the prospect of not seeing him again. He assured them he would keep in touch and had been told by the Fa'ahlima that he was allowed to write to them and call them whenever he wanted to. On his last evening, Narek got up to answer a knock at the door, to find Ka'abash standing there.

"Hello Ka'abash, come in," he smiled.

"Hello Narek. Did I not tell you the year would pass quickly if you focussed on the task at hand?"

"You did Sir, and you were right."

Ka'abash greeted Royden and Telkan and sat down.

"I want you to know I was saddened to learn of Soolian's death," he told them. "Know that I mourned with you."

"Thank you," Royden said.

"Well Narek. Your year is now over and I am here to fulfil the promise given to you by the High Governors when you volunteered. You are now freed from your obligation and all of Fa'ahla gives you blessings for the work you have done here to help bring peace to our world. I have here the location details of Risa Parks so that you may go and find her. She is working in a city a few hundred miles away."

"Thank you so much," Narek said as he took the paper with shaking hands and read it.

'Risa Parks, building 31, dwelling 2. So'ikima female volunteer community.'

"You may use all the Fa'ahla transportation services just as if you were Fa'ahlima," Ka'abash told him. "Here is a travel plan and map. I also have new garments for you to wear," he said as he unpacked a shirt and pants and handed them over. The shirt was white and had two purple diagonal bands from each shoulder that met in the centre of his chest with a large circular symbol.

"This tells everyone you meet that you are a volunteer who has completed his commitment and been given the freedom of Fa'ahla. None of the Fa'ahlima will question you as to why you're not at your work and you will find that everyone will be very friendly to you. As I told you one year ago, you are guests here, honoured guests. You are bringing peace to our world when we could not and you will always be a guest of the Fa'ahlima."

"Thank you Sir," Narek said. "I can't tell you how much this means to me. I can hardly believe that I'm finally going to find Risa soon."

"You have earned it my friend," Ka'abash smiled. "Now," he said as he turned to Royden and Telkan. "You two have a decision to make now that Narek is leaving you. "As you are now just a pair, you can choose now to combine with another pair to make a new group of four. There are three pairs in this community alone. Two of them have lost members in accidents and illness, and the other lost one member to illness and the other completed his five year commitment and has now left to find a new life."

"Well, we're not sure," Royden began.

"Would it help you if I told you that there is also a pair from a neighbouring community that also comprises an Earth man and a Vendalan?"

"Oh, yes it would," Telkan replied. He looked at Royden, who nodded.

"Very well," Ka'abash said. "I will arrange for you all to meet and spend some time together in a week or two. Your housekeeper will let you know when. I will bid you goodbye my friends." Ka'abash stood and looked at Narek.

"Thank you for your service to Fa'ahla Narek. It has given me much pleasure to know you."

"Thank you Sir," Narek replied. "For believing in me a year ago and for helping me. I will never forget your kindness."

The three spent over two hours in silent prayer that evening, beseeching Alima, the god of love and bonding to bring Narek and Risa together for a happy reunion and giving thanks to Salifkan, the god of triumph in adversity for giving Narek strength to endure this past year. When the prayers were finished, all three had tears on their cheeks, a mixture of sadness at their friend leaving them, and joy at the knowledge that the end of his quest was nearby.

Narek was up early with his friends. They had to leave to begin their day's work and he wanted to say goodbye. He handed Telkan his key card and they embraced in the customary way. Grasping their right hands together, they touched their right cheeks and whispered the words of the traditional parting embrace.

"Enkiarae re teliam maiy reil Manuk," they said to each other. "You are taking my love with you brother."

Narek extended his hand to Royden but the big, dark brown skinned man brushed it away and clasped him in an embrace.

"Enkiarae re teliam maiy reil Manuk," He said. "You are taking my love with you brother."

"Enkiarae re teliam maiy reil Manuk," Narek replied with a smile.

"Did I say it right?" Royden grinned and Narek nodded.

"Perfectly, thank you for that. It means a lot that you would take the time and effort to learn such an important thing. I will treasure the memory."

Narek smiled at the men who cheered and waved as he walked towards the perimeter of the community. The guards nodded and smiled as he passed out of the gate and headed south. The journey took three days, due mainly to the location of the Norlode mine being very isolated. Whenever he encountered the Fa'ahlima, they gave him lifts, offered him a meal, something to drink and thanked him for his service to Fa'ahla. When he finally reached a populated area and could catch a hover bus, the driver refused to let him pay for his fare.

"It is a pleasure to drive you my friend," he said. "I will not take money from a Peace Bringer. You sit, enjoy the ride."

As the hover bus approached the large city that lay to the South, the hover buses got more modern and the ride, faster, but always the people treated him in the same way. By the time he stepped off the last bus in the outskirts of So'ikima City, he had not spent any of his own money. All of his travel costs, food, drink and accommodations for the two nights, had been given freely by the Fa'ahlima, who all greeted him like a hero. He drew in a deep breath and felt revived, knowing that somewhere in this very city, Risa waited for his embrace.

"Estriwa allimala Risa re teliam," he whispered into the light morning breeze. "I am here Risa my love."

It did not take long to find his way to the entrance of the female volunteer community, but as he stood looking towards the gate, he thought back to when he was standing at the gate back on Zelidol. A year ago he was desperate and scared, and knew only that he must find Risa, that any risk was worth it. Now here he was at this gate, beyond which she was working, chatting with her friends, not knowing that he was just moments away. He wondered if she still remembered him, if she still loved him and would welcome him into her arms. His heart raced, for he knew that the next few moments would decide his future, whether he was to finally regain the missing half of his soul with her embrace, or whether he would end this day by taking the Tal ak Roi. There was no way for him to know as he stood looking towards the gate, but he sent a last prayer to his gods and vowed to accept his destiny with grace. The blood rushed in his ears as he approached the guards and handed them the letter of introduction given him by Ka'abash.

"You are Narek Jenn," one of the guards said and Narek nodded.

"Yes, I am he."

"You are here for Risa Parks, yes?"

"Yes. Is she here? Can I see her now? Please, it's been so long."

"If only you had got here sooner my friend," the guard on the left said, his face ashen.

"Why? What has happened?" Narek demanded.

"I'm so sorry my friend," the guard on the right added. "There was a terrible accident just one hour ago." Everything went silent for Narek as he heard the words and tried to understand them. It was as if someone had flipped off a vidicom movie, and he was left staring at the guard, his mouth open in shock as time stood still all around him. Somewhere deep inside, Narek's body responded and he dropped to his knees, his head swimming, and vomited into the dust. The guards rushed to his side and crouched down beside him.

"Her group was helping to dismantle a house for searching when the walls collapsed on top of several of the women. We fear they are all lost."

Narek screamed in anguish, his tears splashing onto the dusty road surface, drawing the attention of those nearby, who all stopped to look. The guards each put a hand on his shoulder.

"How can this be?" Narek cried. "After all this time, to lose her like this. How have I failed the gods?"

"Come," the guard on the left said. "You can come and help the party rescue the women. You can find her and spend time with her. Come." They helped him to his feet and he followed them into the community. The women stared as they passed and several times he heard murmurs and saw women whispering to each other. Narek felt self-conscious and was glad when the guards indicated for him to climb into a hover car, and drove through the community to the part of the city that was currently being searched. The women's community was built on wasteland, but soon Narek saw buildings being rebuilt by Fa'ahlima workers and volunteers. Further on he saw piles of rubble where buildings once stood and further still, half dismantled buildings. Beyond that were buildings yet to be dismantled, their empty windows giving the whole place a feeling of abandonment. Narek shivered and looked away as the hover car came to a halt outside the ruins of what was once a large home. A large group of women stood around and many Fa'ahlima personnel worked inside the ruins. Narek jumped out of the car and ran towards the building, followed by one of the guards who spoke to one of the men directing the rescue.

"You are Narek?" the man asked.

"Yes," Narek nodded. "I want to help, I must. Please allow me to help."

"Of course," the man nodded. "Follow me." He led the way into the building and showed him where the accident had taken place. Two adjoining walls and part of the ceiling had collapsed onto the women as they worked. Narek looked at the rubble and realised that it would be a miracle if anyone had survived such an accident.

"Risa," he yelled and dropped his backpack onto the floor. "Risa, I'm here my love. I'm here to rescue you, please don't leave me," he cried as he grabbed rocks and rubble and threw them aside. Twenty minutes later, he uncovered a woman's ankle and the doctor ran over.

"Let me through please," he demanded and reached for the ankle. A few seconds later, he confirmed that the ankle did not belonged to Risa, but that she was dead. Narek cried out in anguish and a woman came up to him and laid a hand on his shoulder.

"I am Lolan and I am in Risa's group. She talked of you so often that I feel I know you. She never stopped loving you Narek."

"She remembered me?" Narek asked and Lolan smiled.

"Yes. She said that she would never take a man to her bed as long as she lived, because there is only one to whom she could give herself, but he has taken another to his side."

"That was a lie," Narek said. "Her sister told her that but it wasn't true. I've loved Risa since I first met her but I was too afraid to tell her. I was afraid she would never want someone like me."

When the woman's body had been uncovered and removed, Narek started picking through the rubble again. After an hour, they found a huge slab of the ceiling lying at an angle, propped up on one side by other rubble and stone. A man yelled from Narek's left.

A.W.O.L

"I have a woman's hand here. Doctor, please." Narek stepped aside to watch the doctor examine the hand to see if the woman was alive or dead. As he did so, the changing light at his feet caught his attention and he saw something that made him cry out.

"Risa? Risa, I see you my love. Hold on a little longer, please. Someone please, Risa is here, look." He held up the tuft of golden hair that poked out from under the slab. "She has beautiful golden hair. This must be her." Narek looked at the doctor who was examining the hand and waited for what seemed like a lifetime.

"It is Risa Parks," he confirmed, "and she is alive." Narek cried out in relief and dropped to his knees, scraping at the stones and dust until his fingers bled. The rescue effort went into overdrive now they knew Risa was alive, and after forty minutes, a lifting machine arrived and they had the slab off in little more than a minute. Narek looked into Risa's face for the first time in over a year. His tears splashed onto her dirty cheek as he gently brushed her hair from her face.

"I am here now my love. We are together now." He stood aside as the doctors worked to get her ready to transport to a hospital, and he was pleased at how carefully and expertly they attended to her. All of the emotions buried inside as he had worked the Norlode mine came rushing out as he sat with her in the hospital transport that raced away from the scene, and he cried, his pent up emotions from over a year of trying to right the wrong that Lorella had done, finally spilling out. Time and again, he told her that he loved her, that he had never wanted Lorella and that he had been working tirelessly for the past year to find her and embrace her. He apologised to her for her suffering, vowed to make Lorella pay for the damage she had done, and as he sat at her bedside in the hospital, he asked her to be his wife.

The days and nights dragged by and Narek stayed by Risa's bedside. Even when sleep overcame him, he refused to be persuaded away from her side and slept fitfully in a chair in her room. The nurses brought him food and drink, which he ate hurriedly, not wanting to be away from Risa a moment longer than necessary. He spoke to her all the time, read her the letters he had written to her during his year of work, and watched as the doctors attended to her needs and monitored her condition. On the fourth day, he finally allowed himself to be persuaded to take a shower and change his clothes. He felt better for a shower and a shave, and a clean set of clothes felt a lot more comfortable.

The nurses offered to wash his dirty clothes and he handed them over gratefully.

"Thank you for your kindness. I'm sorry if I'm being a nuisance."

"You are never a nuisance Peace Bringer," the nurse replied.

As the afternoon gave way to evening, the lack of sleep finally caught up with Narek and he fell asleep, his head on the side of Risa's bed. He awoke during the early hours, awakened by the feeling of something in his hair, and at first did not understand what that feeling was. It took several seconds before he realised that it was fingers in his hair, but once he did, he was instantly alert. He snapped his head up and looked into Risa's open eyes as they gazed down at him.

"Hello Narek," she smiled. "Why are you here? How did you get here? I don't understand but it is good to see you again."

"You're awake, thank the gods," he sighed.

"But why are you here? Is she here?" Risa asked, her eyes welling up. "I don't want to see her if you don't mind, but it is lovely to see you again."

"No my love," Narek said. "She is not here. I read your letter and it broke my heart. I came all this way to find you. The Fa'ahlima said if I worked for a year, they'd let me free so I could find you and tell you of the lie."

"What lie? You came all this way? You've been here for a year? Why?"

Narek burst into tears and kissed her cheek. When he could finally talk, he told her of his journey, from receiving her letter, to finding her buried beneath the slab of stone in the ruins of that house, and everything in between. He told her of Lorella and the lie she had woven and Risa cried as she learned of her sister's true cruelty. Narek admitted to her that he had fallen in love with her the first moment he saw her and how he was too shy to approach her. He begged her forgiveness for his failure and the pain it caused and she gave it willingly.

"You are the only woman I could ever love Risa. I want you and no one else. I came all this way to find you and tell you I love you, please be my love. I beg you."

"I became your love the first day I saw you Narek," she said, "and I'll never be anyone else's."

Risa spent three weeks in the hospital while the doctors fixed the damage done by the falling masonry, and ran all manner of tests to ensure her brain was unharmed from her accident. Narek spent every day with her and slept in an adjoining room every night, and slowly, the pain that separated them began to lessen. The shyness that crippled Narek so, vanished as his heart opened to embrace Risa's own, and he cried with relief and joy as he felt the two halves of his soul embrace and become whole once more. His promise to take the Tal ak Roi faded into the mist and he was happy that his friends Kaylak and Vronil had persuaded him to let them bond their souls with his, and he looked forward to releasing them from that bond when they next met. He was so happy to finally be with Risa, and he did not want to waste a minute ever again, so he took every opportunity to hug her, kiss her, hold her hand or brush a finger down her cheek, anxious that she never forget how much he loved her.

"I hope I'm not smothering you," he said one day.

"Smothering me? Narek, I've dreamed of nothing else since I first saw you. It was agony loving you so much but not feeling able to show you, and I cannot begin to count the number of times I dreamed of you holding me. It will never become a nuisance, not ever."

"When we found you under the rubble, and I thought you were lost, I realised how much my hesitation had cost and I never want to risk such a cost again. I don't want you to spend a moment of your life not knowing I love you."

"Promise me you'll never stop telling me," she asked.

"I promise," he whispered and kissed her.

Ka'abash visited them one day and smiled broadly as he gazed at the couple.

"The love you have for each other is visible for all to see," he said. "I am so happy that you are reunited my friends. This is one of the best things to come from our situation here on Fa'ahla and all our hearts fill with pride at being part of making it happen."

"It is good to see you again Ka'abash, to thank you once again and introduce you to Risa."

"I have come to formally give you both the High Governors' good wishes, and to tell you that they still hold good to their pledge that Risa may leave Fa'ahla with you if she wishes."

"We've discussed this for many days," Narek said as he looked at Risa, who smiled and nodded. "We wish to remain here until all the Ta'ahli have been found and replaced within the tablet. We both want to continue to work, if we may stay together."

"Well of course if that is what you both wish," Ka'abash replied, his eyes wide with astonishment.

"We love your world and you people have been the kindest we've ever met," Narek continued. "We want to remain to see peace return and be a part of bringing that peace."

"Then it shall be done," Ka'abash nodded. "I will arrange accommodations for you and return this afternoon."

True to his word, Ka'abash returned that afternoon with details of their new accommodations.

"You have three choices," he told them. "You can either remain here at Risa's community in the city, or you can go to the Lumua Forest on the southern continent."

"Umm, that's two," Narek said. "You said we have three choices?"

"Ahh yes," Ka'abash smiled. "You could always go several hundred miles north of here and work in a Norlode mine." Narek gasped and grinned. "There is a pair of men who recently lost two of their group, a Vendalan and an Earth man. I'm sure they would be happy to welcome you."

"Oh yes, that's where we want to go," Narek exclaimed. "Unless of course you want to remain in the city Risa? Forgive me, I should've asked you first."

"Wherever you are is where I want to go," Risa replied. "I'd like to say goodbye to my friends before we go if that's allowed but I won't be sorry to leave the city. It's so hot and dusty here."

"Of course," Ka'abash nodded. "I shall arrange for them to visit you at the earliest opportunity."

Risa's three friends visited her in the hospital and they all shared an afternoon of happy introductions to Narek, and sad goodbyes to Risa. They had brought her modest belongings with them for her journey to her new home.

"I know you are a good man Narek," Lolan said. "Be happy for the rest of your lives."

"We will," Narek said. "Thank you all for being such good friends to Risa."

A.W.O.L

The following morning the doctors said Risa was fit to leave the hospital. Narek waited in the corridor while Risa dressed and smiled with relief and happiness. He sent a silent prayer of gratitude to Alima and Salifkan for helping him through this journey.

"Narek Jenn?" a voice beside him said. Narek opened his eyes and saw a Fa'ahlima man smiling.

"Yes, I am Narek."

"I am here to shuttle you to your new accommodations."

Narek and Risa were met by a Fa'ahlima escort who introduced himself as Ki'welo.

"Welcome Narek and it is a pleasure to meet you Risa. I am pleased that you are recovered from your accident. Come, let me show you to your accommodations."

The single storey building offered everything Narek and Risa could wish for. Situated just outside the men's community, it afforded them privacy and kept to the single gender rule. Risa blushed when she saw the single bedroom with a large bed and Narek kissed her cheek. When they were alone he took her into his arms and held her for long moments, enjoying the feel of her body against his own, and the thrill of desire coursed through him. He lifted her chin and kissed her passionately and as he drew away, he felt his spots throb all down his neck, chest and spine.

"Narek," Risa said as she looked at him. "Your spots are black, I remember them as brown."

"They are brown normally," he said and blushed.

"So why are they black and why are you blushing?" she grinned.

"When a Vendalan man is ready to take a mate, his spots begin to darken and become more prominent," he explained. Risa touched a finger to his neck and he closed his eyes as his body responded. "They turn black because I desire you so," he whispered.

"Make love to me Narek," Risa said. "I've wanted you for so long."

Narek smiled and swinging her up into his arms, carried her into the bedroom. For hours they explored each other's bodies, neither feeling any shyness or embarrassment. Narek tasted every inch of Risa's body and she teased him mercilessly by caressing his spots with her fingers and tongue. When he could stand it no longer he knelt between her thighs and hoisted her up onto his lap, lowering her gently onto his full length. She groaned with pleasure and pulled him to her as she began to move rhythmically. Narek moved with her, matching his thrusts to her movements and suckled her nipples as they both rose to a shattering climax. After dozing a little, Narek loved her again, this time sliding between her thighs and gazing down at her as she lay beneath him. She grasped his backside and pulled him in hard as she rose up to meet his thrusts. With a sudden cry, Risa's back arched and Narek felt her grip him rhythmically as he gently continued thrusting. The pleasure was almost too much to bear, but he held back until her body stopped convulsing, then lowered himself onto her and held on tight as he moved within her. He nuzzled her neck and thrusted slowly, wanting this perfect moment to last forever. When he could not hold on a moment longer, he thrusted purposefully and as his body released inside her, he whispered her name and told her he loved her.

Telkan answered the knock at the door and stood, open mouthed with shock.

"Manuk. Kaskirae pen chiwey, li estrillie Risa. Estriwa maitiliok ruliksi reilichi," he exclaimed. "Brother. You have returned to us, and you have Risa. I am overjoyed to see you both."

"Kiana Manuk, kaskira maiy re teliam li estrima maseyi ku lostra," Narek replied. "Yes brother, I have returned with my love and we are together at last."

"Hey who's there Telkan," Royden said as he appeared at the door. "Holy shit it's Narek. Well Manuk, welcome back. And you found her," he said, smiling at Risa. "Wow it's good to see you sweetheart. This guy here drove us crazy for a whole year; all he ever talked about was you."

"Hey now buddy," Narek said and everyone laughed.

"Come on in, we need to celebrate this. Telkan, how about opening that bottle of wine huh?"

"Great idea," Telkan nodded, heading towards the kitchen.

"Has Ka'abash been back to you both about joining with another pair yet?" Narek called.

"Nope, not yet," Royden replied as he set four glasses down on the table.

"Well he will do soon, and when he does, you're to accept okay?"

"Huh?" Telkan frowned. "What are you telling us Manuk?"

CHAPTER FIFTEEN

The sun rose over the Norlode Mine men's community and Narek kissed Risa awake.

"Good morning my love," he whispered into her ear and smiled as she stirred.

"Is it time to get up?" she yawned and kissed him.

"Umm, no," he replied, "but it is time to make love to me." He nuzzled her neck as he let a hand trace its way down to her breast and tease the nipple. She responded by caressing the spots on his neck, just under his ears where he liked it the most and watched as they quickly darkened to black. Not an inch on their bodies was left unexplored with eager fingers and tongues, and as she sat astride his lap and moved her body in time with his thrusts, she realised she was truly happy for the first time in her life.

They had settled into a happy routine since moving into their own dwelling just outside the perimeter of the men's community and they both enjoyed their daily life. The Fa'ahlima were good friends and despite Risa being the only woman volunteer, she was not the only woman in the community. Many Fa'ahlima women worked in the shops and other facilities built for the volunteers, and she had many women friends whose company she enjoyed. Some of them taught her to cook traditional Fa'ahla meals and Narek, Royden and Telkan were willing guinea pigs on the evenings she tried out the recipes. As the months went by, one by one, the remaining Ta'ahli were found, and there came a time when only one remained to be discovered. The Keystone still eluded the searchers and without it being returned to its position at the very centre of the tablet, the sacred frieze would never be complete, and true peace would never return to Fa'ahla.

One year and seven weeks after Narek and Risa joined with Royden and Telkan to complete their group of four, the Norlode mineshafts and tunnels were officially declared as having been fully searched. Two more of the Ta'ahli stones had been found in the mine, and the two discoverers, as was Fa'ahla tradition, were given the choice of ending their work for good and either leaving Fa'ahla with their blessings, or remaining there as much honoured Peace Bringers. The vast majority chose to remain on Fa'ahla and many of these chose to continue the work, such was the friendship between the Fa'ahlima and the volunteers.

Since the mine tunnels and shafts were now cleared, the search was extended to the area beyond. A long bluff curved around, many hundreds of feet high and groups of specially trained volunteers climbed and search the natural crevices in the cliff wall. The remainder searched the rocks at the foot of the cliff and gradually, inch by inch and day by day, they worked their way along the miles of bluff. One afternoon, not long after their mid-day meal, the four were searching amongst a pile of rocks from some long forgotten rock fall, when something caught Narek's eye. The rocks were all a uniform, mottled grey, with paler lines meandering through, but something white drew his attention and he bent to look closer.

"Hey what's this?" he muttered as he bent to scrape away the gravel and dirt that partially covered it. Instinctively he drew his hand away as recognition embraced him, a frisson of fear coursing through him. The smooth white of the skull looked stark against the grey of the rocks, and when he knew what it was, Narek was startled.

"It's a skull. There's a body here guys," he said as Risa, Royden and Telkan bent to look.

The Fa'ahlima came running over and the four heaved the rest of the rocks away to reveal a skeleton, clad in the tattered remains of a long garment. A necklace revealed a symbol and some Fa'ahlima writing which none of the four friends were able to read. A Fa'ahlima man took it over to the sunlight to examine it and the four watched as his eyes widened and his jaw dropped open.

"What?" Royden asked. "Come on; don't keep us in suspense here. What does it say?"

"Tell us," Narek urged.

"This is the symbol of the Acolytes, those who train under the High Governors and one day, replace them."

"So this is the body of an Acolyte?" Risa asked and the Fa'ahlima man nodded.

"Yes it is, but that is not what is so shocking."

"So?" Telkan almost yelled, raising his arms to the sides to emphasise the point.

"It says Acolyte Ma'imosh, son of Chi'ondol and Da'atma, gives his life to the service of Fa'ahla." The four were silent; jaws open wide and unable to speak for several moments.

"You mean this is the guy who stole the Ta'ahli?" Narek said and the man nodded.

"Yes. You have found the one who committed this dreadful crime and brought war to our world. His bones will forever hang in the Sha'yve as a reminder to all future generations of Governors of how fragile a thing peace is, and how hard we all must work to maintain it."

"Wow," Narek hissed as he bent to look at the skeleton. These bones were the reason Risa ran away, and why he had to chase all over the galaxy to find her. He was angry and wanted to scream at this dead man, but then he realised that he was also the reason he and Risa had months of a joy he could never have imagined a person could experience, and he was grateful. His anger melted away as he put a hand gently down onto the ribs and said a silent prayer to Shashowan, to bring the soul of this man to peace. As he lifted his hand away, the tattered remains of the garment fell away and Narek's gaze fell upon the Keystone lying serenely within the body cavity. It was several seconds before he realised what it was he was looking at, and once he did, he hesitated before daring to touch it. All sounds from the other workers, the wind in the trees and birds calling above, faded to silence as he realised the last of the Ta'ahli were now found. A tiny dot in the centre, from which many lines ran to the edges, was the only design upon the stone and Narek thought that perhaps the lines represented the sun's rays. The ramifications of this moment, for everyone on this planet, hit home and he burst into tears.

"Hey what's up baby?" Risa said as she went to him

He stood, wiping his eyes with his free hand and turned around to face them, his other hand held out in front. The group crowded around to see, and as they realised what they were looking at, all gasped in shock. Hands went to mouths and everyone looked at everyone else, and all had tears in their eyes. Someone shouted for the Fa'ahlima to come and see, but Narek hardly heard, the keystone in his hand weighed almost nothing, but what it meant for everyone on Fa'ahla was immense. He knew this was a seminal moment in not only his own life, but that of everyone on the planet, and the fact that so much depended upon something so small, was both ironic and deeply profound.

"Come," the Fa'ahlima man said, grabbing Narek's elbow and urging him to follow. "Come, you must ring the completion bell. The blessings of all Fa'ahlima upon you Peace Bringer." He bowed his head, the tears still evident on his face and urged him to follow. Narek followed him to the centre of the community where a tall tower stood, upon which was the siren that rang to announce the discovery of another of the sacred Ta'ahli.

"That button you see is the discovery bell that you have all heard. Every time one of the Ta'ahli is found, all discovery bells on Fa'ahla ring to tell the people about the new discovery. This time, you will ring the completion bell and all over Fa'ahla, the people will know that the search is over, that the Keystone has been found. Lift the cover and press the button within."

Narek lifted the flap he saw on a small box above the button that rang the discovery bell and found a bright yellow button within. He pressed a finger to it and the siren sang a new song, a song that no one on Fa'ahla had ever heard. All the workers stopped; this was a sound they had not heard before and all were curious. Amongst them, the Fa'ahlima all dropped to their knees and wept. After several seconds, the electronic message was passed from community to community, tower to tower and within ten minutes, all towers on Fa'ahla were singing this new song of peace. The Fa'ahlima wiped their eyes and passed the word to the workers and soon, the word Keystone and gasps were rushing along the bluff, swiftly followed by cheers and whoops of celebration. Royden and Telkan raised Narek onto their shoulders and he held the Keystone aloft for everyone to see. The cheering did not die down for many minutes and within an hour, the party started.

The Keystone was taken by the Fa'ahlima, secured within a metal box and guarded by four armed guards. The details from the tag around Narek's neck were entered into the record as the discoverer, and both began their journey to Mount Tuliash and the Sha'yve where the High Governors were already waiting to receive it. In a tiny workshop at the base of the mountain, stonemasons began working on the final statue that would join the others in the Hall of Discovery at the side of the Sha'yve. The scan taken of Narek as he first journeyed to Fa'ahla and needed new garments, was displayed upon the wall, and as night fell, the masons got to work. Anyone passing by during the night would hear the sound of metal on stone and the happy songs of the masons as they laboured on this happiest of days.

Back at the Norlode mine, the party continued well into the night and it was in the early hours that Narek and Risa returned to their dwelling and made love, and then, as the dawn rose on this first day of peace on Fa'ahla, they slept until mid-morning. In the days following the discovery of the Keystone, all the volunteers were given new garments made from the finest materials, and a huge bonfire was made of all their working garments. Each was given a brooch, made of the most valuable precious metal to be found on Fa'ahla. The circular brooch showed the central portion of the image from the Ta'ahli tablet, the divine spark at the centre of the Fa'ahlima creator's energy body. Narek recognised it as the same symbol upon the Keystone and understood the symbolism of the lines, emanating from a central point.

The brooch given to Narek was the same, but had a tiny oblong replica of the complete Ta'ahli tablet hanging beneath it. He pinned it to the centre of his new garment and wore it with pride. On the tenth day after the discovery, the journey away from the Norlode mine began, and all the workforce were shuttled in relays to new accommodations that had been erected for the completion ceremony in the town at the foot of Mount Tuliash. All of the Fa'ahlima motherships, the Shi'maqs were recalled and all returned to their home world at top speed, the new volunteers aboard them unaware that they were now spared the work of searching for the Ta'ahli. They would instead be offered the opportunity to return from whence they came or remain on Fa'ahla to help with the rebuilding of the cities.

The bones of Ma'imosh were interred within a niche in the East wall of the central hall of the Sha'yve, as a reminder to all of the fragility of peace and how easily it can be destroyed. The Ta'ahli tablet adorned the top of the central ottoman but still missed its Keystone. That was to be Narek's task to replace it, and for three whole days he was instructed in the long ceremony that would culminate in the completion of the tablet with the placing of the Keystone at its centre. He had not learned the Fa'ahlima language as they had chosen to use the common tongue, and he had to learn the specific moment when he was to step forward to replace the Keystone. Over and over again, he listened as the Fa'ahlima went over the words with him so that he would recognise his moment. He sighed with relief when the High Governors promised they would also give him a visual signal, a nod of the head, just in case his nerves made him forget what he was to listen for.

He was nervous but immensely proud as he walked behind the High Governors up the long trail from the foot of Mount Tuliash to the Sha'yve. He carried the Keystone within its transparent box and the crowds that lined the trail cheered and threw flowers as the procession passed. Many shouted their blessings and many had tears on their cheeks. Risa, Royden and Telkan followed behind Narek, as part of his group of four, they were equally rejoiced as co-discoverers and all three grinned from ear to ear. Behind them, the entire volunteer workforce of the Norlode Mine strode proudly and behind them, thousands of others followed. Fa'ahlima and volunteers alike, all wanted to get a good position to witness the completion ceremony. The media crews were everywhere, sending the ceremony all across Fa'ahla to those who could not make the journey and in public buildings, city centres, parks and gardens all over the planet, giant vidicom screens were erected and huge crowds, both Fa'ahlima and volunteer, sat and celebrated.

The ceremony took many hours, but Narek was proud as he stepped forward at the correct moment and, taking the Keystone from its box, gently replaced it in the centre of the Tablet atop the central ottoman. As the tablet was completed, sirens and horns sounded and the people cheered. All across Fa'ahla, anything that could make a noise was doing so, horns and sirens, whistles and flutes and all voices on the planet were celebrating. The ships upon the oceans sounded their sirens, the Shi'maqs in orbit around the planet sounded theirs, and it seemed as if the entire Fa'ahla system was rejoicing the return of peace to their world. The statue of Narek was placed with the others in the Hall of Discovery, so Fa'ahlima for generations to come could make pilgrimage to the Sha'yve to give thanks to the discoverers who brought peace back to their world.

The oldest of the High Governors stepped forward when the cheering died down.

"We, the Fa'ahlima, give our blessings and gratitude to the Peace Bringers who have given their service to Fa'ahla. We, in our jealousy and hunger for power, brought our world to its knees, and only through your effort and sacrifice has peace been returned to us. We have learned our lesson and will bear the shame of our actions for as long as Fa'ahlima live upon this world. All Peace Bringers, those who celebrate with us today and those who have gone before who now rest in the Hall of Peace Bringers, have the love and friendship of all Fa'ahlima. Fa'ahla is a new world today, one governed by a single, united political party with one goal, to ensure that peace is maintained on Fa'ahla. You who have so tirelessly toiled to bring peace back to us will search no more, for the quest for the Ta'ahli is at an end." More cheering, more sirens and more tears rippled their way around the entire planet and Narek and his friends knew they had never before witnessed such a profoundly important event and were proud to be a part of it.

The weeks that followed were busy ones on Fa'ahla. The volunteers were all given the choice to return from whence they came or remain on Fa'ahla and become citizens. The majority chose to remain and many wanted to help with the rebuilding, such was their love for their new friends and many had been on Fa'ahla for years and regarded it as their home. Fleets of Shi'maqs began the process of taking those that wished to leave, to the worlds from which they volunteered and all were proud at being the first ever to return after volunteering with the mysterious Fa'ahlima. They took with them not only a fortune paid to them for their work, but also the love and blessings of their new neighbours.

The day came when the four friends had to decide what they wanted to do, stay or leave.

"I want to stay," Royden said emotionally. "I've met a girl, another volunteer and we want to stay here and help with the rebuilding. I met her when we went to that party that Narek didn't want to go to, and we've kept in touch and spent time together on our days off."

"That's wonderful," Narek said. "I wish you both every happiness."

"What about you?" Royden asked. "What are you guys doing?"

"We've talked about it," Narek said, looking at Risa, who nodded, "and we're returning to Luzel 2. I committed a grave offence by going AWOL from the military and it weighs too heavily upon me. I want to return and face my punishment."

"And I want to return and face Lorella," Risa said. "I want to look her in the eyes and tell her of the love Narek and I share, and I want to see her shamed for what she did."

"What about you Telkan?" Narek asked. "Are you going or staying?"

"I would like to return with you Narek, if that's possible. Could I get work on Luzel 2 do you think?"

"Of course manuk," Narek smiled. "We will find work for you and you can keep Risa company while I fulfil my sentence."

"We'll both be looking for work," Risa said. "I doubt my old job will still be available."

Narek, Risa and Telkan embraced Royden and his girlfriend Shola as they said their goodbyes. The group had formed a strong bond during their time together and it was a sad occasion for them to be parting.

"Be happy, all of you," Royden said. "Don't waste a moment ever again okay?"

"We won't," Narek said. "We absolutely won't. Have a wonderful life together you two, you hear?"

When the goodbyes were done and the tears wiped from their eyes, Narek, Risa and Telkan boarded the shuttle for the short journey to the Shi'maq that lay at anchor in orbit and waited to take them home to Luzel 2.

The shuttle descended through the clouds towards Base 7 on Luzel 2 and Narek was getting nervous.

"You know Risa," he said. "I will probably be arrested the moment I leave the shuttle, so don't start panicking okay? Don't think you'll never see me again or anything and you won't be on your own. Telkan will be with you."

"*Shra lai mirulik Manuk. Laiwa re shinal,*" Telkan replied. "I will look after her brother. I give you my word of honour."

"*Swan kiahi,*" Narek nodded. "Thank you."

"Don't worry Risa," Telkan said. "I'll look after you."

"Thanks," she smiled. "How do I say thank you in Vendalan?"

"*Swan kiahi,*" Narek replied. "You want to learn the language?"

"Yes," she nodded. "Yes I'd like to, if you're happy to teach me."

"Then we will," Narek said.

"*Swan kiahi,*" she said.

"Okay, here we are," Narek said as the shuttle came in to land within the military compound. Welcome to Luzel 2 Manuk."

Ka'abash approached and went to the hatchway. As it began to descend, he turned and smiled.

"Knowing you has brought me much pleasure my friends. Are you ready?" Everyone nodded.

He led the way down the ramp, the three following close behind. Narek saw the Base Commander, Major Cable, with four of the military security force and knew he was to be immediately arrested. He took a deep breath and tried to remain calm. Risa squeezed his hand.

"Welcome to Base 7," Cable said to Ka'abash, who put a hand to his chest and bowed his head in response.

"Thank you my friend for allowing me to land. I am here to return two of your personnel to you, and another who wishes to make this his home."

"Thank you Sir," Cable said. "I am pleased to have my people back and delighted to welcome a new friend to the base."

"I wish to say, before I depart," Ka'abash said, "that these three friends have done Fa'ahla the greatest service in the history of our world. It is only through their perseverance and sacrifice that peace has now returned to my world and my people. All of Fa'ahla blesses them and it will bring us much sorrow to know that they are to be punished."

"I give you and your people my word of honour," Cable said, "that Sergeant Jenn is only to be punished for the misdeed he committed as one of my soldiers and nothing more. It is a military rule that I do not have the power to break."

"I understand rules," Ka'abash said. "I assume that you do however, have the power of interpretation?"

"Oh yes Sir," Cable grinned. "I do indeed."

"Narek, my friend," Ka'abash said as he turned away from Cable. "I will honour your memory Peace Bringer. Live in peace and be blessed."

"Thank you Sir, for everything," Narek said. "We will not forget our time on your world and our memories will be happy ones."

"Risa," Ka'abash said as he took her hand. "When I first met Narek and saw the pain in his eyes as he told me of losing you, I knew this was a bond that even our creator dare not break. It brought me much joy to hear of your reunion. Enjoy your life together and make the fullest use of every moment. Live in peace and be blessed."

"Thank you Sir," Risa replied. "For bringing us together and for making us feel so welcome."

"Telkan," Ka'abash smiled. "The quiet one. How you have grown in confidence since you took those first steps into my ship. I looked at the tears in your eyes and saw a broken man and I feared you would never smile again. How you have changed my friend. Live in peace and be blessed."

"Thank you Sir," Telkan said, "for taking me in when I just wanted to die before I'd begun to live, and for giving me something to live for again."

Ka'abash nodded and smiled at the three friends, then turned and walked back into the shuttle.

"Sergeant Jenn," Cable said. "I have to arrest you now, you know that don't you?"

"Yes Sir," Narek said and saluted.

"Relax Lashen. Listen, you went AWOL. That's a crime and you know it. However, I have been fully informed of all the circumstances surrounding your decision to leave and with the Fa'ahlima having spoken on your behalf; I don't feel the need to be harsh with you."

"Thank you Beganzi," Narek replied.

"You will have to spend a few hours in military custody though," Cable said. "Just until I give you a formal interview and deal out your punishment etc, you know the drill. Take him away guys." The four armed military security men escorted Narek across the base and into the security headquarters. Risa put a hand to her mouth and began to cry. Telkan put his arm around her shoulder.

"Fear not Risa, I am here to take care of you."

"Don't you worry Risa," Cable said, "he's gonna be fine and you'll be together again real soon okay? Now, introduce me to our new friend."

"This is Telkan Preel," she replied, "and he wants to come and live and work on the base if that's okay."

"Welcome Telkan," Cable said as he extended his hand, which Telkan shook. "My name is Adrian Cable and I'm the Base Military Commander. "It's always nice to have another Vendalan here. I'm sure we can find some employment for you somewhere and there's a few new apartment units gone up just a few weeks ago. You can move straight into one."

"Thank you very much," Telkan smiled.

"Your old apartment is vacant again Risa," Cable told her, "so you can move right back in if you want to. We have all of your belongings stored here in one of our old ammunition storage units."

"Thank you, that would be nice. I loved that apartment."

"The new apartment units are right behind the stores building, so Telkan will be nearby so neither of you need feel lost. Now, as for a job, how about being our stores department head?"

"But that's Lorella's job," Risa said, her eyes wide at the suggestion.

"Correction," Cable smiled. "It was Lorella's job. She's no longer on Luzel 2 so her job is now vacant and you're the best qualified. Gage is now working your old job and says he doesn't want Lorella's old job. That would then mean that Gage's old job as stores hand is now vacant, so Telkan here can take that position."

"She's not here?" Risa asked.

"No," Cable replied. "As soon as the men came back without Narek and told us what happened and why, everyone started to avoid her like the plague, and her social life took a nosedive. Word gets around y'know and it started to be bad for business, so her boss took her aside and umm, suggested she leave. A couple of months later she took off with some engineer on a low budget passenger liner and she's never been seen since. It came out after she'd gone that she'd been doing a bit of prostitution on the side, and Base 7 was the source of some gossip for a while. I know she's your sister but we're not unhappy she's gone."

"Oh my god," Risa exclaimed. "Who's been doing her job then?"

"We got someone from base 16 who was newly qualified and fancied getting a bit of experience in a position of responsibility. We always told him it was temporary; we never allowed ourselves to doubt you would one day return with my Sergeant."

"Thank you," Risa replied. "I don't know what to say, I've caused so much trouble and you've been so kind."

"Now stop that my girl," Cable encouraged. "Lorella has gone, Base 7 now has a good reputation again, I have my best Sergeant back and you're home where you belong. That seems like a good day's work to me."

"I'm happy to be back," she smiled.

"So, would you like the job?"

"Well yeah," Risa nodded. "I could do it standing on my head and I know Telkan will make a fine stores hand."

"Indeed that is a wonderful opportunity Sir," Telkan nodded. "Thank you for your kindness."

"No problem. Now come with me and I'll make a couple of calls and then get some guys to help shift your stuff back into your old apartment Risa. Then I'll have a word around and see what we can rustle up to furnish your new place Telkan. How long is it since you ate?"

Narek saluted Major Cable, before turning and leaving the office. Once outside he grinned and sighed deeply, happy to be back in his familiar territory again. As he walked the corridor, he heard boot steps coming towards him and turned to find Kaylak and Vronil staring wide eyed at him.

"Manukichi," he grinned. *"Estriwa maitiliok reil ruliksi pirasti,"* he said as he embraced them both. "Brothers. I am overjoyed to see you again."

"Ruligul estriya pashilam mei estrima maitiliok damesh kaskirae," Kaylak said. "We saw you were under arrest but we are overjoyed that you have returned."

"Manuk. Swan coyan romskal ordeyn reliopaofas. Anyelitcha skantol," Vronil said. "Brother. Much time has passed since you left. We thought of you every day."

"Niahaof kiyo sakrichi skanlok li en leiwama swan kirama. Risa me telari li estriwa mekriyol pirasti," Narek told them as a tear ran down his cheek. "I felt

your souls every moment and they gave me much strength. Risa loves me and I am whole again."

The three walked across the military compound and Narek saw a group of soldiers approaching.

"Good afternoon Sarge," a voice said. Narek turned and gasped when he saw Calin Talko standing before him.

"Calin? Calin Talko?" he asked.

"You remember me? I'm happy to see you again Sarge. It gives me the opportunity to thank you at last for what you did for my family."

"You are all together now?"

"Oh yes, we got here safely thanks to you. Mother was treated in the hospital here and they did an operation on her that made her so much better. She now needs just a small amount of different medicine and she's a whole new person."

"That's wonderful news," Narek said.

"And thank you for what you did for me too Sarge," Calin said. "Best thing you ever did was fix up that punishment for me. It changed me. Changed me for the better. I decided to join up and I've enjoyed every moment of it. When I think I could've ended up a criminal in a gang or even murdered by another gang, I thank the universe for you Sarge."

"You did the work Calin," Narek said. "Well done. I'm proud of you."

"Thank you Sarge."

Gage whooped when he saw Risa enter the stores and almost dropped the box he was carrying.

"My eyes deceive me," he said. "I see it but I don't believe it."

"Believe it buddy," she grinned. "Good to see you again Gage. Give me a hug."

"Oh Risa," he grinned as he hugged her. "I cried for ages when you left like that. We all cried. All except her. No one could think why you would just up and leave like that, but when Narek went nuts in the bar that night, everyone began to realise what was up. My heart broke for you. I'm so glad you're both home."

"Thank you," she said. "And I see you got my job after all."

"Yeah," he blushed. "Do you umm, want it back now?"

"No, don't worry," she grinned. "I'm taking Lorella's job and Telkan here is taking your old job. Say hello to Gage, Telkan, he'll be your first line boss and he will answer to me."

"Welcome Telkan," Gage smiled as they shook hands. "The job's real easy. You'll pick it up in no time."

"I'm happy to meet you Gage," Telkan replied. "I'm sure the job can't be as hard as hauling rocks."

"Huh?" Gage asked as both Telkan and Risa burst out laughing.

Narek was relieved of his position for three months and sentenced to do community work around the base for the period. He did not mind at all, he was able to move into the apartment with Risa and it was easy. Cleaning up, loading and unloading of cargo, taking care of livestock, refuelling the ships and any other jobs around the base that needed doing. He did them all with a smile, and when his three months were up and he regained his rank and position, he was ready to return to his real work. The night before he took a unit of men on a week of advanced survival training, he took Risa into his arms and hugged her tightly. Winking at his three Vendalan friends who had enjoyed dinner with them, he took a deep breath.

"Risa my love. Will you join with me in marriage?"

THE END

Merita King

COMING SOON

The Trials of Nahda

You know the difference between fantasy and reality, right?

Sam Sinclair thought so too, until his boss sent him to Nahda, to arrest a museum researcher for stealing an ancient artifact.

Until the pair find themselves trapped deep below an abandoned fusion reactor, Sam had never had occasion to doubt what was real and what was not.

As events unfold, forcing him to embrace the possibility that what he always believed to be just fantasy, could indeed be very real, his life comes crumbling down around him.

Finding himself now a fugitive of the law, left for dead by his prisoner, and still trapped within the underground city, Sam struggles to accept the evidence of his own eyes.

Some things are impossible aren't they? Sam thought so too, but what he experienced forced him to look at the universe in a different light.